"If we must dawdle in the library, let's make it for a worthwhile purpose."

Caught off balance, Leonora lurched into his lap. Though part of him would have liked to throttle her, another part thrilled to the sensation of her in his arms. In a deft motion that would have done credit to a trained pickpocket, he plucked the spectacles from her nose and the combs from her hair, tossing them onto the table.

"I've worked hard for you this week, Miss Freemantle. I think I deserve a reward."

He hushed her inarticulate sounds of protest with a forceful application of his lips.

She froze in his embrace, her whole body going temporarily slack. Surrendering before his onslaught. Falling open. Inviting him deeper.

Then, with a shift so sudden it robbed him of breath, Leonora pried herself from his arms and slapped him soundly.

"How dare you, Morse Archer!"

* * *

The Wedding Wager
Harlequin Historical #563—June 2001

Acclaim for Deborah Hale's recent books

The Bonny Bride
"…high adventure!"
—*Romantic Times Magazine*

A Gentleman of Substance
"This exceptional Regency-era romance
includes all the best aspects of that genre…
Deborah Hale has outdone herself…"
—*Romantic Times Magazine*

"…a nearly flawless plot, well-dimensioned characters,
and a flame that will set your heart ablaze
with every emotion possible!"
—*Affaire de Coeur*

My Lord Protector
"Invite yourself to this sweet, sensitive, moving and
utterly wonderful tale of love from the heart."
—*Affaire de Coeur*

THE WEDDING WAGER

DEBORAH HALE

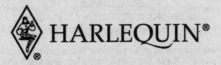

HARLEQUIN®

TORONTO • NEW YORK • LONDON
AMSTERDAM • PARIS • SYDNEY • HAMBURG
STOCKHOLM • ATHENS • TOKYO • MILAN • MADRID
PRAGUE • WARSAW • BUDAPEST • AUCKLAND

ISBN 0-373-29163-9

THE WEDDING WAGER

Copyright © 2001 by Deborah M. Hale

Please address questions and book requests to:
Harlequin Reader Service
U.S.: 3010 Walden Ave., P.O. Box 1325, Buffalo, NY 14269
Canadian: P.O. Box 609, Fort Erie, Ont. L2A 5X3

For my parents, Ivan and Marion MacDonald,
who taught me so many important lessons,
and for my sons, Brendan and Jamie Hale,
who picked up where they left off.

Chapter One

**Bramleigh Military Hospital for
Enlisted Men
1812**

The whole place smelled of men.

Leonora Freemantle could almost feel her nose twitch and her muscles tense, like a hare or hind scenting predators on the wind. Looking neither left nor right, she strode down the ward behind Matron. As she passed bed after bed of convalescing soldiers, she sensed their covert glances, heard their muttered quips.

"Looks like Matron's got a new dragon-in-training, lads."

"D'yer reckon she's sucking on a lemon?"

"Puts me in mind of me old drill sergeant."

The derisive snickers dogged Leonora's footsteps. Thrusting out her chin and stiffening her spine, she fiercely resisted the urge to adjust her spectacles and straighten her bonnet. They might take it as a sign of weakness. Never would she give them the satisfaction of thinking she cared for their opinion in the least.

Still, she could not quench the blistering blush that seared her face. How long had some of these men been without a woman? Yet they still found her laughably unappealing.

At least they were honest about their feelings. One could not say the same for most of their sex. That, Leonora had learned from bitter experience.

Matron veered into a small common room, heading straight for a clutch of men crouched in one corner. Leonora heard the muted click of dice tumbling along the hardwood floor. A shout went up, followed by a flurry of muttered curses.

"Knicked-it again, Archer!" cried one of the spectators in tones of grudging admiration. "Damned if you ain't the luckiest elbow-shaker I've ever seen."

At the mention of that name, Leonora perked up her ears. If this was the Sergeant Archer she'd come to see, it was encouraging to know he liked gambling.

The thrower scooped up his ivories with a practiced motion. "Luck's got naught to do with it." A note of teasing laughter warmed his words. "It's skill, my boy, simple as that."

"Ser'nt Archer!" Matron descended on the players like a terrier into a chicken coop. "How m'ny times have I told ye? Thar's to be no gamblin' in the hospital!"

The sergeant rose to his feet, unfolding the long, lean-muscled body of a Rifleman. For an instant he winced, as though the movement hurt him. Then his features blossomed into a smile of devastating charm, which he fixed upon Matron.

Leonora's sensible, bluestocking heart began to flutter in a most unnerving fashion. Nothing in Cousin Wesley's letters from the Peninsula had prepared her for the sight of his sergeant.

Stop it! she willed herself. *Stop this foolishness, at once!* Her traitorous body mutinied. Her breath quickened.

Why should the sight of this man affect her so? Leonora asked herself as she watched him jolly Matron into a mood of exasperated tolerance. She hoped an intellectual consideration of the problem might bring her insurgent emotions back under control.

Why him? She'd seen far handsomer specimens—at least by the standard of the times. Smoother, blander, more uniformly proportioned.

There was nothing smooth or bland about this man's face. Every feature was bold and definite. The nose and chin jutted out as though hewn from golden-brown stone, ready to take on the world. The wide, bowed mouth looked capable of a vast spectrum of expression, while the dark eyes wielded a provocative, penetrating gaze.

On a face less striking, the emphatic black eyebrows would have dominated. On Sergeant Morse Archer, they harmonized into an aspect of arresting appeal.

"What have we here?" He turned his piercing, hypnotic eyes upon Leonora, one full brow raised expressively.

Their color was a dynamic melding of green, brown and gold, Leonora realized as Sergeant Archer stepped toward her. For the first time in many years she yearned to be beautiful. His striking good looks made her all too aware of her own shortcomings. Though she told herself it was the height of folly, she could not help wanting him to like what he saw.

Matron answered his question. "A visitor for ye, Ser'nt Archer. Now mind yer manners."

At a look from the sergeant, his gambling companions rapidly dispersed. Matron took up a post just outside the door. Whether she meant to guard the privacy of their conversation, or to act as some sort of chaperon, Leonora was not certain.

"What can such a lovely lady want with the likes of me?" asked Sergeant Archer once the room had cleared. His voice was as rich and mellow as well-aged brandy. Once again he unleashed his potent smile.

A shiver of icy wrath went through Leonora. *Lovely lady?* The liar! Did this cynical charmer expect her to lap up his spurious flattery? As she pulled off her glove, she longed to smack it against his cheek. Remembering how desperately she needed to win his cooperation, she curbed her ire and thrust out her hand for him to shake.

"Sergeant Archer, I'm Leonora Freemantle. I believe you know my uncle, Sir Hugo Peverill. I've come to make you a proposition."

She could tell her words unsettled him, though he made a determined effort to hide it. Those expressive brows drew together and his mien darkened like a summer sky before a storm. His deep voice rumbled with the muted menace of distant thunder.

"Go away, Miss Freemantle. I'm not interested in your *proposition.*"

He tried to execute a crisp pivot on his heel. Apparently his wounded leg refused to cooperate. His stern frown crumpled into a grimace of pain as he staggered.

Before she had a chance to think better of it, Leonora reached out to steady him. The sleeves of his coarse-woven shirt were rolled up to the elbows. As she grasped his bronzed forearm, she felt the taut power of his muscle, the disconcerting warmth of his bare skin and the provocative caress of his dark body hair.

A jolt of mysterious energy surged in her. From the sensitive tips of her fingers and the palm of her hand, it radiated up her arm—to her throat and her bosom and the pit of her belly.

She hated it.

How dare this exasperating creature provoke her so? Even as he dismissed her without hearing a word she'd come to say. Long ago she had vowed never to submit to a man's whims. She had no intention of starting now. Not with her whole future at stake.

When he tried to wrench his arm away, she tightened her hold. "I'll let go when you agree to hear me out, Sergeant Archer."

Animosity warred with amusement—every nuance of the battle showing on his vigorous, mobile face. Amusement won.

A row of square, even teeth flashed briefly in a fiendish grin. "This could turn out to be a very *interesting* day, if I choose not to listen."

Leonora's cheeks smarted. She knew what he would say next. Her own thoughts had raced ahead to the same conclusion.

"Not to mention an even more interesting night." A warm, infectious chuckle bubbled up from some well of humor deep within him.

Abruptly, Leonora released his arm. Tears of impotent fury prickled in the corners of her eyes. She refused to let them fall. Why had Uncle Hugo chosen this infuriating man as the subject of their wager?

As he limped toward the door, she leveled a desperate parting shot at his back. "Strange. I didn't take you for a fool, Sergeant."

Her words found their mark. He hesitated in midstride, and his shoulder blades bunched, as though he had just taken a blow between them.

Leonora pressed her momentary advantage. "In my experience, only a fool shuts his ears to a proposal that might benefit him."

Though he continued to face the door, Morse Archer

lobbed his reply back at her. "When a woman like you comes with a proposition for a man like me, Miss Freemantle, it isn't often to *his* benefit. At least, not in the long run."

A shriek of vexation rose in Leonora's throat, but she stifled it—barely. She'd assumed Morse Archer would leap at the opportunity she offered him. Instead he had thrust her into the role of supplicant. One she abhorred.

It made her twice as determined to win Uncle Hugo's wager and free herself from the need to go cap in hand to a man ever again.

"Pray, what do you mean by *a woman like me,* Sergeant Archer?"

"Don't be thick, woman." He rounded on her. "I mean a lady of your class." The disdain in his voice was palpable.

At last—a scrap of leverage to use on him.

"Would it surprise you to learn that I care no more for the notion of *class* than you do?"

"It would."

Drawing an unsteady breath, Leonora forced herself to look squarely into his penetrating gaze. "I believe all that separates the so-called upper and lower orders of our society is education."

"Do you then?" He crossed his arms over his chest in a pose that demanded, *And what's that to me?*

At least he made no further move to quit the room.

"I do. That is why I'm here. Uncle Hugo thinks I'm a crank, as does nearly everyone else of my acquaintance."

One mercurial brow lifted a fraction, as if to cast his opinion with the rest. Leonora hurried on, before he took a notion to dismiss her again.

"My uncle has set me a wager, to test the validity of my theory."

At the word *wager,* she sensed a subtle air of interest from Sergeant Archer.

Eagerly, she explained the plan. "I have three months to educate a common soldier and pass him off as a gentleman officer during a Season at Bath. If I win the bet, Uncle Hugo will finance a school for indigent girls, of which I shall be headmistress."

"And I'm the common, ignorant soldier you plan to work your magic on?" The question sounded innocent enough, but the subtle curl of his lip conveyed scorn.

"If by *magic* you mean something easy or illusionary, you're mistaken, Sergeant. It will be three months of very hard work for both of us. In the end, I believe you'll find the result worthwhile. Will you do it?"

He smiled now—with his lips at least. "No, Miss Freemantle. I will not." His tone and posture were a parody of high courtesy. "Now please be so kind as to go away. You've taken up quite enough of my time for one afternoon."

Didn't he recognize the chance she was offering him? Couldn't he see the noble cause it would serve?

"Are you devoid of ambition, man? Not the least bit interested in improving yourself?"

The insincere smile disappeared. Nostrils flared, he bore down on her like a charging bull. Against her will, Leonora retreated a step before his menacing advance. He stopped within a whisker of her, so close she could feel the heat of his breath on her face. He spoke with muted intensity, his whisper more intimidating than most men's thunderous bluster.

"I have plenty of ambition, Miss Freemantle. On *my* terms. I happen to like who and what I am. So you can keep your *improvements.* I don't need you or anyone else turning me into some mincing, mutton-headed gentleman."

Leonora held her ground. Somewhere deep within her, she fought to quench a flicker of admiration for Morse Archer's pride and independence. Remembering all she stood to gain…and lose, she forced herself to try one last time.

"Please, Sergeant. If not for yourself, think of my school."

"Where you can turn wholesome farm girls into useless debutantes? An admirable cause, to be sure."

With all the dignity she could muster, Leonora replied, "I don't expect you to understand my motives. No one else does."

"The trouble is, I understand all too well, Miss Freemantle. I know all about having the charity of my *betters* crammed down my throat and having to tug a forelock and say 'Thankee, ma'am', even while I choke on it."

His words smote her. Her school would be nothing like what he described…or would it? "We are not talking about charity, Sergeant."

"Aren't we, Miss Freemantle?" His burst of rage seemed to collapse on itself. Slowly he turned away from her and hobbled toward the door.

For a moment Leonora just stood, watching him go. Limp and spent, she felt as though she'd been buffeted by a violent storm. As she gathered up her courage to once again run the gauntlet of stares and whispers in the ward, she wondered how her uncle would react to this turn of events. He'd been so adamant on engaging this particular man.

Well, she had tried her best to recruit Morse Archer. He had refused. Uncle Hugo would simply have to pick someone else.

In some ways it was a pity. The sergeant seemed to possess a degree of intelligence, and his speech was not too rustic. Taken together with his arresting physical presence, it would not have been difficult to pass him off as a gentleman.

All the same, Leonora found herself breathing a sigh of relief. The last thing she needed was to spend three months in the close company of a man like Morse Archer. So stubborn. So intractable.

So compelling.

Morse watched Leonora Freemantle stalk off the ward, clearly oblivious to the winks and elbow digs with which the men greeted her departure. Turning to the window, he continued to stare after her as she climbed into her barouche and drove away. He wanted to make certain she was gone.

Or so he told himself.

"Give the ivories another rattle, Sergeant?" A young corporal from Morse's regiment flashed a hopeful grin. The lad's right arm had been severed below the elbow, but he'd learned to throw the dice pretty well with his left hand.

Morse shook his head in the manner of an elder brother who had better occupations than entertaining the little ones in the family. "You heard Matron, Corporal Boyer. No gambling on hospital property. I'm in hot water enough with the army. No need to go courting more."

Boyer flashed him an awkward grin, then ambled off. This was the first time Morse had referred to the Board of Inquiry, though the matter must have been common knowledge among the convalescing soldiers at Bramleigh.

There was a good chance he would end up cashiered. Dismissed from the army in disgrace. Thinking of the Board made Morse think of the miserable retreat from Bucaso. His leg throbbed, just above the knee, where a French bayonet had pierced it.

During the British retreat from Bucaso.

Limping over to his cot, he sank down on it, stretching out his long frame. His heels projected two inches past the end of the thin mattress. To distract himself from the pain in his leg and the equally painful memories of that last rearguard skirmish, Morse turned his thoughts to Leonora Freemantle.

The gall of the woman! To stroll in like Lady Bountiful with her Christmas basket and offer to turn him into a gentleman. In the instant before she'd opened her mouth, something about her had attracted him. Now Morse was damned if he could decide what it might have been.

She had little in common with the type of woman he usually favored. In the first place, her figure was too lean and angular for his taste. He seldom paid much heed to women's clothes, but in her case they were too ugly to ignore. He often noticed women's hair, but Miss Freemantle had kept hers pulled back so severely and covered by her bonnet that he could not have sworn as to its color. There might have been something to her eyes—color or clarity, but tight little spectacles detracted from their modest charms.

Altogether a prim, bluestocking spinster.

None of these had roused Morse's antagonism, though. Her voice had done that.

Since joining the army, during his service in India and Spain, he'd seldom had occasion to hear an English lady speak. There was only one female at the Bramleigh hospital—if you could call her that. Matron, the old gargoyle, spoke in Cornish dialect so broad Morse often had trouble understanding her. Nothing in her gravelly voice evoked painful memories. Morse could not say the same for Leonora Freemantle.

To make matters worse, her first words to him had concerned a proposition. True, it was not the kind of proposition Lady Pamela Granville had made him on the day before he enlisted. The emotional echo stung just the same. It had made him resist Miss Freemantle's offer even before he heard it. Now, as his leg throbbed and he tried to block out the persistent din of the ward, Morse wondered if he'd been a fool to reject her proposal out-of-hand.

His other options were depressingly limited. He couldn't stay on at Bramleigh much longer, since he was past danger of amputation and he could use the leg, however haltingly. Even if the Board of Inquiry didn't drum him out of the service, he could not go back to soldiering. The doctors were optimistic that his mobility would return with time. Until then, his lameness would make it all but impossible to find the sort of job his limited education had equipped him for.

The dinner bell rang. With a weary sigh, Morse hauled himself up from his cot and joined the tail end of the queue headed for the refectory. There, he spooned the tepid, watery stew into his mouth with little interest or enjoyment. Boyer and a few of the other lads from his regiment took their places with Morse at their accustomed table. In one way or another, they were all casualties of the retreat from Bucaso.

They were the lucky ones.

"Yer comp'ny didn't stay long, Sergeant." There was an implied question in Boyer's innocent remark. "Not exactly your kinda woman, were she?"

The men exchanged grins all around the table. Their sergeant's way with women was a point of pride among his men. They knew he had a taste for pretty, plump, saucy barmaids. They also knew he seldom had trouble attracting them.

Without glancing up from his stew, Morse cut their amusement short with a single muttered sentence. "The lady was Lieutenant Peverill's cousin."

A muted *"Oh"* rose from the men, breathed with obvious regret and perhaps a little shame. The late Lieutenant Wesley Peverill had enjoyed universal esteem among the enlisted men in his company. None more than his sergeant—Morse Archer.

Just then, Morse realized what had drawn him to Miss Freemantle in the instant before she spoke. It was the likeness to her cousin. Lieutenant Peverill had been a short, slight man with a deceptive air of delicacy. Yet that unpromising frame had housed the guile of a serpent, the tenacity of a badger and the courage of a lion. For as long as he lived, Morse Archer would rue his young lieutenant's senseless death.

He had glimpsed something of Lieutenant Peverill's cleverness and ferocious bravery in the woman. She had stood her ground and peppered him with every scrap of ammunition she could muster. When he'd turned on her with the full force of his wrath, she had scarcely flinched. He'd been skeptical of her claim that social class meant nothing to her. Now, remembering her kinship to the lieutenant, he could believe it.

Boyer spoke up again. "Came to thank ye, did she, Sergeant?"

Morse nodded. "Something like that."

The men knew Sir Hugo Peverill had called on their sergeant soon after they'd all arrived at Bramleigh. The old man had come to thank Morse for risking his life to rescue the lieutenant from certain death. Unfortunately, the young man's wounds had proven too grave to survive. But his heartbroken father had cherished the small consolation that the lad had died and been buried at his home in England rather than some shallow, unmarked grave in Portugal.

Sir Hugo had offered Morse money, a job, anything he might ask. Morse had declined with rather ill grace. He took no pride in his actions during the retreat. His desperate charge into a forest of French bayonets had been too little, too late. To accept a reward for it only compounded his sense of guilt.

Apparently the wily old Sir Hugo was unwilling to take no for an answer. Thus the transparent stratagem of this *wager* with his niece. Morse did not go so far as to suspect Leonora Freemantle knew it was a ruse. She could not have entreated him so passionately unless she believed it to be genuine.

Gnawing on a crust of hard bread, Morse imagined the food he might have received at Sir Hugo's estate, Laurelwood. When rations had been tight in Portugal, Lieutenant Peverill had often waxed lyrical about the contents of his father's larder and the talent of his kitchen staff. More such stories recurred to Morse as he lolled around the ward after dinner feeling curiously restless.

That night he dreamed of a fine, fat feather bed made up with linen that smelled of sunshine and clover. A warm, cheery fire blazing in the hearth. A plump roast goose laid out on the sideboard with all the trimmings, its skin brown and crisp over juicy dark meat. Morse woke to find his mouth watering.

No doubt about it, Laurelwood would have made a soft billet for the next three months, while he recovered the full use of his leg. A snug roof over his head. Meals the like of which he hadn't eaten in years. And nothing required of him but to suffer the tutelage of Sir Hugo's bluestocking niece. For a wonder, the idea rather appealed to him.

It was too late now, though.

No doubt Miss Freemantle had gone straight out and acquired a more willing subject. A sharp fellow who didn't let pride and foolish memories blind him to a good thing.

Morse recalled his father's gruff admonition. ''When a man's got nothing, he can't afford pride, son.''

He also remembered the bitter elegy he'd muttered over

the unmarked graves of his family. "When a man's got nothing, pride's all he *can* afford."

One of these days, Morse Archer decided with a rueful shake of his head, his misbegotten pride was going to land him in serious trouble.

Chapter Two

"Dash it all, Leonora. Don't keep me in suspense any longer, my dear." Sir Hugo Peverill glanced up from his eager ingestion of the roast goose, an expectant gleam in his eye. "How soon can he come?"

To delay her reply, Leonora pretended an intense concentration on her dinner. She was hungry. It had been a long, cold ride to Bramleigh and back, with only her indignation to keep her warm on the return journey.

"Well? How soon?" repeated Sir Hugo.

Still, Leonora hesitated to speak the words. She was no coward. Cousin Wesley had often claimed she possessed more courage than a field officer—denying society's expectations by remaining unwed and devoted to her scholarly pursuits.

It was one thing to deny society. Quite another to deny Sir Hugo when he took hold of an idea. Leonora often compared her late aunt's husband to a Royal Mail coach. Thundering toward his destination. Waving away objections like the Royal Mail speeding through toll stations. Impatient of the slightest delay or detour.

He wouldn't be happy with the detour she was about to

deliver him. No sense in forestalling the inevitable, however.

"He isn't coming, Uncle." Though she tried to sound indifferent, Leonora braced for the backlash. "We'll simply have to find someone else. I'm certain there are plenty of men with the sense to recognize a unique opportunity when they're presented with one."

"Not coming? Ridiculous. Rot!" Sir Hugo's white sidewhiskers bristled aggressively and his prominent Roman nose cleaved the air. "Of course he's coming."

Leonora almost expected him to add, *Sergeant Archer just doesn't know it yet.*

She shook her head. "No, Uncle. He was quite adamant on the point. I had a devil of a time even persuading him to give me a hearing. When I finally won the opportunity to state my business, he accused me of trying to cram charity down his throat."

"Then you must've gone about it all the wrong way." Eerily pale blue eyes shone with a glacial light that terrified many people. "Knew I should've gone with you. You're a fine filly, Leonora, but you don't reckon with the importance of a man's pride."

Leonora pushed her plate away. Her stomach suddenly felt sour. She longed to remind Sir Hugo that she'd seen her family's fortune decimated, all in the name of assuaging male pride. Noting how the ruddy flesh of his jowls had taken on a deep mulberry cast, she refrained from engaging him in a full-scale argument.

For all his overbearing will and eccentric whims, he was a warmhearted, generous creature. With only a tenuous claim of kinship by marriage, he had been more of a father to her than any of the men her mother had married.

"Don't get yourself into a state, Uncle." She did her best to soothe him. "Can't we just find someone else? I don't believe Sergeant Archer will do it no matter who asks or how we coax him. He's an impossibly stubborn fellow.''

''Stubborn?'' Sir Hugo brandished his bread knife like a sword. ''Poppycock! Resolute, you mean. It took a resolute character to defy orders and take on a dozen Frenchmen with bayonets to save Wesley.''

Leonora could well picture Morse Archer fighting off an entire French battalion. It was no stretch to conceive of him defying orders. The difficult part was imagining him doing all that for the sake of someone else.

Long ago, she had reconciled herself to the notion that human beings were selfish creatures at heart. The sergeant had struck her as a man well accustomed to looking out for himself. She had tried appealing to his sense of altruism by mentioning her school. He'd been positively insulting in his refusal, with more cant about unwanted charity.

The truth suddenly dawned on Leonora. ''That's what this wager is about, isn't it, Uncle Hugo? Not me and my school. You're just using them as an excuse to repay Sergeant Archer.''

''Harrumph! Excuse? Repayment? Nothing of the sort!'' Sir Hugo took a deep draft of his wine, avoiding Leonora's gaze.

''He wouldn't accept your help when you offered it outright.'' She persisted. ''So you hit on the idea of this wager. You might have been frank with me.''

A look of relief came over Sir Hugo's florid features. An unusually forthright man, he could not have enjoyed misleading her.

''I'll own that was part of it. I hadn't much hope of Wes getting off the Peninsula alive. You'll never know what it meant to me, having him here at the last. There's scarcely enough in this world I can do to repay Archer for making that possible. Wish I could make him understand.''

He spoke that last sentence on a sigh heaved from deep

within his stout frame. Leonora could almost feel the weight of his debt on her own heart.

"I can't say I care to be manipulated like this, Uncle," she chided him, but gently. More in hurt than in anger. "I thought you were in earnest about our wager."

"So I am, my dear. Whatever gave you the notion I wasn't? I take our wager very seriously indeed." His gaze rested on her with tangible fondness. "I want to see you settled and happy with a good man and a brood of lively young ones I can spoil rotten in my dotage."

"Uncle!" Leonora could not keep a hint of asperity from her voice. "We've been over this territory a hundred times at least. You know I'd never be happy in a marriage, any more than Wesley would have been happy as a civilian."

Too late, she clapped a hand over her mouth. Not for anything in the world would she add to her uncle's pain.

Sir Hugo replied with a long, level look. "How happy do you think he is now, eh?" he asked at last. "I should have done more to dissuade Wes from taking a commission. I'll not sit by and make the same mistake with you, my dear. Just because Clarissa never met a blackguard she wouldn't marry is no reason to condemn our whole sex…"

"I'll thank you to keep my mother and her *men* out of this," Leonora snapped.

Her uncle held up his hands in a parody of surrender. "No need to till that ground again. I'm only saying—since I haven't been able to convince or cajole you—I've been driven to the extremity of this wager. If you fulfill its conditions, I'll endow that school you're hankering after."

"And?" prompted Leonora.

"And," he grumbled, "provide you with a settlement that ensures you never need to marry."

The very thought made a smile of contentment blossom on Leonora's face.

"Just be sure you don't forget your part of the bargain." Sir Hugo stabbed the table with his forefinger.

Her budding smile withered, as if by a briny blast from the North Atlantic. "I'm not apt to forget, Uncle."

How could she with stakes as high as her future happiness? Lose the wager and she had sworn to marry a man of her uncle's choosing. If she had not wanted her school so desperately she never would have agreed to Sir Hugo's terms.

"Another thing you'd better remember is that I have the sole right to choose the subject for our wager. I won't settle for anyone but Morse Archer."

"But, Uncle, I told you…"

"So you did. Now I'm telling you, Leonora—if Archer won't agree to come, the wager's off."

"You can't mean that." Leonora blanched. Without this one chance, however slim, she'd never have her school.

"I assure you, I do mean it. Now, don't look so stricken, child. I'll go along with you, and between the two of us I'm sure we can win Sergeant Archer 'round. Why don't you spruce yourself up a bit for our visit. Haven't you any colored gowns?"

She wanted to protest that her appearance was the last consideration likely to sway Sergeant Archer. A maypole tricked out in ribbons was still a stick.

"Gray's a color, Uncle."

"'Tisn't. Not in a gel's frock, anyhow. Neither is black, brown nor that dull green. Do something with your hair, while you're about it. Can't you twist it up some way to make it curl?"

"Yes, Uncle." Leonora sighed. There was no talking sense to him in such a mood.

She did not look forward to her return visit to Bramleigh. Sharing the same room with two of the most exasperating men she'd ever met, Leonora wondered how she'd resist the urge to knock their heads together.

When Lieutenant Peverill's father and cousin tracked him down on the hospital grounds, Morse was hobbling along a mud-churned footpath with a stout tree branch for support.

It was a cold winter for Somerset, even to people who hadn't spent a decade baking in the heat of India and Iberia. Experiencing his first English winter in ten years, Morse felt the cold more keenly than he'd expected. Be that as it may, he could not stand being cooped up in the ward a moment longer.

He was an outdoorsman, a man of movement, a man of action—well suited to life in the Rifle Brigade. Whether the army discharged him or not, the time had come to hang up his green jacket. He would miss it.

In spite of the danger, the bad food, the miserable pay, the heat, the flies, the hatred of the local people, the blinkered stupidity of the officer corps and the occasional loneliness. It was all he had known for ten years. He felt rather empty and adrift to think of leaving it all behind. All the more, when he considered the bleak future that lay before him.

"Halloo! Sergeant Archer!"

Morse glanced up to see Sir Hugo Peverill bearing down on him, Leonora Freemantle coasting along in her uncle's wake. Without quite realizing what he was doing, Morse found himself approving the way she walked. Chin up. Eyes firmly fixed on her target. No mincing along, fussing about the mud that might spatter the hem of her cloak and gown.

"Wondered if we were ever going run you to ground, man." Sir Hugo gasped for breath.

With a start, Morse realized what they must want with

him. The notion of three months at Laurelwood lured him like a beacon in an otherwise murky future. If only his cursed pride would not rear up and spoil everything.

Morse extended his hand. "Good to see you again, sir."

"Indeed. I believe you've met my niece, Miss Freemantle." Sir Hugo pushed the young woman forward by the elbow, until her hand met Morse's.

Their previous interview flashed in Morse's mind. He remembered the touch of her hand on his bare arm, and the crude jest he'd made when she would not let him go. Little wonder she thought he could do with some gentlemanly polish.

Determined to show her he was not devoid of manners, he bowed over her hand. "I have had that pleasure."

The wind had whipped a few spirals of dark hair loose from beneath her bonnet—a less severe piece of headgear than she'd worn on her previous visit. The cold had coaxed an engaging spot of color into the ivory flesh over her high cheekbones. Her spectacles had slipped down to the tip of her nose, leaving unguarded a pair of most attractive gray-green eyes.

Eyes that shot him a look of censure, which he could not fathom. What had he done wrong now?

She snatched her hand back, as if she feared he might bite it. "You did not appear very pleased with our first meeting, sir."

Morse felt his own cheeks tingle. Perhaps it was time to come in from the cold. "I must beg your pardon for that, miss. There are days this place would try the patience of a saint. I'm sorry you had the misfortune to catch me on a bad one."

Sir Hugo clapped his niece around the shoulders, but he addressed his words to Morse. "Only natural, my boy. Of course, Leonora will pardon you. She's one of those rare females who doesn't hold a grudge."

"Rare, indeed." Morse smiled again into those gray-green eyes, hoping to make peace.

Leonora Freemantle replied by abruptly jamming her spectacles back into place. It was as though she had slammed a heavy door in his face. Morse took an involuntary step back.

Sir Hugo raised a hand to anchor his hat against a strong gust of winter wind. "We'd like to talk to you again, if we may, Sergeant?" He shouted to make himself heard over the rising rush of the wind. "No sense freezing our giblets out here, though. If you're not ready to go back in just yet, perhaps we could take a little drive around the neighborhood?"

"Very well, sir." It had been many a year since he'd driven in a good carriage.

"Capital!" Sir Hugo flashed an open, appealing grin.

It reminded Morse so forcefully of his young lieutenant that a choking lump rose in the back of his throat.

Sir Hugo pivoted and strode toward the driveway, calling back over his shoulder. "Lend the sergeant your arm, Leonora. This ground looks uneven."

She shot Morse a look that might have been apology or defiance—it was difficult to tell behind those grim spectacles.

Then she took his arm, as bidden.

Morse fought back a smile that tickled at the corner of his mouth. Plenty of women would have been delighted to take his arm. Leonora Freemantle looked positively martyred by the effort. No question that she was an unusual creature, unique in his experience. That novelty attracted Morse. He wouldn't mind getting better acquainted with her.

"Go ahead and grin, Sergeant." She kept her eyes fixed straight ahead. "I know you want to. Enjoy my humiliation."

"I don't understand what you mean, miss. You don't look much humbled to me."

Between the sturdy fabric of his greatcoat and the thick wool of her pelisse, there was no real contact between his arm and hers. Not like their previous meeting, when she'd clutched his bare arm with her naked hand. As a vivid memory of that instant rose in his mind, Morse felt a queer rush of heat that defied the bitter wind. He found himself counting back, trying to recall when he'd last had a woman.

Before he finished his count, they reached the carriage.

"Come along!" Sir Hugo sang out, motioning to them through the open door.

Again Leonora Freemantle spoke, as though she had hoarded her words till the last minute so there would be no time for discussion.

"You needn't have begged my pardon, Sergeant. I am the one who owes you an apology. Of everything you said to me when we last met, it appears you were right in almost every particular. Save one. My school will not be charity—at least not of the wretched type you've experienced. I beg you to reconsider helping me."

Morse understood about pride. He could appreciate what it cost her to speak those words. If only she'd left him with a moment to reply. The best he could do was a little show of gallantry, helping her into the carriage. As he caught a glimpse of one trim ankle encased in a fitted leather boot, Morse felt that confounded surge of warmth again.

Impatient with himself, he tried to tamp down the feeling. It did not yield to his control.

Climbing in behind Miss Freemantle, he sank gratefully into the seat opposite her and Sir Hugo. If he'd needed any reminder of the comfortable life he could expect at Laurelwood, the elegantly appointed interior of the barouche provided it—in spades. Mahogany, oiled and polished to a gleaming finish. Fine brass fittings. Supple leather upholstery.

Reaching up with his ivory-handled walking stick, Sir Hugo rapped on the ceiling of the carriage. Without a moment's hesitation, the barouche rolled smoothly away on the frozen road.

Sir Hugo fixed his intent gaze upon Morse. "I'll come to the point straightaway, Archer. No shilly-shallying about. I know you military chaps haven't much patience for that. The fact is, Leonora and I need you most desperately to help us with our wager."

"Yes, well…sir…as a matter of fact…I must tell you…" Morse groped for the words that would allow him to accept Sir Hugo's largesse while surrendering as little of his self-respect as possible.

"Say no more, my boy," interjected Sir Hugo in a manner that brooked no gainsay.

Both his tone and the *my boy* set Morse's oversensitive pride abristle, though he tried in vain to quell the feeling.

"I know just what's on your mind," Sir Hugo continued. "My niece and I can hardly expect you to relinquish several months of your life, not to mention putting all your plans in abeyance, while we settle a philosophical conundrum of no consequence to anyone but ourselves."

When the older man paused for breath, Morse tried to voice his objection. "No, no, Sir Hugo. That's not—"

Sir Hugo raised a stout hand to bid Morse be quiet. "Hear me out, young fellow. At least don't refuse us until you've heard the compensation I mean to offer you."

Morse wanted to laugh. Compensation? They meant to pluck him out of the cold, hungry, jobless life that awaited him, and cast him into the lap of luxury. Now, on top of that, they proposed to *compensate* him for doing it. He was hard-pressed to imagine how they reckoned to sweeten the pot. Curiosity, together with his respect for Sir Hugo, kept him from interrupting further.

"If you'll agree to help us," said Sir Hugo, "I'll engage on your behalf the best legal counsel money can buy. I'll also bring to bear every scrap of influence I can muster. No false promises, of course, but I should be very much surprised if the Board of Inquiry doesn't throw out your case."

Morse felt his jaw go slack. What could he say? Here was Sir Hugo offering to smooth out all the wrinkles of his life as casually as a housemaid straightening the bedsheets.

As he struggled to find his voice, Miss Freemantle spoke. "Don't forget the rest, Uncle."

Morse could not believe his ears. There was more?

"Of course, my dear." Sir Hugo took a deep breath. "My niece advises me that you should have a stake in the success of her little experiment. An inducement for you to give it your best effort."

Morse experienced a momentary pang of affront at the notion that he would ever give less than his best. Sir Hugo's next words drove the slight from his mind.

"If you succeed in passing yourself off as a gentleman officer at Bath, I'll see you set up somewhere that a man's caste isn't of such consequence. Any British colony you want to name—the Caribbean, North America, Botany Bay. I'll wangle you a decent grant of land and provide you with gold to buy equipment, stock and seed. Whatever you need. That should make it worth your while putting up with our foolishness, what?"

His generous mouth spread into a broad grin as he waited for Morse's answer.

Morse clamped his own lips together, to keep from saying the first thing that came into his mind.

Damn! He'd managed to curb his pride enough to accept

Miss Freemantle's original offer. Now, with the kindest intentions in the world, Sir Hugo had heaped a double helping of charity on top of the first. Much as the prospect tempted him, Morse knew it was too rich a dish for him to stomach.

"It's a generous offer, sir." Morse strove to keep his temper in check. The old man meant well, after all. He just didn't understand. "But I can't accept."

The curve of Sir Hugo's smile pulled straight and taut. The color began to rise in his face. He looked like a man struggling to contain an outburst.

Morse was suddenly aware of Leonora Freemantle, too. She looked quite stricken. Though why the founding of a school should mean that much to her, Morse could not fathom. Neither could he fathom the unaccountable urge he felt to take her in his arms and comfort her.

He wished he could find it within himself to oblige them. To oblige himself for that matter. If he could have contrived some way to appease his damnable pride, he'd have leaped at Sir Hugo's offer.

"Are you mad, boy? How can you think of turning up your nose at—"

"There, there, Uncle. Don't fret yourself." Miss Freemantle patted his arm.

She cast Morse a look as frigid as the crust of snow that blanketed the surrounding fields. Perhaps he'd only imagined her instant of vulnerability. "It's clear Sergeant Archer does not feel himself equal to the challenge of our wager."

Her words struck Morse like a leather glove whipped across his cheek. His pride, already piqued to quivering pitch, dove to take up the gauntlet.

"Challenge? You call that a challenge, to masquerade as some arrogant puppy of an officer? I've suffered enough of those fools that I could do it tomorrow, without your three months' tutoring.''

She appraised him with her eyes, and he returned the insult. Somewhere within him, Morse felt a flash of admiration for a worthy opponent and a yearning to win her admiration in return.

''Prove it, Sergeant. Take the wager.''

''I have nothing to prove to you, or to anyone else, Miss Freemantle.'' Morse felt reason and control slipping from his grasp like a greased rope, but he could not tamely swallow this woman's baiting.

''Admit it, Sergeant. You haven't the nerve to try.''

''I never heard such confounded rot.''

''It isn't rot.''

''''Tis.''

''Then you're up to the challenge?''

''Bloody right.'' The words were out of his mouth before Morse realized what he'd said. He saw a flicker of triumph in his opponent's striking eyes. ''I mean, no. I can't. I could, but I won't.''

''Now, now, Archer,'' interjected Sir Hugo. ''Don't tell me a Rifleman would go back on his word. You accepted. Heard it with my own two ears. I mean to hold you to it.''

Part of Morse longed to call back the acceptance he'd flung at Leonora Freemantle during their childish tit for tat. The greater part surrendered to a wave of relief that she had galled him into doing what he'd wanted to do all along.

''Since you've left me no choice, how soon can we start?''

Sir Hugo appeared to rouse himself from his amazement at Morse's abrupt turnabout. ''If the sawbones at Bramleigh will pronounce you fit enough, we can load your gear and be back to Laurelwood in time for tea.''

Morse stared at Leonora Freemantle with a gaze that held its own challenge. "That suits me."

His stomach growled just then, though the others politely ignored the sound. The notion of tea at Laurelwood set his mouth watering, and his stiff muscles yearned for the luxurious embrace of a feather bed. After a hard decade of soldiering, surely this Rifleman deserved a soft billet. Then he noticed Leonora Freemantle eyeing him with the speculative gaze of a drill sergeant sizing up a raw recruit. A shiver of apprehension ran through him.

Or was it excitement?

Chapter Three

A soft billet?

For the hundredth time in the past fortnight, Morse gave an ironic groan at the thought of that rose-colored dream. Rolling onto his stomach, he clamped the feather bolster over his head almost tight enough to suffocate him. It still wasn't enough to drown out the persistent tapping on his door.

"G'way, Dickon!" he hollered at the young footman. "Give me a few more minutes' sleep."

His plea was futile, and Morse knew it.

The tapping stopped, but that only meant Dickon had let himself in. As he'd been ordered to by that she-devil. Morse clamped his fingers onto the thick linen of the pillowcase.

It was no use.

Dickon, who must have weighed twenty stone, had fingers the size of country sausages. He removed the pillow from Morse's head with a restrained but irresistible force.

"Time to get up, sir," he rumbled in an apologetic tone. "Don't make me douse ye with the cold water, like yisterday."

With a growl of resignation Morse struggled out of bed

and let the footman help ready him for the day. It was a ritual he detested. More than ever, at this frigid hour long before dawn. However, Leonora Freemantle insisted he become accustomed to dealing with servants. Morse had discovered that, in all matters pertaining to him, Miss Freemantle's word was law.

Law be damned—it was tyranny!

"Dunno why you take on so, sir." Steaming water splashed into the washbasin from the kettle Dickon had brought with him. "When you was a Rifleman, didn't you have to be up at dawn?"

"Well…yes." Morse muttered the grudging admission as he took a chair and let Dickon lather him up for his morning shave.

An hour before dawn to be precise. Sir John Moore—God rest his soul—had drilled that habit into his Riflemen. Daybreak was often a time the enemy chose to attack, hoping to gain the advantage of surprise.

"But that's not the point."

As the big footman shaved him, employing an unexpectedly deft touch with the razor, Morse mulled over his grievances against Leonora Freemantle.

Contrary to what he'd expected, meals at Laurelwood were tortured affairs involving the proper deployment of a bewildering array of cutlery and crystal. If he made so much as one hapless mistake in the choice of his fork, Miss Freemantle was not above depriving him of whatever dish he was about to eat. Worse yet were the endless hours each day sitting at a desk, staring at a book until his eyes fairly crossed. Laboring over a piece of written work with his pen clenched almost to the breaking point.

"It all comes down to this, Dickon." Morse rinsed the residue of soap from his face. "I'm not much good at taking orders."

"G'way, sir." The footman handed Morse a pair of

buff-colored breeches. "Soldiering all those years and no good at taking orders?"

A piece at a time, Morse donned the articles of clothing Dickon held out for him. The apparel was all well tailored in the finest quality fabrics. When he glanced in the mirror, Morse grudged a fleeting grin at the fashionable dandy who stared back at him.

Still, his body itched for the old green jacket that had once marked him as a member of the elite Rifle Brigade.

"A green jacket's different, Dickon. The redcoats are drilled to follow orders without a second's thought, but a Rifleman's trained to think for himself. For all that, I was still a bit too independent for the Rifles. It landed me in trouble more than once. I'm well enough off if I respect the ability of my superiors and see the sense in what they're asking me to do. To take senseless orders from a fool who ranks me, though—that's my notion of hell."

Sticking a finger under the edge of his stock, he tugged in vain to loosen the wrapping of linen that hugged his throat like a noose.

"Buck up, sir." Dickon nudged him, flashing a broad wink. "It's Wednesday night, remember?"

"Wednesday night." Morse savored the words. The tension that bunched his shoulder muscles began to ebb.

Wednesday and Saturday nights were his only respite from the tyranny of General Freemantle. Without them, Morse was certain he'd have chucked the whole business, in spite of his debt to Sir Hugo.

True to his word, the old man had managed to dissuade the Board of Inquiry from pursuing charges against Morse, letting him muster out with no fuss.

"Think you can liberate us another few pints of that fine ale?" Morse asked the footman.

When Miss Freemantle went into the village on Wednesday and Saturday evenings, he took the opportunity to sneak off with Dickon for a pint or two in some deserted cranny of the house. While they drank and ate whatever cold collation Dickon could forage from the pantry, Morse told stories of his adventures as a Rifleman in the Fourth Somerset Regiment. It felt good to bask in the footman's soldier-struck admiration. In fact, it was almost enough to buttress Morse against Leonora Freemantle's persistent assault on his self-assurance.

"Better'n that sir. Do ye fancy a drop of hard cider?"

"Don't I just! Could do with a drop this very minute."

Dickon nodded his massive head in sympathy. "Be off, now, sir. Miss Leonora will be waitin' on ye. I'm apt to catch the edge of her tongue if yer late. It's the oddest thing. Before you came to the house I never heard a cross word from her. T'was all *Would ye be so kind* and *Might I trouble ye for this or that.* This past fortnight, though, she's been as cranky as a badger sow."

An involuntary smile rippled across Morse's lips. He was certain it would be his last before nightfall. No doubt, Leonora Freemantle could badger with the best of them. Not to mention carp, reproach and downright bully.

Army life had been hard and dangerous by times, Morse admitted to himself. Apart from the pitiful pay, it had not been entirely thankless. He'd earned his promotions, won the affection and respect of the men in his command, gained the trust of his superiors—at least those superiors whose opinion mattered to him.

At *Camp Laurelwood,* however, he was reminded day and night that he could do nothing right.

Morse forced his feet down each step of the darkened staircase toward the library. Every soldier's instinct in him shrank from tardiness. For ten years it had been dunned into him that he must be where he was expected, when he was expected, no matter what. The lives of his comrades might hang in the balance. He couldn't make himself believe it was of any consequence whether he started lessons now, or two hours from now. It was all a pack of nonsense anyhow.

With a grunt of disgust, he thrust open the library door.

Heaving an exasperated sigh, Leonora glanced at the mantel clock. Once again Morse Archer was a quarter of an hour late for their prebreakfast lessons. This, in spite of her having sent Dickon to wake him half an hour early. Little wonder General Wellington's Iberian campaign was all but lost, if he was commanding an army of surly idlers like her *star pupil*.

Drumming her fingers on the desktop, Leonora eyed the Latin grammar, open to a pitiful tenth page. Every day they slipped further and further behind on her meticulously constructed timetable. She had tried everything she could think of to challenge the man, but he obstinately refused to learn the most rudimentary Latin declension. His knowledge of English history was appalling. He couldn't tell Agincourt from Hastings, and she sometimes wondered if he knew that Henry the Fifth came before Henry the Eighth. As for his ignorance of literature...

She could have forgiven the man if he'd proven an obvious dullard, incapable of learning. But that was not the case. In his dinner table conversation with Sir Hugo, she caught glimpses of the knowledge he'd gained while soldiering abroad. Morse Archer was too clever by half. If only she could curb his stubborn refusal to apply himself.

She'd tried everything short of cajolery. For some reason she could not bring herself to use a soft approach with him. Perhaps because his physical presence unnerved her so. Often when she should have been correcting his atrocious penmanship, she found herself instead staring at his hands. Blatantly staring at his powerful, shapely hands. Imagining them taking steady aim with his rifle, clamped around a bottle of Spanish wine or spanning the waist of some sultry Dulcinea.

Then he would glance up and catch her watching him. And his eyes would twinkle with mockery. Leonora willed herself to think of something else before she gave way to a shriek of vexation. Distracting her thoughts was no easy matter. A nauseating lump of panic rose in her throat as she pictured the days and weeks slipping away with so painfully little to show for them. Despite his hollow boasts to the contrary, at the rate he was going Morse Archer would not pass for a butler let alone a gentleman.

And when the petty nobility of Bath laughed him out of town, she would have to forfeit the wager. Marry a man of her uncle's choosing. Surrender her dream of a school. Abandon the academic pursuits that were her only joy in life.

A briny mist stung her eyes.

Impatient with herself, Leonora pulled off her spectacles and roughly employed the cuff of her sleeve as a hand-kerchief. Not since the youngest years of her childhood had she allowed anyone or anything to drive her to tears. She was not about to yield that honor to a man like Morse Archer.

The library door burst open. Shutting it behind him with a bang that reverberated through the room, Morse lumbered over to the table and dropped heavily into his seat.

With a hiccup, somewhere between a gasp and a sob, Leonora pushed her spectacles back on again and stiffened her posture.

"If you learn nothing else from me in the next two and a half months, Morse Archer, I trust you will at least cultivate the civility of knocking before you barge into a room."

He glared up at her, one eyebrow cocked insolently.

"Why should I waste my time knocking? Weren't you expecting me?"

Leonora made herself glare back, hoping he would not notice the redness of her eyes. "I was expecting you a full quarter of an hour ago, as you should be well aware. That does not excuse the rudeness of your conduct. As penalty for lateness, we will work an additional half hour before taking breakfast."

She ignored the groan with which he greeted this news. "And as penalty for your lapse in manners, I will expect you to spend an additional half hour reading history this evening before you retire."

For some reason Morse showed no obvious dismay at this second punishment. Leonora was tempted to raise it to an hour.

"We have wasted quite enough time this morning. May I remind you that we have only ten weeks remaining until we must go to Bath. Let us begin with a review of yesterday's Latin lesson. Translate the verb *to eat,* and conjugate it in the present tense if you please."

"To eat?" Morse lounged back in his chair, not so much as glancing at the book open before him. "Last night's dinner was so long ago, I'm not sure I recall the meaning of that word in English, let alone Latin."

"Keep this up," shot Leonora, her patience worn to a thread, "and it could be several hours before you get the chance to refresh your memory. Kindly apply yourself to the lesson and provide me with the translation and conjugation of the verb."

Morse slammed his Latin grammar shut. "This is lunacy. Your wager is to pass me off as a gentleman soldier, not the Arch-bloody-bishop of Canterbury! If you'd just let me—"

"That is quite enough, sir!" Leonora's simmering resentment threatened to boil over. "I am the teacher here.

This wager is to test *my* skill. You understood that when you agreed to take part. *I* decide upon the curriculum. *I* choose the subjects. *I* set the lessons. You'd do well to master the role of pupil before you try usurping mine. Now let's get on with it."

She reopened the book and thrust it under his nose. If he insisted on behaving like a spoiled child, that's how she would treat him from now on.

"Conjugation of the verb *to eat,* repeat after me…" She pointed out each word as she read it.

To her amazement, Morse did repeat after her. However, he did so in a flat, apathetic tone that left no doubt he'd forgotten each word the moment it left his lips.

For the next two hours Leonora persevered, bending over her pupil, straining to avoid any physical contact between them. As her outstretched finger glided beneath each line of text, she spoke the words of a dead language. Morse parroted her in a voice that sounded all but dead.

Her back and shoulder began to ache. Hunger gnawed at her innards. Worst of all, a painfully acute awareness of Morse Archer—the sight, sound and scent of him—set her senses aquiver. By half past eight, she wanted nothing more than to pick up the heavy Latin grammar and hurl it through the library window.

"Celo, celare, celavi, celatus." Morse heard the words coming out of his mouth, as though from a distance. The page of Latin grammar was there before him and his eyes were open, but he did not see it.

"Habeo, habere, habui, habitus." So much of army life had been numbingly boring physical routine. Morse had fallen into the habit of letting his hands or feet go through the familiar motions, while his mind fixed on some point of interest.

"Audio, audiere, audivi, auditus." His speech organs

produced the words by rote, while Morse found himself absorbed in the contemplation of Leonora's hand.

Her fingers were slender and tapered. The nails were neatly kept, like five tiny translucent seashells. For all its daintiness, it was neither weak nor vapid. Instead it moved with an expressive, purposeful grace, which Morse found fascinating and strangely beautiful.

He scarcely realized what he was doing when his own hand reached for hers. She froze. With a stifled gasp, her recitation of Latin verbs ceased.

Once, in India, Morse had handled a priceless religious artifact, exquisitely carved in luminous pale jade. He held Leonora's hand with the same breathless reverence, savoring its warmth and smoothness. It seemed the most natural impulse in the world to lift it to his lips in homage.

His curious trance shattered when Leonora ripped her hand from his grasp.

She found her voice again. "What is the meaning of this? How dare you take such liberties?"

Her face a livid crimson and her eyes gaping wide, she backed toward the door.

"I was just noticing what lovely hands you have." Morse wondered that such a little thing had obviously upset her so. "I didn't mean to offend you."

She stared at her hand as if she was seeing it for the first time, and was not pleased in the least with what she beheld. "You would do well to take more notice of your studies, Sergeant Archer, and less of my...person." The last word came out in a strangled squeak.

Morse endeavored to suppress a smile. He had never imagined his icy, implacable martinet could appear so flustered. And over such a trifle.

"Since you are obviously not...attending to the lesson, perhaps we had better adjourn...for breakfast. Afterward,

I expect you to read the next twenty pages of Mr. Butler's *Hudebras.*''

Morse opened his mouth to ask where she would be while he was reading. Before he could voice the question, though, Leonora had slipped out the door and fled.

She never did come to breakfast.

For the first time since setting foot in Laurelwood, Morse was able to relax and enjoy a meal in peace. As he tucked ravenously into a plate of eggs and broiled veal kidneys, he pondered the unaccountable events of the morning. What was there in an innocent touch and a trifling compliment to throw Leonora Freemantle into such a bother? He had no success in puzzling it out.

After a leisurely breakfast he returned to the library and found it deserted. For lack of any better diversion, he did read a few pages of *Hudebras.* When it failed to stir his interest, he got up and walked over to the window.

The bright winter sunshine and the steady drip of water from the eaves told Morse the day must be mild. Reasoning that a bit of fresh air might revive his powers of concentration, he called for his hat, greatcoat and walking stick.

Ambling along the path between high cherry laurel hedges, Morse found himself able to bear more and more weight on his injured leg. With a bit of regular exercise, perhaps he would regain his former easy stride.

By the time he returned to the house, he was in a better humor than he'd enjoyed since coming to Laurelwood. Whatever he had done to disrupt the endless routine of lessons, it was well worth trying again. If compliments flustered Leonora so... Morse chuckled at the very thought of how she'd respond if he called her by that name. Surely she had other features he could admire the next time he needed a respite from his studies.

Her slender, graceful neck, for instance. If he nuzzled

her sensitive nape, she might take to her bed for several days with a fit of the vapors.

Morse grinned to himself, anticipating her reaction.

Immensely pleased at the cleverness of his plan, he took up his book again and devoured nearly a hundred pages of it by teatime.

Chapter Four

He had *kissed* her hand.

Several hours later it still tingled faintly and the memory of Morse's lips on her skin continued to prompt a most ridiculous blush in Leonora's cheeks. She had retreated to the sanctuary of her bedchamber, not trusting herself to face him again that day. On no account must that man see the foolish reaction he'd excited in her.

Pacing the carpet runner beside her bed, Leonora tried to dismiss the whole episode for the silly trifle she knew it to be. No doubt Morse Archer had kissed the hand of many a woman. More than their hands, too, unless she missed her guess.

Through the window she spied him striding the grounds of Laurelwood, his limp much less noticeable than when he'd first arrived. Some unaccountable force kept her rooted to the spot, watching Morse Archer until he disappeared from view.

Quite against her will, Leonora found herself slipping into a shameful reverie. Unbidden images cascaded into her mind, piquing her senses. Of all the places on women's bodies where the attractive sergeant *might* have bestowed kisses.

On their lips, of course. Perhaps a bare neck or shoulder had enticed him to nuzzle. Might he have dropped one, delicate as a whisper, upon some pretty ear? Or pressed his face into a head of tousled tresses?

As each notion took hold of her, Leonora's hand—her *kissed hand*—strayed to that part of her own person. Setting her lips aquiver as one fingertip brushed over them, gliding from shoulder, to neck, to ear. Extracting the pins from her hair.

When at last it fell in a fine, ebony billow around her shoulders, her strangely possessed hand reached up and threaded her fingers through the strands. Feeling and appreciating its delicate, silky texture for perhaps the first time in her life.

Catching sight of herself in the looking glass, Leonora almost did not recognize the face that stared back at her. That woman had a strange softness about her features. It made her look far younger than Leonora's twenty-seven sensible years. Even her severe little spectacles could not disguise the dreamy shimmer in her gray-green eyes.

Leonora had seen that look before. Her stomach curdled and her throat constricted at the memory of it.

Mother.

Downy and pensive. Humming a little tune to herself. Fondling a nosegay of posies from her latest admirer. Such looks had meant only one thing. Clarissa Freemantle had welcomed a new suitor into her life. To Leonora, it had always spelled trouble.

Setting her mouth in a taut line, she squared her shoulders and willed that mooning creature in the mirror to vacate the premises forthwith. She would *not* repeat her mother's mistakes, least of all over a shiftless, insolent ex-Rifleman that circumstances had forced upon her.

Leonora thrust her spectacles back up to the bridge of her nose. Plucking a hairbrush from the top of her dressing table, she coerced her locks into submission, plaiting them into such tight braids they made her head ache.

Dickon, the footman, almost dropped his water kettle the next morning when he arrived at Morse's door to find the sergeant already awake.

"Don't just stand there gaping, man." Morse plucked the steaming kettle from Dickon's hand and splashed a generous measure into his washbasin. "Lay out my clothes while I shave."

"I didn't reckon to find you in such fine fettle this morning, sir." The burly footman rubbed his forehead. "Not after the quantity of cider you put away last night and how merry we was making."

Morse worked his shaving soap into a good lather and smeared it on his face, inhaling the tangy aroma. "I've been up before dawn and in the thick of a battle after far worse debauches than last night's wee tipple, man."

He whistled a few bars of a Portuguese drinking song, the words of which he had never understood. "Sometimes a fellow's all the better in the morning for a spot of revelry the night before."

"If you say so, sir." Dickon did not sound convinced. Clearly, he was paying a somewhat higher price for their evening's merriment.

"I do say so, Dickon." Morse rinsed his face and dried it off, flashing his reflection a wolfish grin. He wasn't certain what had brought about his sudden bout of energy and high spirits. Perhaps his congenial evening with Dickon accounted for it. Or perhaps yesterday's unscheduled *holiday* from his studies.

Or could it be…?

The fellow in the looking glass grinned more broadly still. Had he guessed the truth? That, at last, Morse had found himself an effective weapon in his running conflict with Miss Leonora Freemantle.

Until yesterday she had possessed all the artillery, not to mention strategic field position. His only recourse had been a dogged refusal to capitulate. Then, just when he'd thought himself all but beaten, Morse had discovered his own tactical advantage—Leonora's agitated reaction to a little harmless flirtation.

This set them on even ground at last. The prospect of a well-matched contest stirred Morse's blood as nothing had since the rout at Bucaso.

He eyed the suit Dickon had chosen for him. "Don't suppose you can find something more colorful by way of a waistcoat? If a fellow has to act the gentleman, might as well look the part, eh?"

With a glance that questioned if he truly could be Morse Archer, Dickon rummaged in the wardrobe and produced a brocade garment of forest green shot with gold.

Once he had donned his gear, Morse looked himself over in the mirror, approving what he saw. Even that tiny hint of green in the waistcoat reminded him of his Rifle Brigade uniform. It heartened him for whatever battles might lie ahead today.

He let Dickon give his coat a final brush, then Morse descended the stairs to the drawing room as rapidly as his injured leg would allow. Finding the place dark and deserted, he rubbed his hands with gleeful anticipation.

If Sir John Moore had drummed one precept into the minds of the Rifle Brigade, it was the benefit of being first to arrive on the field of battle. One gained superiority of position together with the element of surprise.

Morse lit several candles and picked up the volume of *Hudebras* he'd been reading the previous day. Settling into his chair, he affected an air of one who had been in the throes of diligent study for some time. Fortunately, he did not have to keep up the pose for long before he heard Leonora's footsteps.

Something stirred inside him at the sound, and he had to admit it was more than the anticipation of catching her off guard. His lips warmed at the memory of kissing her hand.

As the door eased open, Morse tried to rein in the eager grin that tugged at the corners of his mouth.

"You are late, Miss Freemantle."

Leonora gasped at the sound of Morse Archer's voice. In the very next instant she berated herself for letting him catch her off guard—again.

"Considering this is the first morning you have managed to arrive on time, Sergeant, it ill-behooves you to criticize."

Blast the man to kingdom come! She had been anxious to reassert her authority this morning and already he had put her on the defensive.

Morse closed his book. Had he read that much since yesterday? She heartily doubted it.

Leaning back in his chair, he swept her with a look that made Leonora break out in gooseflesh from head to toe.

"You mistake me, Miss Freemantle." His tone sounded far too cordial for her liking. The warm baritone wrapped itself around her heart. "I didn't mean to criticize, only to state the fact. If you took a few extra minutes to dress and fix your hair, I would be the last to complain. You look particularly charming this morning."

Her heart hammered and her stomach clenched. How had he guessed that she'd dithered a full ten minutes in her choice of a gown? That, against all logic, she'd spent more precious minutes dressing her hair in a marginally less severe style.

Her feet itched to flee, but Leonora stood her ground.

"I will thank you not to mock me, Sergeant. I am well aware I look a fright this morning."

There'd been nothing she could do to remedy the sleepless smudges beneath her eyes.

"Not that it is any business of yours *how* I look." She strode to the table. "I am here to teach you, not to provide you with an object to scrutinize. Is that understood?"

If she expected his usual surly retort, it was not forthcoming this morning. "I understand you better every day, Miss Freemantle."

She could find no fault with his words, or with the cheerful tone in which they were uttered. Yet, Leonora could not escape the feeling that Morse Archer was having a sharp little jest at her expense.

Retrenching to more solid conversational ground, she pointed to the open book in his hand. "I see you have shown *some* ambition in your reading course."

Teacher's intuition whispered that she ought to appeal to his sense of pride by commending his initiative. Feminine suspicion warned her not to plunge headlong after what was in all likelihood a ruse. "What do you think of Colonel Hudibras's adventures thus far?"

She waited, in smug assurance that he would hem and haw with embarrassment and in the end admit he hadn't read a word.

"It's interesting enough reading, I suppose."

Leave it to Archer to try bluffing his way out.

Before she could devise a probing question to expose his ignorance, he continued. "I don't think much of the colonel, truth be told. Treats that squire of his something shameful. When he made Ralpho take that whipping in his place, I wanted to leap into the book and throttle the blackguard."

There could be no denying his violent indignation. Morse's emphatic brows knit together and his jaw jutted forward. He had read the material, after all. What's more, he had been moved by it.

The notion tugged at Leonora and would not let her go.

In a flash Morse's umbrage changed to chagrin. "I've known too many ranking idiots like Colonel Hudibras in my day," he muttered. For the first time that morning, his gaze faltered before hers.

"I dislike the character quite as intensely as you do, Sergeant Archer," she confessed, taking a seat beside him. What galled her was the colonel's mercenary pursuit of the widow. Like Morse, she had known too many loathsome creatures of that ilk. "Read on and I promise you'll enjoy the part where he gets his comeuppance."

"That I shall." He leafed through the volume searching for his place.

"Would it surprise you to hear that the author is no fonder of Hudibras than we are?" Leonora pulled her chair closer to his. "It was Mr. Butler's intent to satirize the Puritans, who had ruled England after the defeat of King Charles the First."

Morse looked up from the book. "Are you saying there was a time we had no king?"

A lively discussion sprang up between them, about the history of the English Civil War, Cromwell's Puritan Commonwealth and the eventual restoration of the Stuart monarchy. Then they went on to consider the nature of satire and its origins in the Greek literary tradition.

Leonora could scarcely believe it when Dickon gave a tentative knock on the sitting room door and inquired whether they wished to take breakfast that morning, after all. She glanced at the mantel clock, amazed to discover the hands within a few minutes of ten.

"I apologize, Sergeant Archer," she stammered. "I had no idea the time had gotten away from me to such an extent. You'll be starved."

He appeared almost as surprised by the hour as she. "I *am* hungry," he confessed. "Though I can't say I noticed it until this minute. I fear I got caught up in your talk. You have a knack for making this dry-as-dust history and literature come to life, Miss Freemantle."

His dark eyes glowed with admiration. Some long dormant feminine faculty within Leonora assured her it was quite genuine.

Just then she became acutely aware of his knee pressing against hers. How long had *that* been going on? Even through the substantial fabric of her skirt and his buckskin breeches, it had kindled a warmth between them. A rush of that warmth wafted from Leonora's knee to her thighs.

She almost toppled the chair in her haste to put a safe distance between them.

"We had better get to breakfast before everything is stone cold or burned to a crisp." She gasped the words, hard-pressed to catch her breath. "I fear Cook will be cross with us."

She fled to the breakfast room before Morse Archer could reply. By the time he sauntered in, she had regained at least a crumb of her composure. Still, she was too flustered to correct his mess hall manners.

Several times he spoke with his mouth full. He ate bits of ham off the point of his knife. Over coffee, he hunched forward, resting his elbows upon the table. Had she made no headway at all with him in the past fortnight?

For all her disquiet on that score, Leonora had to admit their late breakfast was the most pleasant meal she had passed in his company.

One of the most pleasant she had ever passed, come to that.

Morse Archer picked up the thread of their prior conversation, plying her with any number of thoughtful, pertinent questions about the roots of the English Civil War and its effect upon the Scottish uprising of the last century. Evidently he had been listening to her and retaining what he'd learned. What made *this* morning's lesson so different from those of the past two weeks?

Could it be because…?

Leonora could not deny the eagerness with which he hung on her words. The strange, piquant way he gazed at her from time to time. Was it possible he had taken a fancy to her?

She came to herself with a start, realizing he had just spoken to her. Really, she would have to exercise a good deal more self-control from now on.

"I asked if you would care for another splash of coffee, Miss Leonora."

"I—" No other words would come just then. He had spoken her Christian name for the first time, each syllable gliding off his tongue like spiced honey. She had never thought a word could sound so beautiful.

"Yes—p-please," she finally managed to stammer, though the prim schoolmistress within her protested. The beverage was a stimulant, after all. The last thing she needed at the moment was further stimulation.

Leonora cast about for any topic that promised to distract her from this adolescent preoccupation with Morse. Good heavens! Now she was thinking of him by his Christian name, as well.

"I hope Uncle Hugo didn't miss our company at breakfast." The sentence erupted from her in a breathless rush.

Morse's eyebrows raised. "Did he not tell you he was going off to London? Of course—you weren't at dinner last night. He said he'd be away for a few days. Some urgent matter of business. I'm afraid it'll be just the two of us until he gets back."

An unaccustomed giddiness expanded inside Leonora, as though she was one of those newfangled hot-air balloons inflated too quickly. She tried pulling herself back to earth, without much success.

"We must return to work now, Sergeant Archer." How she despised the beseeching note she heard in her voice.

"That's what I'm here for." He walked around the table and pulled out her chair.

The backs of his fingers grazed her upper arm. Had it been accidental, or deliberate? Either way, it set her head spinning and her breath skipping.

Leonora made a last desperate attempt to regain mastery of the situation, and of herself. Her entire childhood had been spent at the mercy of forces beyond her control. At least she had been mistress of her own feelings—cool and detached where her mother was passionate and imprudent.

Now, this man, with the most insignificant look, word or touch, threatened to overpower her carefully cultivated composure and turn her whole world on its ear.

She jerked her arm away from his hand. "We must return to our Latin studies."

When he met her suggestion with a groan, she flared up at him. "I warned you from the start this would not be a stroll through the park, Sergeant Archer! You boasted you were equal to the challenge, but until this morning I have seen no sign of it. At this rate, we will be laughed out of Bath. You will never see your estate in the colonies and I—"

She bit her tongue. It was none of his business what his indolence would cost her. If he knew, he would only take advantage of the power it gave him over her fate.

Fortunately he quit the breakfast room without asking her to finish her sentence. In all likelihood he did not care a whit about her dire stakes in the wager.

Summoning up every ounce of frosty aplomb she could muster, Leonora stalked off after him. They had dabbled in quite enough sensational subjects for the day. The rest of their lessons would be given over to mathematics, dead languages and anything else she could furnish that might throw cold water on her growing preoccupation with Morse Archer.

Leonora's blatant insult to his diligence kept Morse focused on his studies until almost teatime. To his surprise, he found the Latin beginning to make sense. And he had always been good with numbers, particularly as they applied to situations in real life.

How many rounds could a Rifleman fire in so many minutes? How fast would a company have to march to be at such a place by such a time?

It still irked him that none of their lessons showed any practical application to Leonora's stated goal of passing him off as a gentleman. Several times he had tried getting the point across to her. On each occasion she had almost bitten his head off for presuming to question her authority.

On that score, she put him in mind of two inept officers who'd been his superiors in Portugal. Their blinkered stupidity and blank refusal to accept advice from anyone of lower rank had contributed largely to the fiasco that had ended his military career.

And Lieutenant Peverill's life.

Looking up suddenly from his book, he caught Leonora staring at him. Fresh from thoughts of his young lieutenant, Morse recognized an appealing family resemblance in her face.

"I never served under a better officer than your cousin." He wasn't certain what propelled those words out of him.

To his surprise, Leonora did not order him back to work at once. Neither did she question what had prompted him to speak of the lieutenant for the first time since coming to Laurelwood.

"Cousin Wesley mentioned you in his letters. I think he would be pleased to know you're here."

Her little chin, so intrepid for all its delicacy, betrayed a subtle quiver. Behind the bastion of her spectacles, Morse thought he spied a fine mist rising in Leonora's eyes.

Ordinarily, Morse Archer was not a man who had any patience for tears or overwrought outbursts. Yet something launched him out of his chair and to Leonora's side. His hands closed over her shoulders.

"I'm sorry I mentioned him. I didn't mean to distress you, honestly."

At the slightest provocation he would have taken her in his arms. But Leonora gave him no opportunity. And no quarter.

Twisting free of his chaste touch, she flew to the opposite corner of the room and pretended an exaggerated interest in whatever she saw out the window. The steady drip of icicles melting from the eaves, perhaps.

"You have worked well today, Sergeant." She did not bother to turn and address him face-to-face. "As a reward, you are excused from lessons for the remainder of the day."

Earlier in the week Morse would have welcomed the news with a whoop of glee. Now he cursed himself roundly. What should have been a reward felt instead like…exile.

Chapter Five

Leonora listened to Morse's retreating footsteps with an exasperating mixture of relief and regret.

If she had not fled the warm invitation of his hands upon her shoulders, if she had not dismissed him from the room with her next breath, she might have surrendered to her impulses. She might have pivoted into his powerful arms and wept a woman's weak tears against his sturdy shoulder.

The prospect tempted her, as much from curiosity as...anything else. She had no experience of seeking comfort from another person. Mother had always been too much in need of support herself to lend it elsewhere. And Leonora would have died under torture before betraying a hint of weakness to any of her detested stepfathers. By the time she had come to live with Aunt Harriet and Uncle Hugo, she was well past the age for tearful outbursts.

Yet somewhere in the mists of early memory there lurked the phantom fancy of a comforting embrace. The faint musk of horses and tobacco. The croon of a deep, affectionate voice. The subtle scratch of a serge coat against her cheek. It had been her one and only experience of security.

And it had been ripped away from her long before she was able to understand why.

Since then she had learned to rely upon herself alone. Not upon her looks, as she had seen some foolish women do. In time, creamy skin would wrinkle. Bright eyes would lose their sparkle. Shiny hair its luster.

Intelligence, determination and self-control—these would stand the test the time. Neither were they a happy accident of nature. They could be learned and properly cultivated in any girl so inclined.

Leonora returned from her reverie to find her hands balled into tight fists. So tight, in fact, that her fingernails bit into her palms.

She was determined to cultivate those serviceable virtues in other young women whom fate had placed at a disadvantage. In her school, she would recover the kind of security she vaguely recalled from her childhood.

But how would she ever win her school if she didn't coax a better effort out of Sergeant Archer? He had shown some improvement today, in his attitude at least. Would it be enough?

"Oh, Wes," she whispered. If her cousin's spirit lingered anywhere in the mortal world, it would be here at Laurelwood. "You won his devotion and disciplined him into a good soldier. What am I doing wrong?"

No answer came. Nor had she expected one, being too fiercely practical to believe in communication from beyond the grave. Still, Leonora could not help feeling there was a lesson to be learned from Cousin Wesley's style of command.

Though, what it was, she had yet to fathom.

"Up early again, sir?" Dickon handed Morse the kettle. "If you don't mind my saying so, it makes a pleasant change from having to drag you out of bed."

"Pleasanter for us both, Dickon." Morse began to whistle a marching tune as he shaved.

"If you don't mind my asking, sir—" the footman delved in the wardrobe for Morse's clean linen "—what brought on the change?"

Morse's razor froze in midstroke. He scrutinized his reflection in the glass as though to ask *that* Morse Archer to explain himself.

When the fellow unhelpfully mimicked his own puzzlement, Morse was forced to stammer, "I—couldn't say—for certain."

Recovering a shred of his old sangfroid, he added, "Just bowing to necessity, I suppose. Or getting used to the new routine. There wasn't any need to get up early at the hospital."

Dickon appeared satisfied with the explanation, for he nodded and continued his work without further comment.

Resuming his shave with a somewhat less steady hand, Morse was less convinced by his own rather lame reasoning. Bowing to necessity did not explain the recent lightness in his step or the merry tune that hovered on his lips of late, begging to be whistled. His inexplicable eagerness to begin the day must be more than merely adapting to a new routine.

He continued to puzzle the matter as he dressed. Conflicting impulses jousted within him. One urged haste, to get his clothes on and proceed downstairs as quickly as possible. The other counseled patience. Take his time in tying his stock. Let Dickon buff his boots properly. Arrive for his morning studies looking his best.

As he set off for the library, at last, a disquieting thought struck Morse. If he hadn't known better, he might have suspected he was trying to make a favorable impression on Leonora Freemantle.

But that was rank nonsense.

First of all, he had long since ceased to *strive* for any woman's regard. The kind of female he liked, Morse attracted and won effortlessly.

Which led to the second consideration—Miss Leonora Freemantle was anything but the kind of female he usually preferred. She was too bookish, too determined.

Too challenging.

Was there such a thing? The notion brought him to an abrupt halt halfway down the stairs. All his life he had thrived on challenge and novelty. But not where women were concerned!

And besides, what would Miss Freemantle want with a chap like him? Ill-bred. Uneducated.

Even if he did fancy her—which he most emphatically did not—he could not afford to dally with a woman above his station. Not again.

So Morse told himself as he slipped into the study, uncertain whether to encourage or to suppress his eagerness to begin the day's lessons.

"Early two days in a row, Sergeant Archer?" Leonora's voice startled him. Roused him? "To what do we owe this unexpected development?"

Morse felt his cheeks begin to sting. A reaction to the shaving soap, perhaps?

No. It was more than that. Like any opponent worthy of his steel, Leonora had neatly turned the tables on him. Yesterday he had mounted a surprise attack, exploiting his advantage of being first to take the field. She had not let him enjoy that superior position for two days running.

In spite of himself, a grin of something like admiration rippled across Morse's lips. He recalled a word Lieutenant Peverill had sometimes used when an opponent proved wilier than he'd expected. *Touché.*

Touché, Miss Freemantle. Touché, indeed.

Too late, Morse tried to cover his confusion with a

scowl. "Why am I early? Perhaps because I want to win that bet with Sir Hugo as much as you do. Have you any idea what a fresh start in the colonies would mean to a man like me?"

Leonora stepped forward into the dim light of a single candle. No doubt about it—she'd been lying in wait to surprise him. Her smile, a rare and unexpected favor, erased Morse's annoyance.

"I think I have quite a good idea what it will mean, Sergeant. That is why I suggested it to my uncle. I hope the knowledge and skills I can impart to the girls at my school will provide them with similar opportunities."

The notion seized Morse and all but throttled him. "You suggested Sir Hugo offer me an estate in the colonies?"

She nodded. "Someone had to. Uncle is the most generous man in the world, but he can also be the most selfish in some ways. Or maybe *selfish* isn't the right word. Just unimaginative when it comes to understanding what other people want."

Her voice died away to a bemused murmur. "He can't fathom why they should want anything but what he wants *for* them."

And what did Sir Hugo want for his bluestocking niece that she didn't? Morse found himself wondering.

Leonora seemed to become aware of his presence again, as though she'd been musing out loud. She blushed, a rosy cast Morse could easily detect even in the dim light of the library.

He detected other things, as well.

Like the wistful luster in her gray-green eyes. Perhaps it was the soft green shade of her gown that set them off so becomingly. This was the first time he'd seen her in anything but the dullest of dark hues. Lighter ones suited her complexion and coloring far better.

Why would a woman go out of her way to look unattractive, when in fact—?

"Sergeant Archer?"

Morse suddenly realized she had spoken his name for the second time. "Sorry. Woolgathering. The early hour, I expect. You were saying?"

"I was saying, perhaps we should take our seats and apply ourselves to today's lesson. If we wish to have any hope of winning the wager, that is."

"Of course." Morse had the unpleasant sensation that he was losing command of the situation, and himself.

Then he remembered his secret weapon.

Striding toward their study table, he tried to disguise the hitch in his step. With a flourish, he pulled out Leonora's chair and beckoned her to sit.

"To be frank, Miss Leonora, the inducement of your uncle's wager is only part of my impatience to begin work this morning."

Casting him a wary glance, she took the seat he offered. "Indeed? And what might the other part be?"

Morse settled into his usual place on the wider side of the table. During the course of yesterday's lesson, his chair had migrated to his teacher's end of the table.

Now as he leaned close to her, he spoke in a quiet voice that suggested intimacy. "Can you not guess…Leonora?"

The catch in her breath betrayed the lady's awareness of the missing *Miss,* and all that its absence implied.

Before she could respond, Morse supplied the answer. "It's a rare dolt of a fellow who wouldn't grasp at the chance to spend all day in the company of such a fetching lass."

Some scrap of insight warned Morse he was venturing far too close to the truth with his flattery.

Another thought drove that one from his mind altogether. What if Leonora reacted to his comment as she had to his previous liberties—bidding him away, or bustling off herself?

That *had* been his original plan, hadn't it? Yet, at that moment, nothing could have been farther from Morse's desire.

To his massive relief, Leonora dismissed his fawning with an ironic lift of one brow and a toss of her head. "Really, Sergeant, we must put you to work with a dictionary. A woman of twenty-sev—of my years, hardly qualifies as a *lass*."

Touché again, Leonora!

"That's as may be. What man in his right mind wants the company of a simpering miss?" Morse took up his Latin grammar, suddenly disinclined to press his advantage and risk frightening her away.

Why did it frighten her? he wondered—the romantic attentions of a man. Indignation or outrage, he could have understood from a woman of her character. Her anxious agitation puzzled and intrigued him.

As did the lady herself.

Though clearly reluctant to pursue their conversation further, Leonora Freemantle could not resist a parting comment. "In my experience, a simpering miss is precisely what most men do prefer. Now if you will indulge me by turning to page forty-three, Sergeant Archer. Perhaps we can attempt a short translation of Livy."

Not content to let her have the last word on *most men*'s taste in women, he muttered, "More fools, them."

Almost as if he meant it.

Of course he hadn't meant it.

Leonora reminded herself of the obvious several times as she and Morse struggled over the Latin translation.

Still, part of her felt ridiculously grateful he'd said it—sincere or not.

How many times a day, during her girlhood, had Mother admonished her to get her nose out of a book, lest she never land a husband?

Every time, Leonora had clenched her lips to keep from hurling a disrespectful retort. If her mother's later husbands were representative of the marriage pool, she would prefer to not *fish* for one at all.

Little had Mother guessed that she had taken the warning as wise counsel. Everything Mother cautioned to avoid—unflattering clothes, spectacles, too much book-learning, Leonora had taken pains to acquire. For a husband was obviously someone to be eluded at all costs.

All the same, something in her had hungered for the occasional pretty gown, the odd dance at a ball. Even, now and then, the counterfeit flattery of a handsome man.

Thinking of handsome men...

To her dismay, Leonora found herself hovering over Morse's broad shoulder, prompting him when his translation faltered. The muted scent of his shaving soap and the rich cadence of his voice set her senses reeling.

They made her long to lean closer still, until she succumbed to the invitation of his thick, chestnut hair—running her fingers through it, or nuzzling it with her cheek.

And if she did—how might he react? What might he do in return?

Certainly Morse Archer had betrayed more interest in her than any other man ever had. Even before she'd begun making subtle *improvements* in her appearance. Apart from his rapidly healing leg injury, he was a healthy, vigorous, virile specimen of manhood. One who'd been denied the company of women for some little time. Yet she had no fear of catching him for a husband.

The notion took Leonora's breath away.

That was the subject of the wager, after all. He was abetting her quest to avoid marriage. And if they failed, she would have to marry some aristocratic half-wit of Uncle Hugo's choosing.

With a shudder of distaste, she banished that thought from her mind. Her preoccupation with Morse Archer had a will of its own, however. It would not be banished.

So Leonora reached a compromise with herself.

Uncle Hugo would be gone for a few days. Apart from the servants, she and Morse had Laurelwood to themselves. Perhaps tonight, after dinner, she might invite him to take a glass of port with her in the drawing room. They could put their studies aside and simply *talk*. About his experiences as a soldier. His plans for the future. Suddenly she was hungry to know everything about him.

Or she might offer to play the pianoforte. She imagined Morse sitting beside her, or leaning over her shoulder to read the words from her sheet music.

An unguarded sigh escaped from between her lips.

"Is something wrong?" Morse turned, then, to look at her.

Leonora knew she should pull herself away. Stand straight. Take a few steps back.

Her body refused to cooperate.

It hung there, bent over Morse, scant inches separating them. They could not have held that position for more than a few seconds, Leonora later reasoned. But in that time, as his eyes locked on hers and the brief space between them fairly shimmered with heat, it took all the self-control of a lifetime to not trespass that tiny distance and press her lips to his.

A tentative tap on the library door boomed like a cannonade in Leonora's ears.

Seized by a spasm of shame, she wrenched herself away from Morse and called, "Yes. What is it?" in a high, breathless voice.

Dickon pushed the door ajar and peeked in. "Pardo

me, miss, but you did give orders I was to knock if you and Sergeant Archer hadn't come to breakfast by nine.''

Had she said that? Leonora's thoughts whirled so that she could not swear to it.

"Thank you." Her words came in little gasps. "We'll be along in a moment."

Morse rose from his chair and stretched. The way his muscles bunched under the tight fabric of his breeches made Leonora's mouth go dry. There were so many things she didn't know about men. And until this week, she hadn't cared to find out. Now her freshly whetted curiosity knew no bounds.

"I think you could do with a good plate of breakfast and a strong cup of tea." Morse cast her a solicitous look. "You don't seem quite yourself this morning."

It was all Leonora could do to keep from agreeing vocally.

She wasn't herself. At least not the *self* she had shown the world for the past two decades.

Morse Archer's obvious interest in her, and her curiosity about him, had kindled some long-quiescent ember of whimsy and excitement within her. Suddenly she was most anxious to see where it might take her.

Acting on a daring impulse, she reached for Morse's arm. "I am feeling a trifle light-headed." No lie, that. "Will you be so kind as to steady me on our way to breakfast?"

Her request appeared to catch him off guard. "I—don't see why not," he sputtered.

"We must make an effort to polish your social graces, Sergeant. The polite reply to a lady would have been, 'I'd be honored, miss.'"

An embarrassed grin made him look endearingly boyish. "I *am* honored, Miss Leonora. Happy to be of service."

She laughed. For the first time in how long? "You're a quick student when you choose to be, Morse."

The intimacy of his Christian name was out of her mouth before she realized it. The word felt very much at home on her tongue.

For a wonder, he politely refrained from comment, pulling out her chair from the breakfast table and making sure she was well settled before taking the seat opposite her.

Morse tucked into breakfast with his usual relish. Scarcely a wonder after the poor food he must have suffered during his days as a soldier. For her part, Leonora could not summon up much appetite.

Perhaps the odd sensations she was experiencing were only the symptoms of some malady, after all.

Chapter Six

"**Y**ou're looking very...well, this evening, Miss Free-mantle." As he watched Leonora descend the staircase, Morse congratulated himself on his restraint.

Part of him wanted to pay her a much more extravagant compliment. Tell her that the warm rose hue of her gown brought matching roses to her cheeks. Mention how the candlelight played frets of gold and copper through her loosely pinned hair.

Some wiser instinct urged caution. He did not wish to frighten her away tonight.

"Why, thank you, Sergeant Archer."

Was it his imagination, or did she stand a little straighter, hold her head a fraction higher?

She awarded him a smile, glancing up suddenly through dense dark lashes. In any other woman, Morse might have suspected a hint of mischief or flirtation in such a look.

"Whatever slight indisposition I suffered this morning, I appear to have recovered."

"Then you won't need my arm to steady you?" Morse cocked his elbow anyway.

"Perhaps not." A teasing note warmed her words. "May I take it just the same, simply because I wish to?"

The corners of Morse's lips spread wide. "The best reason in the world for doing anything."

They strolled into the dining room, where the long mahogany table had been set quite differently than for past meals. At those, Sir Hugo had occupied the head of the table while Morse and Leonora sat opposite each other halfway down the length of it. Tonight, their places had been set at one end, near the hearth, leaving the rest of the table empty.

Morse held Sir Hugo's accustomed chair for Leonora. "Well, isn't this cosy."

Unfurling her napkin across her lap, she spoke without looking up at him. "While Uncle is away, I thought we might relax our formality a little. After your diligent work today, you deserve a pleasant evening."

Barely suppressing a sigh of satisfaction, Morse took his own seat. He had this skittish filly eating out of his hand.

"I can imagine few pleasanter ways to spend an evening, than in your company, Miss Freemantle."

She raised a brow. "Polishing your social graces, Sergeant?"

Morse grinned. "You said I should."

Glancing down as the fish course was placed in front of him, he assessed his array of forks.

With exaggerated care, Leonora picked one up. "Begin at the outside and work your way in. When in doubt, watch your table companions for a cue. Now, let us have no more lessons for this evening. Tell me something about yourself, Sergeant. I know you served under Cousin Wesley with the Somerset Rifles. Were you born and bred in that part the country?"

"Aye...that is...yes, Miss Freemantle. Near Pocklington. Been Archers thereabouts for as long as anyone can recollect. My folk weren't like yours—traveling from a great family seat in the country to a town house in London or Bath for the winter. We stayed put. I'm the first of my family to ever have gone abroad.''

She flinched at his words and the color drained from her face. ''Don't disdain permanence, Sergeant. Many people would envy you a place to call home.''

''Not if they saw it they wouldn't.''

Morse could not keep a note of bitterness from his laughter. His family's tenant cottage, with its smells and drafts that had contributed to the deaths of his three younger sisters—it would have fit inside Laurelwood's vast dining room with space to spare.

''Is that why you chose to enlist, then? So you could travel far from Somerset?''

Now Morse flinched, remembering what had driven him into the army. ''You might say so. A chance to get away from the past. I don't suppose you can understand that, can you, Miss Freemantle?''

She laid her fork down upon the plate and waited for the serving girl to remove them. Then she looked up at him. ''I may understand better than you think. I envy anyone who feels no need to escape his or her past.''

With a wide sweep of his arm, Morse indicated the damask draperies, the marble mantelpiece, the highly polished sideboard. ''What could anyone want to escape in all this?''

After a long look Morse could not interpret, Leonora stretched her lips into a fleeting grin. ''What, indeed? If you do not wish to dwell on your childhood, perhaps you might tell me about your days as a Rifleman. When did you meet my cousin Wesley?''

Eager for any distraction from painful memories, Morse seized her question. ''In India. Did he never tell you the story?''

For a wonder, it did not bother him to speak of Lieutenant Peverill in India. Perhaps because the lad had been so much alive then, with years ahead of him. Or perhaps it was the bond of affection he shared with Leonora for her cousin. Could she be coaxed to share some stories from their childhood?

Indeed she could.

So passed one of the most enjoyable dinners Morse had ever eaten. As an audience for his soldiering stories, Leonora proved superior even to Dickon. The way her eyes trained upon him, her apt questions and perceptive comments, all made him feel proud of his modest accomplishments and minor adventures.

And when she spoke of long-ago summers spent in the country with her cousin, Morse almost felt himself a part of their merry escapades.

He watched with jealous eyes as the serving maid removed his final plate, thinking it a shame this meal must end.

Leonora seemed to divine his thoughts. "I know we must be up early tomorrow to resume our studies. But if you would care to join me in the drawing room, I could play for you on the pianoforte. A gentleman should cultivate some knowledge of music, after all."

"I should like that very much."

Morse caught himself staring at her hands again. For the first of many times that evening.

He had always liked a nice tune, but never before had he heard such music as Leonora played on the pianoforte. Her supple fingers danced across the ivory keys, coaxing forth rich harmonies, some sad, some sweet, that caught Morse by the heart and held him. At times she seemed unaware of his presence, lost in the golden echoes of her art. If he had ever thought Leonora lacked passion, he now knew better.

As the final notes died to a whisper, they both stirred from their trance.

She glanced up at him, a bright blush staining her cheeks. "I fear I am boring you, Sergeant."

"No." He strove to frame words of praise half fine enough, but failed. "Not in the least."

He was only a common soldier, after all. One of the *other ranks*. A mere servant of his superior officers. How could he hope to appreciate such refinements as learning and art?

Leaning over to the canterbury stand that held her sheet music, she spoke in a tone of apology. "I do know some livelier tunes—old ballads and such. Will you look and see if there's anything here you might know? We could sing together."

She slid down the bench to make room for him.

"Most of the songs I know are fighting or drinking songs." Reluctance and eagerness tugged Morse in opposite directions, but he left his armchair and joined Leonora at the pianoforte.

"What about this one?"

She had played only a few notes when Morse cried, "'The Merry Milkmaids'! I do know that one."

He began to sing the words and she joined him. Then she struck up another familiar old tune, and another.

Many of them were about love, Morse realized, conscious of his leg pressed against Leonora's. Often, love gone wrong.

Amarillis told her swain,
That in love he should be plain,
And not think to deceive her...

The notion pricked Morse's conscience, but he shrugged it off. He'd never claimed to love Miss Freemantle. As for his sham wooing, he had the uncomfortable sense it was becoming too much in earnest.

* * *

"'Amarillis told her swain...'" Leonora found herself humming the tune as she hurried back to Laurelwood from her Wednesday evening class. Her conscience bothered her a little for having dismissed the girls early, but what use was it trying to teach them if she could not keep her mind on the lesson?

Perhaps, if Morse had not retired for the night, she would invite him to join her at the pianoforte again. Or he might enjoy hearing her read aloud from an English translation of *Don Quixote* or one of those stirring tales by Mr. Scott.

The flesh of her leg warmed in anticipation of the contact between them as they shared the pianoforte bench or the chaise. Her pace quickened.

They had spent such a congenial evening the night before. As a result Morse had been far more attentive and manageable during today's lessons. In her urgent need to win the wager, she was prepared to exercise every possible advantage. And that included Morse Archer's dangerously flattering admiration for her.

Letting herself in the side door, Leonora laid her book satchel on a narrow table by the door. She pulled off her bonnet and gloves, listening of any sound that might betray Morse's whereabouts.

She checked the drawing room, but found it empty. The library, likewise.

"Has Sergeant Archer retired for the night?" she asked Maudie, the parlor maid.

"I don't believe so, miss." The girl stared down at the carpet runner.

"He doesn't appear to be anywhere on the main floor. Did he go out, by any chance?"

"No, miss. I'm quite sure he never went out."

Was the girl simply being unhelpful or downright eva-
sive?

"Not here. Not off to bed. Not gone out. You have
given me a good account of where Sergeant Archer is *not,*
Maudie. Now, if you know, will you kindly inform me
where he *is.*" She spoke more sharply than she meant to.

The parlor maid took a step back, blinking rapidly.
"Well, miss, he and Dickon may be up in the west wing.
They sometimes go there of an evening when you're off
to the village."

"Do they, indeed?" She would have to have a word
with Morse about becoming too familiar with the servants.
"I don't know why you didn't say so first as last. Thank
you, Maudie."

"You're welcome, I'm sure, miss." The girl bustled off
below-stairs as though she feared further interrogation.

Leonora kept on her cloak and hunted up a candle to
light her way in the chill darkness of the west wing. The
rooms there had not been open for the better part of ten
years, when Aunt Harriet was still a vital force at Laurelwood, hosting house parties for her son and her niece.

Now, Leonora's breath and her soft-slippered footsteps
seemed to echo in the cold stillness.

Far down the corridor, light spilled out from an open
doorway. The sound of male voices lured Leonora.

Until Dickon lured him up to the west wing, Morse
moped about Laurelwood that Saturday evening. With
Leonora off on her mysterious biweekly visit to the village,
he'd been forced to eat dinner alone. For some reason the
boiled beef had completely lacked savor. Even his favorite
almond pudding had failed to rouse his appetite.

Afterward, he'd wandered into the drawing room and
picked out a few tentative notes on the pianoforte. But it
hadn't been the same without Leonora's company. He'd

glanced at the pedestal clock beside the door, wondering what hour she would be home.

Morse caught himself in a sigh.

Was it one of contentment? In the past few days Laurelwood had become everything he'd envisioned when he'd first accepted Sir Hugo's invitation.

Or was it regret that, one way or another, this very pleasant idyll would come to an end at last?

"Oh, there you are, sir." Dickon ambled into the drawing room, a promising looking jug tucked into the crook of one arm and a small covered basket suspended from the other. "Have you forgot what night it is?"

"Not by a long shot, Dickon." Morse forced a hearty note into his reply. True, he was well aware of it being Saturday. His rendezvous with the footman had slipped his mind, though.

"Cook let me have a brace of wee game pies for our tuck-out." Dickon's florid face positively glowed. "Got her fair eating out of your hand, Sergeant. I've never seen the beat of you for getting your way with contrary women."

There was no question the young ox meant it as a sincere compliment. For some reason, it made Morse squirm.

"Rounded up something tasty to wash those game pies down?" he asked with a show of interest. In truth, an evening of drinking and carrying on with Dickon held rather less than its former appeal.

Dashed if he could cipher why.

"More of that good hard cider, Sergeant." Dickon glanced down lovingly at the jug. "It did put you in a fine fettle last time. Fair cured you of sleeping in, too."

"Good medicine, that." Morse feigned a chuckle as the pair of them headed upstairs. Oh, well, at least it would provide him with *some* way to pass the time this evening.

And perhaps Dickon's cider would prove effective medicine to treat whatever was ailing him of late.

They made themselves at home in a deserted sitting room not much bigger than a cupboard. While Dickon got the coal fire burning, they alternated swigs from the cider jug to ward off the cold. Before long a feeling of warmth crept through Morse's flesh, though he was not certain whether to credit the fire or the drink. This particular batch had been well fermented.

Dickon leaned back in his chair and took a long pull from the jug. "Ah, that's good stuff! There's them as say cider drinking is bad for a body and I'll own cider drinking killed my grandsire."

Before Morse could croak out an expression of sympathy, the young footman leaned toward him and landed a solid nudge in the ribs with his great elbow. "Mind, it took all of ninety years to do it!" He threw back his big, blunt head and roared with laughter.

Morse joined in, though his ribs protested. He glanced toward the window, wishing it overlooked the driveway, so he could watch for Leonora's return.

Dickon broke out the game pies, which were the last word in savory pastry. Lieutenant Peverill had often sung their praises to Morse during the Peninsular campaign, always with an edge of longing in his voice. In some strange way, Morse felt it his duty to relish this one, on the lieutenant's behalf. Hard as he tried, he could not work up an adequate pitch of appreciation.

"What's this?" exclaimed Dickon. "Can't eat it all, sir?" His own pie was now only a pleasant memory.

Morse flashed an apologetic grimace. "I must have eaten too much beef at dinner." A bald lie, that. He'd scarcely worried down a slice. "If you have room for the rest of mine, go ahead and clean it up."

"I do hate to see it go to waste." Dickon devoured

Morse's leavings in two great bites, perhaps to forestall a change of heart in the matter.

They drank until the cider jug became perilously light to heft. When Dickon urged him to recount more of his soldiering exploits, Morse obliged, though with rather less enthusiasm than on previous occasions. They sang a song or two, though Morse's voice rang out less lustily than it once had.

"Ye know, Morse," confided Dickon at last, in the slow, earnest manner of an inebriate confidence. "I thought ye had her dancin' to yer tune, but now I see ye're in a bad way yerself."

"Wha' bad way?" Morse bristled. "I'll have ye know, I'm in right fine fettle, I am."

Dickon gave his big head a ponderous shake from side to side. "No ye ain't neither. Off yer feed. Jumpy as a wet cat. Why, ye can't even prop'rly enjoy gettin' drunk. I've seen them signs before an' I know what they mean right enough."

"Yer daft." Morse drained the cider jar dry. "Or drunk."

The feeble jest made him laugh immoderately. His head was spinning and his loins ached with the need for a woman. Though what he might be capable of doing with one in his present condition, he could not answer for.

Just hold her in his arms perhaps. Or lay his head upon her bosom and be lulled to sleep by the gentle rhythm of her heart and the cherished melody of her voice.

"I ain't that drunk," protested Dickon. "And I know what's what as well as th' next fella. Ye got a fancy for Miss Le'nora, Morse Archer. Ain't no use denin' it, neither. I've seen the way ye make calf eyes at her, an' how ye hold her chair. Ye mus' be hard up for a woman, is all I can say."

"Get it through yer thick skull, Dickon." Morse pulled

himself erect in his seat and tried very hard to not slur his words. "I do *not* have a fancy for Miss Leonora High-and-Mighty Freemantle. If I act p'lite around her it's just 'cause I'm tryin' to act like a gen'leman."

Dickon only laughed. "Pull the other one, Morse! Ye plaster yerself up against her ev'ry chance ye get. Bet ye've kissed her, too, haven't ye?"

Morse opened his mouth to deny it, but the words would not come. Instead he fell into a reverie of kissing Leonora's hand, and what it might be like to kiss her elsewhere.

"There! Ye see?" insisted Dickon, vindicated. "It ain't a crime, Morse. Bit foolish is all, her being so much above ye."

Dickon's words lit a fire of indignation in Morse. He jumped from his chair, then staggered. Grabbing the mantelpiece to steady himself, he glared at the footman. Surely, Dickon could not be right? He was not some amusing young yokel smitten to the heart with a woman far beyond his grasp.

Not any more. Never again.

"Ye got it all back'ards, dunderhead." He marshaled his most contemptuous look with which to skewer Dickon. "I'm not struck on her. What fella with sense would be? No, I'm jus' jollyin' her along, the way I do with ol' Cook, so she'll forget that damned Latin and 'rithemtic once in a while."

Dickon's eyes widened and his mouth rounded into an admiring little circle. "Ye don' say."

"I *do* say." Morse warmed to his explanation. This would shut Dickon up about him fancying Miss Freemantle. "Matter a fact, when I've had my fill of the lessons, all I have to do is put an arm 'round her waist or give her a little kiss on the hand. She bolts like a hare and lessons are over for the day."

As those words left his mouth, Morse thought he heard a noise in the corridor.

A mouse, perhaps. They were rare around Laurelwood, but he'd seen at least one. Morse took a staggering step toward the door to investigate.

"Ain't ye the scoundrel, though." The admiration in Dickon's tone belied his words. "An' here all this time ye had me hoodwinked."

"That'll teach ye to underes'tmate a Rifleman."

Pulling open the sitting room door, Morse looked out into the darkened corridor. A flash of something caught his eye as it turned the corner, but that was all.

With a shrug, he turned back to Dickon.

Then he heard the distant noise of a slamming door.

Chapter Seven

Slamming her door with a fury that rattled its hinges, Leonora flung herself onto the bed, where she erupted in a volley of sobbing.

That scoundrel! That bounder!

Had she learned nothing from her mother's miserable example? All men were the same. At least all the handsome, charming rogues who set lady's hearts so easily aflutter.

How could she have been so foolish as to suppose Morse Archer any different from the rest of his duplicitous ilk?

To think she had dismissed her class early and hurried back to Laurelwood to spend time with him. His absence from the library and the drawing room should have alerted her that something was not right. That and the stricken look of the housemaid she'd questioned.

Still, she'd been more curious than alarmed or suspicious.

Why had she stolen upon them so silently? Eavesdroppers never overheard any good of themselves, it was said. Perhaps she had hoped to hear something good, in spite of the old saying—a declaration of Morse's feelings for her. A drunken one, to be sure, but no less heartfelt for all that.

Well, she had heard Morse Archer's declaration. His confession that he'd been callously leading her on as a means to shirk his studies. Leonora wasn't sure which enraged her more—his deception or his indolence.

With balled fists she hammered at her pillow, wishing Morse Archer's face could feel the sting of every blow.

What galled the most, Leonora admitted to herself, was that she had been so easily duped, so naively carried away by her adolescent infatuation. She, above all women, should have known better than to trust such an attractive, engaging rascal of a man.

By degrees her sobs subsided, though the crushing weight on her heart and the vague nausea in her belly persisted.

It was not as though she wanted Morse Archer to fall in love with her.

Leonora tipped a measure of cold water into her washbasin and dabbed a handkerchief in it.

She had seen too much to ever believe in the fantasy of romantic love. Besides, he clearly disdained her world and the things she held most dear. Had an honest physical attraction, man to woman, been so very much to expect?

Apparently so.

Catching a glimpse of herself in the glass, Leonora winced. Her eyes were bloodshot and swollen. Her face an ugly patchwork of snow white and livid crimson blotches. Strands of her fine dark hair had come loose and straggled about her face in a decidedly unbecoming fashion. And she had been witless enough to delude herself that a man like Morse Archer genuinely fancied her?

A hiccup of bitter laughter broke from her lips.

What ludicrous irony—all these years she'd labored to maintain a dowdy facade, when she hadn't needed it at all.

Leonora Freemantle at her best was still in no danger of attracting a husband.

She pressed the cold, moist linen to her eyes, hoping it might relieve the sting of more tears than she'd ever cried all at one time.

As she mulled over the events of this week, knowing what she knew of Morse Archer's despicable scheme, her passionate anguish slowly congealed into cold wrath. How dare he have used her so badly after the opportunity she'd offered him and the effort she'd expended to help him improve himself?

Well, no more. She was done with him.

As soon as Uncle Hugo returned, she would inform him of Morse's conduct and ask him to call off their bet. If he refused, she would even capitulate and accept her penalty. Nothing could be worse than having to continue tutoring Morse Archer, knowing what he truly thought of her.

Bad enough that she would have to continue until her uncle got back from London.

As she readied herself for bed, knowing the hope of sleep was futile, Leonora made grim plans for that odious interval. Until he could be properly ejected from Laurelwood, she would make Morse Archer's life hell.

And if he should try any of his counterfeit wooing on her?

The Rifleman had better be prepared to take cover!

What had come over Leonora? Morse asked himself for the hundredth time in the past two days. He'd seen nothing of her on Sunday—not that he'd been in much condition to enjoy her company, he admitted sheepishly.

Monday morning he'd hastened to the library, eager to begin lessons. Only to discover the congenial Leonora of the previous week had been supplanted by his old nemesis.

The relentless, humorless, thoroughly heartless General Freemantle.

"Elbows *off* the table if you please, Sergeant Archer. This is not a mess hall." Even from the far side of the library, the look of disdain she cast him could have flayed the skin off an army mule.

"The Battle of Hastings did not end the War of the Roses. It *began* the Norman Conquest, a good four hundred years before that." The asperity of her tone left Morse without doubt that she had never encountered such a dunce.

If he hadn't known better, he'd have sworn she was retaliating for some wrong he'd done her. But that was absurd. If anything, he'd gone out of his way to be amiable of late.

Though Morse shrank from admitting it, even to himself, this sudden unwelcome change in Leonora puzzled and grieved him.

Had she decided he was too coarse and stupid to win her silly wager? Had she grown offended by his familiarity, considering him socially *beneath* her?

By Wednesday noon he'd had quite as much of General Freemantle as he could stomach.

"Kindly redo this translation from Tacitus." She crushed his painstakingly copied paper into a ball and tossed it onto the fire where it blazed to ash before his eyes. "I can make nothing of these chicken scratches you pass off as writing."

Morse sat back in the chair and crossed his arms before this chest. "If you want a fresh copy, you can go whistle for it." He cast her a forbidding look that would have sent the men of his command running for cover.

Leonora stood her ground and shot back one of equal venom.

Taking a clean sheet of paper from the corner writing

desk, she held it out to him, speaking in clipped, precise tones. "You *will* make a new copy, Sergeant Archer. One that is legible and accurate. Furthermore, you will stay in this room until it is finished. If dinner is over by then, it will be your own lookout."

Her spectacles had slipped down her nose to reveal those intriguing eyes, and a becoming flush had crept into her cheeks. Damn, but she could be a fine-looking filly when she chose. And a spirited one.

Her obvious contempt for him smarted all the more because he had foolishly let himself care for her opinion. He'd given her a weapon to use against him and she had exercised it without mercy.

Well, two could play at that game.

Making as if to snatch the paper from her, Morse clamped his fingers around Leonora's wrist and pulled her toward him. Stifling his anger, he flashed her a wicked grin. "Come now, pretty teacher. If we must dawdle in the library and miss supper, let's make it for a worthwhile purpose."

Caught off balance, Leonora lurched into his lap. Though part of him would have liked to throttle her, another part thrilled to the sensation of her in his arms. In a deft motion that would have done credit to a trained pickpocket, he plucked the spectacles from her nose and the combs from her hair, tossing them onto the table.

"I've worked hard for you this week, Miss Freemantle. I think I deserve a reward."

He hushed her inarticulate sounds of protest with a forceful application of his lips.

She froze in his embrace, her whole body going temporarily slack.

It had been far too long since he'd kissed a woman, and never one less ardent than he. Perhaps it was the novelty that made Morse savor his kiss with Leonora.

She tasted of tea. Hot, strong, black tea. With lemon. Her lips had a warmth and provocative softness he never would have guessed to look at her.

At first they surrendered before his onslaught. Falling open. Inviting him deeper.

His body turgid with desire, Morse plunged.

Then, with a shift so sudden it robbed him of breath, Leonora pried herself from his arms and slapped him soundly on the cheek.

"How dare you, Morse Archer?" She leaped to her feet and groped on the table for her spectacles, replacing them with the air of a warrior hefting his fallen shield.

They did not slam into place quickly enough to disguise the film of moisture in her eyes. The sting of her blow almost brought an answering tear to Morse's.

"If you suppose this show of impropriety will get you excused from retranslating Tacitus, you are quite mistaken." As she backed away a safe distance from the table, she twisted her hair tightly. Then she jammed a comb in place with a savagery that made Morse wince.

"I have been fool enough to fall for your callous ploy once too often." When she drew breath, Morse detected the ragged suggestion of a sob.

"I assure you, I have learned wisdom, since. Now get to work if you expect to dine this evening!" She marched to the mantel and pointedly turned her back on him.

Morse sat in stunned silence.

How had she found out? Had he been *that* transparent? The notion disturbed Morse, for it suddenly dawned on him that his campaign of romantic attentions had not been all bluff.

Hot on the heels of shock came shame. The way Leonora had presented it, his clever plan sounded cowardly and dishonorable.

Lieutenant Peverill would never have approved.

Almost against his will, he got to his feet and approached her. "Leonora, I—"

She must not have heard him coming, for she started when he spoke and touched her shoulders. With a swiftness of reflex any Rifleman might envy, she pivoted and pulled free of his hands.

"Don't imagine you can win back my trust with more of the same guile, Sergeant."

In that brief instant of contact between them, Morse had felt her trembling. Now she betrayed no hint of it. Reluctant to show weakness before the enemy, perhaps? It sparked Morse's admiration almost as much as it wounded him.

He had never wanted them to be enemies.

"And spare me the insult of an explanation." She tried to back away from him, but found herself trapped against the mantel. "My eyesight may be weak, but I trust the acuity of my hearing. I overheard you boast to your boon companion, Master Dickon, how you had set about to *charm* your way out of lessons. Perhaps it's time you learned it takes more than a handsome face and glib tongue to get on in this world."

Before Morse could recover from the dismay of being denounced, or contrive any sort of accounting for his behavior, a great commotion erupted in the entry hall outside the library.

Dogs barked. A familiar genial voice boomed. The air filled with the sounds of luggage being carted into the house.

Leonora took a deep breath and expelled it in something like a sigh. "Uncle is back, at last. Recopy the translation or not, as you wish, Sergeant Archer. As far as I am concerned, this wager is finished. Even I cannot teach a pupil so intractable he would stoop to toying with a woman's affections. I wash my hands of you."

She slipped under his arm and threw open the library door. "Welcome home, Uncle Hugo."

Morse scarcely heard their exchange of greetings and news. Leonora's final words whirled in his thoughts, condemning him. His pleasant sojourn at Laurelwood was over and he had been the sole architect of his eviction.

And what would he miss the most?

In that grim instant Morse realized it was the boon of Leonora's company.

Enveloped in Uncle Hugo's hearty embrace, Leonora fought back yet more tears.

How glad she'd be when Morse Archer was out of her life for good and all, along with the turbulent emotions he provoked in her.

If only she could convince her heart of it.

"How could you have gone off to London without a word to me?" She gave her uncle a thorough scrutiny from head to toe. He looked well enough. His air of self-satisfaction bordered on smugness. "You didn't need to consult a physician, I hope?"

"A leech?" Sir Hugo removed his hat, mussing the half-dozen long hairs he kept combed over his bald pate. "Oh, my, no. Whatever gave you such a preposterous idea? Why, I'm fit as a fiddle."

An apoplectic fiddle troubled by the gout, Leonora thought, but did not say so.

"Went up to town on a spot of business." He unwound his muffler and began to unbutton his greatcoat. "Though it soon turned into pleasure. Will you look who I met up with in my travels?"

He stepped aside to give her an unobstructed view of a person standing behind him.

It was a man—of sorts. Very tall and spindly. Dressed with more flamboyance than discretion. The creature responded to Leonora's glance with a guileless grin. Or perhaps *witless* was a more accurate description.

With a forceful hand on her back, Uncle Hugo propelled Leonora toward him. ''Now, don't say you've forgotten Cousin Algie?''

When she responded with a blank look and an embarrassed shrug, he augmented the introduction. ''You remember—Algie Blenkinsop, a distant cousin of mine and a friend of Wesley's from school. The lad's heir to his grandfather, Lord Biggleswade, and one of these fine old days he'll come into Laurelwood, too, thanks to the entailment. Algie, surely *you* recollect my niece, Leonora Freemantle?''

''Mr. Blenkinsop, of course.'' Leonora thought she recalled the name—vaguely. Wes had spent a good deal of time at school rescuing the hapless fellow from some trouble or other, as she recalled. So this was the person who would inherit Laurelwood in Wesley's stead.

Algie Blenkinsop took the hand she proffered, pumping it up and down with a force that set her quivering. ''Miss Freemantle, I should say I remember you. Deucedly good to meet you again. I was up to Laurelwood once with Wesley on holiday. You trounced me roundly at chess, as I recollect. And whist. And backgammon. Say, are you still as clever as you used to be?''

An unoriginal pleasantry caught in Leonora's throat, suddenly constricted with panic.

The beaming of Sir Hugo's ruddy countenance. The entailment of Laurelwood. Algie Blenkinsop's gaze of dumb adoration, not unlike an overgrown greyhound. There was no question in Leonora's mind—Mr. Blenkinsop would be her uncle's choice of a husband should she lose the wager.

The pair of them were looking at her, expecting some manner of reply. When all Leonora wanted to do was hurl herself onto the floor and wail.

"Welcome home, Sir Hugo." Morse Archer's voice from the library door gave her a moment to compose herself.

For an instant Leonora was so overwhelmed with gratitude she would have forgiven him everything. Then she remembered what Morse's lack of diligence would cost her.

Her heart hardened against him even more.

"Archer, my boy." Sir Hugo beckoned him close for an introduction. "Algie, this is Morse Archer. He was one of Wes's comrades in arms against Bonaparte. A stout member of the Rifle Brigade, don't you know. He's been doing a spot of convalescing with us since he was discharged from the army."

Algie exclaimed his pleasure at meeting Morse and shook his hand as thoroughly as he'd shaken Leonora's. "Sir Hugo promised me plenty of agreeable company if I should come for a few weeks' visit. I just know we'll have a jolly time together."

Leonora took grim glee in watching Morse squirm. Then she considered the *jolly time* she'd have to endure for the rest of her life as Lady Biggleswade. Suddenly she understood the desperation that might lead a wild animal to gnaw off its own leg to escape a snare.

But this snare was one of her own devising.

If only Morse Archer had not proven so impossible. If only she'd discovered the key to winning his loyalty.

"I must go tell Cook you've come home with, er... company, Uncle Hugo."

It was a transparent excuse to get away. By now there could not be a servant in the house ignorant of their master's return. Leonora didn't care. She dared not stay another minute in the company of these three men who had unwittingly conspired to ruin her life.

Uncle Hugo with his well-meaning desire to see her

married off and mistress of his beloved Laurelwood in the years to come. Morse Archer with his stubborn refusal to apply himself. And Mr. Blenkinsop...the chinless ninny who might well be glad of any wife desperate enough take him.

"You do that, child." Uncle Hugo exchanged a suggestive look with his guest. "My niece has a good head for all the details that go into the smooth management of a house."

"Capital." Algie bobbed his head. Did that absurd grin never leave his face? "I look forward to renewing our acquaintance during my visit, Miss Freemantle."

When she had not the courage to summon more than a pained smile in reply, Uncle Hugo answered for her. "Oh, I expect you'll be getting acquainted with Leonora very well indeed, Algie. I just know the pair of you will get on."

If she had not been certain he was motivated by only the tenderest feelings for her, Leonora would have sworn Uncle Hugo was taking pleasure in tormenting her. Before she disgraced herself by breaking down entirely, she turned her back on the men and fled to the kitchen.

Morse had the uncomfortable conviction there was more going on than the simple introduction of a houseguest. But for the life of him, he could not fathom what.

Leonora wore an even more stricken look than when she'd given him his dressing-down in the library. Sir Hugo's usual heartiness had taken on a gloating edge. What could he possibly have to gloat over?

As for Algie Blenkinsop, he was clearly the sort of aristocratic boob Morse had long despised. Everything in life handed to them on a silver platter. Trained from the cradle to expect deference from anyone *beneath* them. Too arrogant to recognize their own stupidity—even when it cost better, abler men their lives.

The notion that Blenkinsop would inherit Laurelwood in Lieutenant Peverill's place stuck in Morse's craw till he almost gagged on it.

Perhaps it was just as well he'd be shipping out of Laurelwood soon. Whatever his uncertain future held, at least he would not have to suffer the tedious company of Algie Blenkinsop.

As soon as he could make a polite excuse, Morse slipped away to the library. There he labored over his Latin translation until his eyes fairly crossed and his fingers cramped around the pen.

He left the exercise for Leonora to find, hoping she would read an apology in every meticulously written word.

Dressing for dinner that night, he wondered if he would be allowed to take away the fine clothes Sir Hugo had purchased for him. Morse scrubbed at the ink stains on his fingers. They stubbornly resisted his efforts.

Over and over, he reviewed Leonora's edicts regarding table manners. He hoped to conduct himself impeccably that evening—for perhaps his last meal at Laurelwood. Then Leonora might see that he had learned something from her, after all. Even if it was far too little and far too late.

To his surprise and dismay, she did not put in an appearance at dinner, nor was there a place set for her. At first Morse wondered if she was too upset to face him again. Then he realized it was Wednesday evening.

What was this mysterious errand that took her into the village two evenings a week? She had never volunteered the information and Morse had been too glad of the respite from lessons to question his good fortune. Now, with his time at Laurelwood running out, the matter was suddenly very important to him.

Making his excuses to Sir Hugo and his guest, Morse left the table at his earliest opportunity. Bundling up in his greatcoat and beaver hat, he borrowed one of Sir Hugo's walking sticks and set off for the village.

The unseasonably mild night held a distinct promise of spring. Morse inhaled a deep draft of the moist, loamy air that smelled of quickening life. This was a time for new beginnings, yet his heart labored under a burden of regret.

Perhaps it would ease once he'd had a chance to talk with Leonora.

He owed her a sincere apology.

What's more, he owed her the truth.

Chapter Eight

Leonora looked around the cramped little vestry room at the dozen village girls who made up her class. "I know it's earlier than usual…again, but I'm afraid we must conclude our studies for the evening."

From their places around two rickety tables, the girls glanced up at her without a word and closed their books. The genuine regret on their young faces flattered her, even as it provoked a pang of guilt. She had sent them away prematurely on Saturday, too, in her rush to get back to Laurelwood. And Morse Archer.

What a fool she'd been!

In contrast to that stubborn, underhanded Rifleman, it was a joy to teach students like these. So eager to learn, so appreciative of the opportunity she afforded them. But tonight she could not keep her mind on the lesson no matter how hard she tried. Her concentration was continually buffeted by questions and worries about her future.

She had fondly hoped some of the girls in her class might attend her new school once she got it going. With that dream now dashed, she could only wonder whether Mr. Blenkinsop might allow her to continue teaching this class.

Her mood had obviously communicated itself to her pupils, for they donned their wraps in somber silence. Since this might be one of her last classes with them, Leonora regretted even more the necessity to dismiss them early.

"May I have a word with you, miss?" Elsie Taylor edged toward the small table Leonora employed as a desk. The eldest and brightest of her scholars, Elsie was a tiny wren of a girl whose dark eyes held a world of curiosity and whose oft turned and patched clothes belied a natural refinement of manner.

"Surely, Elsie." Leonora scoured up an encouraging smile and tacked it in place.

"Girls," she called out to the rest of the class. "Don't forget to read the next two chapters of *The Pilgrim's Progress* before Saturday and be prepared to discuss Christian's experiences in Vanity Fair and Lucre Hill. Keep in mind what I told you about allegories and see if you can come up with some examples from your own life that relate to Christian's journey thus far."

The girls took up their twopenny editions of Bunyan, which Leonora had purchased from her own meager resources. If she could not continue to teach them herself, she wondered if someone else might be found to take on the task. If Mr. Blenkinsop was very rich, perhaps he would allow her to buy books and supplies for the class, at least.

As the last of them filed out with a subdued word of farewell, Leonora turned to her star pupil. "What can I do for you this evening, Elsie? Are you through *The Pilgrim's Progress* already and want to start on something more challenging? I can lend you my own copy of *Gulliver's Travels* if you promise to take very good care of it. It was the last Christmas gift I received from my cous—"

The girl shook her head. "It's not that, Miss Freemantle,

though I thank you kindly for the offer. I'm sure it's a fine book."

She held out her copy of Bunyan. "So was this. I *am* finished with it, but I'll not be borrowing anything new."

To Leonora's puzzled look she replied, "My auntie's found me a place in service at a big house in the West Country where she's the head house parlor maid. I'm to start as a scullery maid, but I can work my way up. Saturday will be my last class, as I'm catching the post coach on Sunday. You won't mind my coming then, I hope, miss? Even if I don't mean to continue?"

"Of course not, Elsie. Do come, by all means." Leonora tried to disguise her disappointment lest it distress her young friend. Behind Elsie's matter-of-fact announcement, it was plain she did not relish what the future held in store for her. "You are welcome to keep your copy of *The Pilgrim's Progress* as my parting gift. I can tell you from experience that it improves upon successive readings. And thank you for giving me advance notice of your departure from our midst. We shall all miss you and hope you will enjoy your new situation."

Precious little fear of that, Leonora reflected to herself as Elsie thanked her for the book and took her leave. A scullery maid's job was one of the dirtiest, most thankless and most wearisome in any household. Up before dawn to light the kitchen fire, not to bed until the last cook pot from dinner was scoured clean. The poor girl would have little opportunity to keep up her studies, even if she was so inclined.

If only Elsie could have stayed on in the class for a few more months, Leonora reflected. A well-worded letter of character from her might have secured the girl a junior teaching position at some charity school. Not well paid, to be sure, but the kind of work she could enjoy and take pride in.

Packing her satchel, spirits sunk even lower than when she'd arrived, Leonora regretted the loss of her wager. Every bit as much for her pupils' sakes as for her own.

By the time Morse discovered Leonora's whereabouts, a tiny cupboard of a room in the vestry of the local church, the girls were already filing out, singly and in pairs.

As he waited for Leonora outside on the brightly moonlit night, he hunted up Lieutenant Peverill's tombstone in the churchyard and doffed his hat out of respect. The icy breeze ruffled his hair.

Paying him no mind, the girls hung about for a few minutes talking freely of their class, their teacher and their disappointment at another evening's early dismissal.

It pricked Morse's conscience to think how he'd relished a premature end to his own lessons. How he'd connived to bring it about, while others hungered for the feast of knowledge he turned his nose up at.

From the sound of their voices, he could tell these girls came from families of local tradesmen and tenant farmers. Common folk who could ill afford an advanced education for their sons, let alone their daughters. His own sisters might have grown into girls like these, if they'd lived.

What brought Leonora Freemantle out here, week after week in every sort of weather, missing a hot dinner, when she could have stayed tucked up in comparative luxury at Laurelwood? Why had she labored so relentlessly with a blockhead like him, so she could win the wherewithal to finance a school for girls like these? When, instead, she could have been enjoying a round of house parties or tricking herself out for a Season at Bath to snare a rich husband?

Clearly he had underestimated her, just as he had once underestimated a certain boyish lieutenant who'd been posted to the Fourth Somerset Rifles.

A short while after the girls dispersed, Leonora walked through the vestry door and closed it firmly behind her. She appeared as unaware of his presence as her students had been. In the white moonlight and the yellow candle glow that spilled from the windows of the old stone sanctuary, Morse watched her.

Her shoulders sagged with a weight of weariness, or perhaps discouragement. Her step was slow, almost tentative, as though reluctant to bear her back to Laurelwood.

A lump rose in Morse's throat as he considered his own shameful contribution to her low spirits.

Stealing up behind her, he lifted the satchel from her hand. "Carry your books, miss?"

She gasped and raised a hand to her heart. "Morse Archer! Whatever in the world are you doing here? It's a wonder you didn't scare me into a fit."

"I don't reckon you scare that easily, Miss Freemantle." He fell into step beside her as best he could. "I didn't want to leave Laurelwood without discovering whereabouts you spent your Wednesday and Saturday evenings. I was almost convinced you must have a secret beau in the village."

She stopped then and turned toward him. The faint light that glowed from houses along the road was not sufficient to show Morse her expression.

"Don't mock me, Sergeant."

Once, it might have been a tart command. Tonight it sounded like a plaintive appeal. Morse's shame threatened to overwhelm him.

"It was only a little jest," he protested.

She began to walk again. "Not a very kind one, under the circumstances."

"Can you slow down a little? My leg's paining like the devil." Morse would not have admitted it to another living soul. What made this woman an exception?

"*You* expressed the desire to accompany *me,* Sergeant, not the other way 'round." Her tone had regained a little of its old pepper, but her gait slackened just the same.

"Will it help if I say I'm sorry?"

Her step hesitated. "For what—the quip about my having a beau?"

"That." Morse swallowed a deep breath and an almost indigestible slice of humble pie. "And for pretending to *be* your beau back at Laurelwood. It wasn't the gentlemanly thing to do, I'll own. But you've known all along I'm no gentleman."

Her reply was the last thing Morse expected. "I think you could be, Sergeant. That's part of what saddens me in all this. I do think you *could* be a fine gentleman if only you *would.*"

Those words, spoken with such a wealth of wistfulness and dashed hopes on his account, caught Morse like a bayonet to the belly.

His armor pierced, a confession gushed out of him. "It won't make a difference to anything, but I want you to know just the same. It wasn't all a bluff, my making up to you. Oh, at first it was, like I told Dickon. But then, once you got off your high horse and acted friendly, I came to enjoy your company, Miss Freemantle. Got so's I looked forward to our lessons in the library and our talks at dinner."

They had left the village behind now, walking along a narrow country lane that ran to Laurelwood. A silence fell between them, punctuated only by their footfall on the firmly frozen road and the whisper of a frosty breeze through the bare branches of the hedgerows on either side.

"I'll miss them," he concluded at last.

More silence. More footsteps. More wind. And the sound of a furtive sniffle, amplified out of all proportion.

Forgetting how Leonora had pushed him away every

other time he'd tried to offer her comfort, Morse reached for her, his hands encumbered by her satchel and his walking stick. When he put his arms around her, she melted against him.

He rested his chin against the peak of her bonnet. "There now, lass. It's not worth shedding tears over a scoundrel like me."

At his words, Leonora pulled back again and began to beat on his chest with her fists. "You? God in heaven, you *are* a scoundrel, Morse Archer! Do you suppose everything a woman thinks or feels revolves around you? Why you conceited, self-important, vainglorious *man.* I'll have you know I have plenty more to cry about than whether or not you make love to me!"

Morse stood there, letting her pummel him. If it helped ease her feelings, why not? He could not decide whether to be relieved or slighted that she wept on account of something other than his behavior.

"Is it your school, then?" Having heard her pupils talk, he could regret the loss of the wager on their account. What he could not fathom was why it mattered so very much to Leonora.

She stopped her rain of blows.

Morse expected her to turn away from him, but she didn't.

As Leonora stood before him, her balled fists opened like reluctant flowers in spring until her outspread hands rested against the breast of his coat.

"It's everything, Morse." She sounded so very forlorn he yearned for her with all his heart. "Did it never occur to you what penalty I'd incur upon losing the wager?"

He thought for a moment. None too clearly, for her nearness and the faint sensation of her touch befuddled him. "Well, you won't get that school you hanker after."

A sound erupted from her, somewhere between a

chuckle and a sob. "That would be a rather one-sided wager, don't you think? If I win, I get my school, if I lose, I don't. What would Uncle stand to gain by offering me a bet like that?"

Morse had never thought of it in quite those terms.

"What *did* you stake?" A sudden ache of foreboding in his wounded leg told him he was not apt to like what he heard.

"Only my freedom. And everything that makes my life worthwhile."

He shook his head. "I don't follow you." Sir Hugo obviously doted on his niece. Morse could not believe he would exact so cruel a penalty.

"It's quite simple really." Her words floated in the darkness, bitter and forlorn as a winter night. "If I win, I get the capital I need to run my school and a sufficient income that I'll never need to wed. Lose the wager and I agree to marry a man of my uncle's choosing and give up my bluestocking ways."

Marry a man of my uncle's choosing. The words reverberated in Morse's mind like a volley of cannon fire at too close a range.

"Blenkinsop!" he gasped. "Is he the man Sir Hugo will have you marry?"

Her hands dropped from his coat, as though she no longer possessed the strength to hold them aloft. "You are quite the logician, Sergeant. Oh, Uncle hasn't come right out and said so, but his motives aren't difficult to divine. He's never made any secret of his hankering for me to catch a husband. Settle down and present him a troop of courtesy grandchildren. Now he's gone one better, making sure I'll never be turned out of Laurelwood. I'm sure he considers it the greatest kindness he could possibly do me."

"All the same—Blenkinsop?" Morse's mouth puckered just saying the name.

"No doubt Mr. Blenkinsop has many qualities that recommend him as a husband in Uncle's eyes. He hasn't a spark of temper, I'm certain."

Morse recalled the flash in Leonora's eyes when she'd crossed verbal swords with him. She deserved a partner with more spirit.

"He doesn't seem the type to squander his fortune drinking, or gambling or keeping other women," Leonora continued.

She made them sound like rare virtues.

"No doubt he'd be a kind father."

The thought of her bearing children by that highborn dimwit made Morse positively bilious. He'd heard quite enough praise for Algie Blenkinsop, modest though it might be.

"That's all very well," he blurted out before she could list any more of the fellow's merits. "He's still not the man for you. You deserve better."

His words rocked Leonora. The earnest conviction with which he uttered them set her heart racing and an unwelcome warmth rising in her face.

"As far as I'm concerned, the best husband in the world is none at all. And that is what I want." Flinging down that bitter declaration, she turned from him and set off walking again. "It's fruitless to discuss, in any case. The wager's lost and there's an end to it. Let's get home before we catch cold."

Behind her, she heard Morse struggling to catch up. Walking into the village could not have done his leg any good. Yet he had undertaken it for an opportunity to apologize.

Grudgingly, she slowed her pace.

In the night sky above them, the wind chased a swath

of cloud across the face of the nearly full moon. Illuminated by the silvery-white light, it looked like the billowing sail of some ghostly barque.

Morse fell into step beside her. "*Is* your wager lost? I mean, have you told Sir Hugo you're prepared to concede defeat?"

Leonora hesitated to answer. The very thought of it made her gorge rise. "I haven't had an opportunity," she said finally. "He and Mr. Blenkinsop arrived just when I had to come away to teach my class."

"In that case, can we have another go at this wager of yours? We both know I wasn't putting forward my best effort, before. If you'll give me another chance, I swear I'll work my heart out for you, Miss Freemantle. Now that I understand exactly what's at stake."

Morse's offer enticed Leonora almost as much as it unnerved her. Could she continue to work with him after the way she'd let him play her for a fool? Could she bear to let her hopes rise again, only to have them dashed if he failed? A month of their three had been wasted—could they make up for that lost time, no matter how hard he was prepared to work?

"Well?" he prompted when the moments passed and he got no answer.

"I'm thinking about it!"

They rounded a bend in the road and Laurelwood hove into view. The light from its windows beckoned them home. Suddenly the only consideration that weighed in Leonora's heart was how empty the place would seem without Morse's presence.

"Very well." She stopped and turned toward him. "I'll give you one more chance. Though I warn you, I have my doubts we can bring it off."

"I accept," Morse replied readily. "On one condition."

Condition? The audacity of the man! Begging for another chance, then setting conditions upon his participation.

"Need I remind you, Sergeant? *You* asked for another opportunity to prove yourself. That hardly puts you in a position to demand concessions."

"I know." The moonlight glinted in his dark eyes like so much devilment. "But I'm asking, anyway. Because I do want to win you this wager and because I think you're going about it the wrong way."

Leonora began to bluster in protest, but he cut her off. "The trouble we ran into before—it's because I'm not good at taking orders."

"There's an understatement if I ever heard one."

"Listen, Miss Freemantle. If you'd been raised on a tenant farm, like I was, always at everybody's beck and call, you might balk at taking orders, too."

This was not the first time he'd spoken of his childhood, always with such bitterness of his tone. Leonora found herself entertaining a hundred questions about his early years. They sounded as disagreeable in their own way as hers had been.

Leonora shivered. "We'll discuss this more once we're warm inside." She started up the cobbled drive.

From behind Morse's words ambushed her. "Do you ride at all, Miss Freemantle?"

What did that have to do with anything? "I used to."

"Then you'll know some horses don't like being curbed too hard." Morse fell into step beside her. "It's apt to make them buck or bolt. You're better to point them in the right direction, then give them their head. They'll gallop you off to your destination without a whit of trouble and faster than a more manageable beast."

"So you're telling me Morse Archer is like a green-broken stallion?" The image stirred her.

"Something like that."

She stole a glance at him, then quickly looked away again. "You feel you're apt to learn faster if I give you more autonomy?"

"If that means letting me have some say in what I learn and how—then, yes."

It irked Leonora to admit a fault. But Morse had frankly admitted one of his. "As much as you dislike taking orders, Sergeant, I feel compelled to give them. For the longest time, there was no regularity in my life—you have no idea how frightening that can be for a child. Once I was in a position to impose some kind of structure upon my little world, I set about it with a vengeance. Perhaps it's time I learned to be less directive."

The last few yards to the front entrance their steps slowed, as if somehow reluctant to leave behind the freedom of the outdoors and the darkness.

"Do we have a truce, then, Sergeant?"

He seemed to mull it over before answering. "A truce—that's a cease-fire between enemies, Miss Freemantle." In the soft glow of the door lamp, he searched her eyes. "I hope we haven't been that. Opponents, maybe, testing each other's steel."

"You found me a worthy opponent?" The notion appealed to her.

"Aye." He smiled. "Though you like to use a barrage of heavy artillery when a single rifle shot would do."

Leonora lifted an eyebrow and fought to stifle the answering smile. "While you favor a sneak attack from the rear." She had to admit, sparring with Morse Archer had a rather stimulating effect upon her.

With a wry chuckle, he conceded the point. "A talent for deception is apt to come in handy during the campaign ahead of us. Take it from a soldier, different fighting styles can sometimes dovetail into the best alliances."

"Allies?" Leonora considered the idea. It sounded uncomfortably like a partnership. Long ago she had reconciled herself to operating alone.

"Very well," she said finally. "Shall we find a quiet spot to sit and discuss our tactics for the coming weeks? Perhaps drink a little toast to our alliance?"

Morse pulled the great front door open and ushered her into the welcoming warmth of the entry hall. "It would be an honor and a pleasure, Miss Freemantle."

The glass of her spectacles fogged up, as they were apt to do when she came in from the cold. Leonora pushed them down her nose and glanced over the lenses at Morse. Perhaps it was only her shortsightedness that lent him such a soft, appealing aspect.

"I declare, Sergeant, you sound more like a gentleman, already."

Chapter Nine

"What, in your estimation, am I doing so very wrong, Sergeant?" asked Leonora as she and Morse settled into a pair of upholstered armchairs on either side of the library hearth, to drink their glasses of port wine.

It went against her grain to *ask* a man's advice on any matter, let alone take it. But she had promised Morse she would try to involve him in the decision-making and she meant to keep her word.

Things would be different this time around. For a start, Morse would know better than to try any more of his sham wooing on her. Why did the prospect leave her with an empty, wistful feeling?

Morse took a slow drink, as though giving himself time to frame his argument. "You wouldn't be doing anything wrong, if we had two years more to prepare instead of two months. The way I see it, you're trying to polish this great lump of coal into a genuine diamond, when all you really need to do is make a paste gem that'll pass casual inspection."

"I'm not sure I see what you mean." Conceding ignorance to a man came almost as hard as soliciting advice.

Yet she couldn't help wishing they had two years ahead of them instead of a meager two months.

In the armchair opposite her, Morse hunched forward, his elbows resting on his knees. The flickering light from the hearth fire made the port in his glass gleam like liquid rubies. It also played over his strong, emphatic features in a way that made Leonora want to sigh with admiration.

Morse Archer was a striking fellow, no question of that. How could she have been foolish enough to think he'd be attracted by a plain, bookish creature like her?

"Take that Latin, for instance," he said. "How many gentlemen have you met who walk around rhyming off all the conjugations of their verbs or cases of their nouns?"

Understanding must have dawned in her expression, for he chuckled. "I've never come across one, either, and don't fancy I will anytime soon. Now and then, you do hear one toss out a quote that shows off his fine education. So prime me with half a dozen handy Latin tags that might cover a broad range of occasions."

"You mean like *aut disce aut discede?*"

Morse's brow furrowed. "Either…learn or…leave?" He cracked a wide grin and winked at her. "Touché, Miss Freemantle. That's an apt quote. Shows what a clever woman you are."

Ovid or Plautus might have supplied her with a fitting proverb about the folly of heeding a flatterer, but at that moment Leonora could not think of one. The mellow tone of *this* flatterer's voice set her thoughts whirling too furiously.

"I haven't time to read all those thick books before we go to Bath, either." Morse gestured toward the floor-to-ceiling bookcases that lined the interior wall. "Though now that you've got me started, I might like to study them at my leisure. For the moment, you can just tell me what's in them and what makes them important for a chap to know about.''

She was beginning to see his point. ''Very well, but what of history...or mathematics?''

Morse glanced back up, flashing a mischievous grin that left her breathless. ''What of them? I know enough ciphering to get by, but I fear I'll always be a dunce at history. I expect there are heaps of gentlemen, well accepted in society, who could say the same.''

Leonora's lips twitched. ''Our Mr. Blenkinsop, unless I miss my guess. Very well, we'll toss away the history books.'' She sighed. ''You don't know what you're missing, though.''

''Why don't you just tell me about it, then? Like with the literature. I remember things I'm told far better than what I read in books.''

Draining the last of her port, Leonora mulled over what Morse had said. She'd noticed something similar among her evening school pupils. A few of the girls learned readily from books, like Elsie Taylor. Others seemed to absorb information better through lectures and discourse. Still others could retain nothing until they'd copied it several times onto a slate.

Her own philosophy dictated that she teach in whatever manner her students learned best. Surely that went for Morse Archer, too?

''With your abbreviated curriculum, we shan't have much to do at all, these next two months, Sergeant.''

He shook his head vigorously. ''That's where your mistaken. I have plenty to learn about the usual pursuits of gentlemen—gaming, hunting, dancing, billiards. They're apt to trip me up far quicker than any amount of Latin or history.''

''Oh, dear.'' Leonora blanched. ''I hadn't reckoned on all that. I know nothing about gaming.''

Except that she hated it. Her second stepfather had gambled away the bulk of her mother's small fortune. How many times had they changed residence to avoid his creditors? Each move to a smaller, dingier house with fewer servants and more vulgar economies.

She'd taken this wager with her uncle only out of dire necessity. How anyone could gamble for amusement, Leonora simply did not understand.

"Hunting is a mystery to me," she added, breaking from bitter memories. "My dancing is not much better, come to that."

A girl who wanted to avoid catching a husband had little use for dancing lessons.

Then inspiration struck.

Leonora sat up straight and snapped her fingers. "We could recruit Mr. Blenkinsop to help! He's not exactly a prime specimen, but there's no doubt he's a blue blood. You might be surprised at what you could learn by watching him."

Morse pulled a face, which made her chuckle.

"Isn't a good soldier supposed to take advantage of every opportunity to further the military goals of his side?"

"Very well." Morse grunted. "I'll make use of him. But I don't have to enjoy it."

As she started to laugh, a great yawn overtook Leonora. Stifling it with her hand, she glanced at the mantel clock "We had better get ourselves off to bed, if we mean to make a fresh start tomorrow."

It had been a long day, during which her spirits had been buffeted this way and that. Riled up by her confrontation with Morse in the library, cast down by Uncle Hugo's return with Mr. Blenkinsop. Revived by Morse's appeal for another chance.

As he followed her up the stairs, Leonora's flesh tingled with the sense of his eyes upon her.

Was it too much to hope life would settle down again?

True to her word, Leonora lost no time in soliciting the assistance of Algie Blenkinsop. The very next morning she broached the idea as they sat eating breakfast.

"We could very much use your help, Mr. Blenkinsop—"

"Oh, do call me Algie," he insisted, beaming at Leonora in a way Morse heartily resented. "I am some relation, however distant, and I'd like us to become great friends."

Biting into his bread with savage force, Morse renewed his vow to see that Blenkinsop should never become more to Leonora than a friend.

"Algie, of course." She fiddled with her fork, clearly aware of the implication of his remark. "As Uncle may have told you, I'm coaching Sergeant Archer for...um... that is, so he can...well..."

"Yes, indeed. Sir Hugo told me all about it." Algie grinned in the older man's direction.

Leonora's face went white as paper, while Morse's breakfast sank to his toes.

"No need to be embarrassed, old fellow," Algie advised.

Heat rose in Morse's face. But it was the heat of rage, not shame. He longed to take Algie's breakfast plate and shove it into his mouth, whole.

"Plenty of chaps hard up for cash and looking to attract a rich wife." Algie forked a great helping of scrambled eggs into his mouth, but kept on talking. "Thank heaven I'm not in that case myself. Hard enough to find a likely gel prepared to say *I do* to becoming Mrs. Algie Blenkinsop when one has pockets full of cash and decent expectations. If I was poor I'd be doomed to bachelorhood for-ever. Ha, ha!'' Tiny fragments of egg showered from his mouth.

Seeing Leonora's jaw hanging slack, Morse realized his was, too. Between his amazement at the story Sir Hugo had concocted, and his ire at Algie's obvious preoccupa-tion with Leonora, he could not dredge up a single word of reply.

''But you, Archer.''

Much as he wanted to hate the fellow, Morse was not immune to Algie's unfeigned admiration.

''You'll have all the romps and chits and green girls in a swoon over you—see if you don't. Still and all, it never hurts for a fellow to polish up the bait before he goes fishing for a rich wife, eh? Jolly kind of Miss Freemantle to lend you a hand.''

If he'd wanted to be kept by a rich woman, he could have—years ago and without the benefit of anybody's tu-telage. Morse knew he didn't dare say it, but conscious that he must say *something,* he managed to concede, ''Haven't been out in society much. Small, provincial school. Then the Rifles. Don't want to disgrace myself.''

''And you shan't, if I can help it.'' Algie cast an ex-pectant look at Leonora that begged a word of approval. Not unlike an overgrown puppy—a slobbery one. ''Just tell me how I can help and I'll be glad to pitch in.''

Though he knew it was a sound idea, Morse could not help but chafe at the prospect of Algie Blenkinsop tres-passing on the privacy of his lessons with Leonora. Not for all the colonial plantations on earth could he have re-turned Algie's guileless, gullible grin. The best he could do was endeavor to not scowl.

''That's awfully kind of you, Mr., er, Algie.'' Leonora didn't look any too pleased at the thought of his partici-pation, either.

Somehow that soothed Morse's resentment.

"Perhaps you could begin by teaching Sergeant Archer—"

"Look here, if you're going to call him Algie, you can bloody well call me Morse!"

"Morse!" cried Leonora, clearly protesting his language.

"Jolly good, Morse!" chorused Algie. "Might as well be on familiar terms first as last, what?"

Morse bit back a retort that he didn't care twopence *what* Algie called him. Yet he flushed with triumph at hearing his Christian name from Leonora's lips—even in annoyance.

From the other end of the breakfast table, he caught Sir Hugo watching the three of them, fairly glowing with satisfaction. Given Morse's fresh outburst, the old man probably considered his wager as good as won.

Don't bake the wedding cake just yet, Sir Hugo. Morse cast him a challenging glare, more determined than ever to prevail.

By the time Saturday evening arrived, Leonora felt justified entertaining a crumb of confidence in her future.

The way Morse had thrown himself into his studies was nothing short of astonishing. Be it Latin phrases, the capitals of Europe or the subtleties of billiards, he approached each with a singular concentration, as though his very life depended upon mastering them.

Leonora needed no reminder it was *her* life, or at least her peace of mind, that hung in the balance. The effort Morse had put forth on her behalf flattered her far more than any of his old mock flirtation.

And yet...

As she waited for the girls in her class to doff their cloaks and cluster around the tables, she could not quench a pang of longing for the meaningful gazes that had really meant nothing. For the accidental touches that had been all too intentional, and the spontaneous kiss that had been coolly calculated.

In the past three days Morse Archer had become a model of propriety—drat him!

Her class was more than usually subdued that evening, perhaps in anticipation of Elsie Taylor's departure. To compensate for their prior early dismissals, Leonora threw herself into an effort to distract their thoughts and lighten their spirits. When discussion strayed from the book they were studying, she let them debate—tossing out a remark now and then to spur them, encouraging everyone to have a say.

At some point during the exchange, Leonora found her thoughts focusing on Elsie, and how the girl might be kept at home a while longer. At least until her school could become a reality.

Then a casual remark from one of her other students gave Leonora her answer. So eager was she to advance the idea with Elsie, that she could barely refrain from dismissing the class early yet again. She checked her impatience by thinking over all possible objections and devising means around them.

"A word before you leave, please, Miss Taylor." The other girls might have marked the animation in her tone or the vitality in her movements, for they bid her good evening with a light of curiosity in their eyes.

The last of them was scarcely out the door when Leonora could contain herself no longer. "Elsie, would your aunt be so very disappointed if you were to find a better situation, closer to your home?"

"There's a cousin of mine would be very happy of the position if I was not able to take it, Miss Freemantle." The girl sounded as if she was working hard to curb her rising hopes. "But I haven't been offered any better situation and my mother says—"

Leonora never did find out what Mrs. Taylor had to say.

"This is your offer, Elsie." She could not hold back another minute. "Uncle has been after me for the longest time to hire a proper lady's maid. I couldn't see that I needed one, out here in the country. But we are planning a sojourn to Bath in the spring and I could do with a little sprucing up. Can you sew?"

"Aye…that is…yes, miss. I made this dress myself." Elsie's words spilled out, quicker and quicker. "Trimmed my bonnet, too. And I can dress hair."

"You're hired!" cried Leonora. "Part of your duties will require you to serve as my teaching assistant for these evening classes—though we mustn't mention that to Uncle. You'll have half a day off a week and you may board at Laurelwood or at home, as you please. Whatever the wages in that other position, let me know and I shall better it by fourpence a week, more if you board at home."

"Are you certain, miss?" Elsie Taylor's eyes grew wide and more than a trifle moist. "Fourpence? Well I never! I know Mum and Papa…I mean to say, my parents, will be glad enough not to have me so far from home. And I cannot say how happy I shall be to stay."

Why had she never thought of such a project before? Leonora wondered, her own happiness very nearly matching Elsie's. Perhaps because she'd never been able to picture herself as a lady who might need a maid?

"I'll be the best lady's maid you've ever had, miss."

No great boast, that, since she would be the first. Out loud, Leonora replied, "I'm certain you shall take me in hand very well, Elsie. I'll expect to see you bright and early on Monday morning."

"Yes, miss. Thank you, miss!" Elsie's feet scarcely

touched the floor as she bolted from the room. To share the good tidings with her friends, no doubt.

Pleased with herself for hitting on such a clever solution, Leonora hummed a little tune as she packed her satchel and—

"Your cloak, miss." There stood Morse Archer, holding it out for her.

Leonora's heart raced. From the surprise of his sudden appearance, of course. "You really must break this habit of stealing up on people, Sergeant. I'm sure it's a handy skill for a Rifleman, but not for a gentleman. What brings you here, by the by? I thought Algie was tutoring you in faro this evening."

She turned her back and allowed Morse to slide the cloak over her shoulders. She was prepared to reprimand him if his hands rested there too long. Or, more forward yet, should offer a squeeze.

He behaved like a perfect gentleman, however. Which did not please Leonora as much as it should have.

"Both faro and macao," Morse replied in a genial tone. "We agreed to a small wager of our own. Winner got to drive Sir Hugo's phaeton into the village to fetch you home."

Leonora busied herself with tying her bonnet, playing for time to temper the foolish smile on her face. Algie had suggested the bet, most likely, she told herself. Counting on Morse's inexperience to give him the upper hand.

And Morse? Well, the cards must have fallen his way. Or perhaps he had made an effort to win. Just to best Algie, for whom he clearly had little use. The opportunity to drive the phaeton might have been a strong inducement, too.

Yet Morse had made it sound as if *she* were the prize. And, try as she might, Leonora could not calm the rapid pulse within her.

* * *

"I'll need a few lessons from Blenkinsop about handling these rigs," Morse confessed as he ushered Leonora out to the phaeton.

Perhaps Algie had deliberately thrown the card match, hoping Morse's dismal performance in carriage driving would diminish him in Leonora's eyes.

Morse shook his head at his own foolishness. Algie Blenkinsop wasn't half clever enough to be so crafty. Besides, what would ever give him the daft idea the two of them were rivals for Leonora?

He hoisted her into the carriage, resisting the urge to hang on to her a trifle longer than necessary. Such behavior would get him turfed out of Laurelwood on his backside. Yet Morse found it deucedly hard to break himself of the habit.

"No question, they're tricky blighters to control." He jogged the reins, almost falling from the high box as the pair of matched bays lurched forward. "Between the height and the lightness of them."

A soft trill of laughter shimmered in the crisp night air like a moonbeam. "There's more to this business of posing as a gentleman than you anticipated, isn't there, Morse?"

He didn't dare take his eyes off the dimly lit road for a moment. And perhaps that was a good thing.

The sight of Leonora in the winter moonlight might have been too great a challenge to his faulty self-control.

"Oh, aye." Without thinking, he slipped back into the rustic idiom of his youth. "I mean—quite. Nothing I can't pick up, though, with a bit of work. I've always liked a challenge."

"Now, there's a discovery that doesn't surprise me in the least." Something about the way she said it, some warm hint of admiration in her tone, made Morse's chest expand until he feared it might pop the buttons on his greatcoat.

One wheel of the phaeton dipped into a puddle, pitching it precariously to the side. Morse leaned the other way and urged the horses to a somewhat greater speed. The maneuver succeeded in keeping the light vehicle upright.

Cursing himself for his lapse in concentration, Morse focused ruthlessly on his driving until they had safely turned up the lane to Laurelwood.

That would show Algie Blenkinsop!

And just to rub it in, should Algie be watching from one of the windows, Morse made rather a show of lifting Leonora down from the phaeton.

To his vast surprise, she clung to him for longer than was strictly necessary.

"I'd like to take advantage of this last moment of privacy," she said.

Morse felt his blood stir, wondering what fashion that *advantage* would take.

"I wanted to tell you," Leonora continued, "how pleased I am with the progress you're making."

It wasn't quite what he'd been expecting, but it dizzied Morse nonetheless. Or perhaps he'd just climbed down too quickly from the giddy height of his perch on the phaeton.

"I promised you I'd give it my best effort, and I meant it…Leonora."

There was nothing he could do to erase his earlier, shameful conduct. The very notion made him shrink within himself as though he'd let down the honor of his regiment. But Morse had sworn to himself that in the coming weeks he would do everything in his power to redeem himself in her eyes.

She gave a little start, as though still unused to hearing him address her that way. A hesitant smile tugged at one corner of her lips, suggesting she did not resent the familiarity.

"So you did…Morse, and I appreciate your effort more than I can say. I was wrong not to have solicited your ideas for our curriculum of studies from the beginning."

Her admission disarmed him completely. Breaking away from their locked gaze, he muttered, "No harm done." His stock felt tight enough to throttle him. "You ought to get inside now where it's warm."

Pulling the front door open, he fairly shoved her inside.

Another moment standing there, he reflected as he led the bays to the stable, and he could not have resisted kissing Leonora Freemantle.

Wager or no wager.

Chapter Ten

What would she have done, if he'd kissed her there in the moonlight?

The question continued to haunt Leonora through the next week as Morse exerted even greater effort in his studies. Ruthlessly focused and businesslike, he gave little indication of being the same charming rogue who had once wooed his way *out* of work.

His table manners were improving slowly, in part because Algie set such a woeful example. At least he'd become astute enough to watch his table companions for cues on which pieces of cutlery to deploy for which course of the meal.

Algie had declared him a natural gamesman—a title that made Leonora squirm. Still, it meant Morse needed only a quick account of the rules and few practice hands to master the most popular card games. His success, at faro in particular, led Leonora to suspect he had a superior grasp of practical mathematics.

His billiard game was improving, thanks to nightly matches with Algie and Sir Hugo. Dancing had proven something of a hurdle, however.

"No *wicked waltzing* for you on that leg, dear fellow,"

Algie pronounced as if it were a death sentence. "Shame, too. The ability to squire a young lady on the dance floor will get you farther in this 'heiress hunting' business than all the billiards and card playing in the world."

"Morse's lameness may play to our advantage, Algie." Leonora corralled the pair of them and Elsie Taylor into the music room for their first lesson.

She called for the gamekeeper, who had a reputation as a fine fiddler. "Rather than try to drill him on all the dances, we can concentrate on a few of the slower ones. If he finds himself confronted with an unfamiliar set when he's out at a ball, he can simply beg off on account of his leg."

"By Jove, you are clever, Leonora!" cried Algie. "Isn't she though, Morse?"

The blatant adoration in Algie's round brown eyes took Leonora aback. For all his lack of discernment, she had become quite fond of him. How could anyone not respond to those unflagging high spirits and that unfailing eagerness to help?

There was not a particle of harm in the dear fellow.

Yet, Leonora could not reconcile herself to the thought of becoming his wife.

"She'd make a fine general," Morse replied to Algie's question.

What made his dark eyes flash so provocatively when he spoke, and his firm jaw clench? He looked so solemn, Leonora could not resist poking gentle fun at him.

"You'll have to devise more poetic compliments than that, Morse, if you expect the ladies to come flocking your way at Bath."

Algie guffawed and Elsie Taylor tried to hide a smile by staring at the floor. Morse cast Leonora a challenging glance and a grin that conceded she'd scored a point off him.

Strangely, her own words struck Leonora less than funny once she'd uttered them. For they conjured in her mind an image of ladies flocking to Morse.

And they would. Game leg or sound, fawning compliments or wry jests.

Pretty ladies, witty ladies, wealthy ladies. Ladies eager to give him what all men wanted from women. And not necessarily with the inducement of a wedding ring.

It should not have mattered to her in the least. But the nauseating void in her stomach, the tightness in her chest and the crushing weight upon her heart told Leonora it did matter.

It mattered far too much.

"I say, Morse." Algie placed his cue ball a precise six inches from the head spot and lined up his billiard shot. "Have you noticed the difference in our Leonora since she engaged Miss Taylor as her lady's maid?"

His ball caromed off the cushions, striking the red, and just missing Morse's cue ball by a hairbreadth.

"Difference?" grunted Morse, bristling over Algie's *our Leonora.* How could he concentrate on making a decent shot with Blenkinsop prattling on like this? "I haven't noticed any difference."

It wasn't true, but he didn't want to dwell on it, let alone discuss it with the likes of Algie Blenkinsop. He'd noticed the changes in her appearance, subtle though they'd been, at first. They were proving a devilish distraction from his studies.

Even Algie's mention of it, just now, devastated his concentration on their billiards match. His cue struck the ball much too hard and a hair off center, sending it in a wild trajectory around the table without so much as glancing either of the other balls. Worse yet, it set up a laughably easy shot for his opponent.

So easy, in fact, that Algie scarcely needed to spare it a crumb of his attention while he continued to talk.

"Not noticed? Clever cove like you? That's rum, I'll say. Most times you have to smash a bottle over my head to attract my attention, but this caught my eye straightaway."

If the ashwood cue in his hand had been a rifle, Morse would have been sorely tempted to raise it and blow Algie Blenkinsop to kingdom come. Bad enough the thickheaded blue blood had the gall to *notice* Leonora, but did he have to rub a fellow's face in it at every opportunity?

In an effort to quench his rising temper, Morse bolted a drink of his brandy.

"You mean, her new clothes?" He begrudged the question, not wanting to encourage Algie in this line of conversation, but unwilling to let himself be thought dense. "Bit more color in them of late."

He tried to shut out any reply from Algie as he set up his next shot.

"Mmm. Take that frock she had on today. Pretty green, like an unripe apple."

When Morse spared a glance at Algie, he couldn't help but notice the fellow's calf-eyed bemusement.

Heaving a sigh of admiration, Algie continued. "It set off her eyes quite splendidly."

Morse had noticed, too. The realization had overwhelmed him like a surprise attack from the rear. But he would not have admitted the fact under torture.

Again his shot went wide. By sheer accident it struck the object ball, but came nowhere near the other.

Algie surveyed the table and clucked his tongue. "Rum luck, old fellow. Your game is off tonight, isn't it?"

With a graceful economy of movement he had yet to demonstrate on the dance floor, Algie tilted his cue over the bridge of his long fingers and made his shot. Up the table, banked off one cushion, striking the red ball, off another cushion and another before striking Morse's ball.

"Carom for me!" he cried.

To add insult to injury, Algie's shot had placed Morse's ball in a tricky corner position from which it would be almost impossible to score.

While Morse did his best to set up this preposterous shot, Algie lapsed back into worshipful contemplation of Leonora. "She has such a graceful step. Don't suppose you noticed that, either, Morse. As finely turned an ankle as I've ever seen on a gel. And I do admire that new way Miss Taylor has done Leonora's hair."

That had not escaped Morse's attention, either. The little village girl had persuaded her new mistress to cut the front part of her hair, rather than dragging it all back tight. Now those fine sable tresses clustered in soft wisps and tendrils around her face, accentuating the delicacy of her features and the stunning beauty of her eyes.

If only he could hold her in his arms, just once, and press his cheek to her hair.

"'Course a chap would be lucky to get a wife like her supposing she was homely as a brush fence," Algie declared, blithely oblivious to Morse's rising vexation.

Too many more such remarks and he'd be lucky to escape a billiard cue getting cracked across his pointy pate.

Morse bungled yet another shot, though he was past caring. All he wanted now was for the match to be over and the besotted Algie Blenkinsop out of his sight for another day.

"Looks are well and good to begin with." Though Algie appeared to be concentrating on his game even less than Morse, he scored another carom with ease. "But a chap's got to remember he'll be married to an old woman for a good deal longer than a young one. A gel like Leonora will look after a chap and see he doesn't get into too many scrapes. And she'll never lack for something interesting to say.''

Morse had never thought about women in those terms. Though it nettled him to admit it, Algie Blenkinsop had a point. Leonora was the type of woman a wise man would want to grow old with.

Gritting his teeth and clutching his billiard cue so hard his knuckles went white, Morse managed to score on his next shot.

Save for his one surprising insight, Algie Blenkinsop was not a wise man. Morse vowed, yet again, that he would do everything within his power to deprive Algie of the chance to grow old with Leonora. Starting with this billiards match.

Before the great pedestal clock in the entry struck midnight, Morse had managed to best Algie Blenkinsop, fifty caroms to forty-eight.

''Another new gown made up, already, Elsie?'' Leonora shook her head in wonder and admiration of the jonquil yellow muslin. ''You *are* a model of industry, I must say. I wish I'd had the good sense to engage your services sooner.''

Blushing at the compliment, Elsie's gaze dropped down to her sewing. ''It's almost finished, miss. I could have it done for you by dinnertime. That is, if you don't need me to make up a fourth for Sergeant Archer's dancing lessons.''

''Not Sergeant Archer, Elsie,'' Leonora corrected her. ''With Bath less than a month away, we must all get into the habit of calling him Captain Archibald.''

Captain Maurice Archibald, they'd decided, sounded enough like his own name, while lending him a more highborn air.

''I'll do my best to remember, miss.''

"Three weeks should give us all plenty of time to get used to it." Leonora fell silent for a moment, puzzling the spasm of dismayed emptiness that rippled through her whenever she contemplated the end of their time together.

Perhaps it was only unease as to how Morse would fare in Bath society.

"I hope he'll be ready in time," she mused aloud.

"Do you think it's right of him to be setting out to deceive a lady into marriage, miss?" asked Elsie.

Leonora detected a subdued note of censure in the girl's voice that her mistress should be working so hard to help him.

"Give Sergeant...I mean, Captain Archibald, the benefit of a doubt. There is far more riding on his success than you might think. In fact, you may have cause to thank him for his effort one of these days."

"If you say so, miss." The girl focused on her sewing once again. "He has the best teachers in you and Mr. Blenkinsop."

"Algie?" Leonora rolled her eyes. "You're right, though, I suppose. He has been a help, in his way, tutoring Morse in all the dissipations of a gentleman."

"He's a fine gentleman himself. Ser—Captain Archibald could learn a good deal just by watching him."

"Really, Elsie." Leonora strolled to the window, where she could see the two men practicing carriage handling in the courtyard. "Morse is twice the man Algie will ever be, regardless of their rank or fortune."

"Oh, I don't know about that, miss." This was the first time Leonora could recall the girl quite so outspoken. "Mr. Blenkinsop isn't as good-looking or as clever, perhaps, but I reckon a cheerful nature and a kind heart are better than any amount of looks or wits."

"Elsie Taylor!" Leonora contemplated the girl in wonder. "Don't tell me you're smitten with Algie Blenkin-sop?"

"Of course not, miss!" Elsie jabbed her needle into the muslin with brutal force, her cheeks suddenly as red as a pair of cherries. "I wouldn't presume any such thing. Especially when it's clear how much he fancies you. I never heard a man go on so about a lady."

Leonora couldn't argue that. It was one of the few things that kept her from liking Algie without reserve.

"Besides, he's a good deal cleverer than you give him credit for," Elsie added almost under her breath.

Turning away to hide a smile, Leonora shook her head. Algie could be far more clever than she imagined him and still not be mistaken for a genius.

"Don't worry about finishing the dress today, Elsie. It looks rather too fancy for dinner at home, anyway. Perhaps I shall save it for an outing at Bath, or..."

An idea germinated in her thoughts and took root. "Your presence as a fourth for dancing would be most helpful, though. Shall we go call the men in from their carriage driving practice and put them to work polishing up their ballroom skills?"

"Oh, yes, miss! I should be ever so glad to help." As Elsie scrambled up from her chair, her sewing cascaded to the floor like a pool of molten butter.

"I hope my pupil will greet the invitation with as much enthusiasm as you do." Leonora chuckled.

As they hurried down the main staircase, Leonora spied her uncle in the entry hall.

"Off gadding again, Uncle Hugo." She fastened the top button of his greatcoat and wound the woolen muffler around his neck. "You aren't courting Colonel Morrison's sister on the sly, are you?"

He pretended to chuff and bluster with indignation, but she could tell the quip amused him. "Nonsense. Courting at my age—nonsense! Glad to see young folk and high spirits back at Laurelwood again. You don't need an old duffer like me hanging about all the time."

So that was it. Leonora wasn't certain whether to swallow a smile or to heave a sigh of exasperation. Uncle Hugo was purposely making himself scarce so as not to hamper Algie's pursuit of her. Perhaps he entertained some vain hope that the impossible creature might win her heart, even if she and Morse ended up winning the wager.

No sense in telling him he could sail away to the South Seas and it would not influence her feelings for Algie Blenkinsop. Or rather, her lack of feelings. If it wasn't what he wanted to hear, the words would go in one ear and come out the other.

"You're *not* old," she said instead. "And we all enjoy your company very much, so you needn't go courting influenza by riding out on an endless round of visits."

Leonora recalled the idea she'd been mulling over on the way downstairs. "Elsie, would you be so obliging as to summon Mr. Blenkinsop and Ser—Captain Archibald in for dancing practice? Promise them a cup of chocolate to warm up before we begin."

As the girl scampered off to call Morse and Algie, Leonora called after her, "If that doesn't budge them, promise brandy."

Sir Hugo chortled. "You know how to manage men, my dear, and that's a fact."

She picked a thread from the breast of his coat. "When I first tried to recruit Morse for our wager, you told me I hadn't a notion how to handle men."

"Well, you've learned in the meantime." Sir Hugo donned his hat. "These lessons of yours must be working both ways."

The idea struck Leonora dumb for a moment. She had

learned a thing or two from Morse Archer—some harsh lessons, others far too pleasant.

As Sir Hugo stepped toward the door, she caught his coat sleeve. "If I'm such a dab hand at bending men to my will, can I persuade you to host a party at Laurelwood in a fortnight or so? We can say it's a farewell to the neighborhood before we go to Bath. Morse is progressing very well, but I would like to give him a chance to test his wings on an audience that won't be too critical."

"Capital idea—capital!" boomed Sir Hugo. "Can't think why the notion didn't occur to me in the first place. We must ask the Misses Maperton and Colonel Morrison's nieces. And that young nephew of Pewsey's who's been staying with him. You write up the invitations, my dear, and I'll give our neighbors plenty of advance notice of their coming. Now I must be on my way before I melt in this coat and muffler."

"Thank you, Uncle." Leonora sent him off with a kiss on the cheek and a sneaking sense of satisfaction that she could manage one man, after all.

"I know it's getting late and you've put in a full day already." Leonora cast Morse a pleading look he could not resist. "We've only got two more days until the party, and only a week after that to get our ducks in a row before we head off to Bath. I want to make certain you have your background well memorized, so no one can trip you up."

Morse gave a weary nod. "Go ahead."

His mind was already swimming with Latin tags and French *bon mots,* not to mention the basic stories from far too many of Old Billy Shakespeare's plays. After a long drive in the phaeton with Algie, then dancing for as long as his leg could tolerate, Morse was ready for a tip of spirits and an early bedtime.

Nothing would induce him to let Leonora down, however.

Particularly not when she appeared to know and appreciate exactly how hard he had been working. Besides that, their time together was running out. Morse found himself clutching at every opportunity for a moment alone with her, no matter how tiresome the subject of their studies.

When she told him about Caesar's conquest of Gaul, or the plots and counterplots executed during the War of the Roses, it all sounded like the most fascinating adventure. When she read to him from the works of the great poets, Morse's soul stirred in response. Even Latin had a pretty sound when it issued from such beguiling lips—one minute firm and resolute, the next softly vulnerable.

"It won't take long, I promise." Her head tilted to one side. Her eyes glowed with empathy and encouragement. "Rather than recite it all by rote, though, we should practice in a way you're likely to encounter at the party or at Bath. Let us pretend I'm a lady to whom you've just been introduced."

Morse's tiredness eased. Flashing her a smile, he sat up straighter on the chaise. The idea of playacting piqued his interest. No question, Leonora was a stimulating teacher—a stimulating...companion. He would miss that companionship, perhaps more than he'd ever expected.

"A pleasure to make your acquaintance, Captain Archibald." Leonora held out her hand to him and batted her eyelashes like a proper vacuous debutante. "What brings you to Bath, pray tell?"

Morse bit the inside of his lip to keep from laughing. With a touch as light as he would have used to handle delicate porcelain, he lifted her hand and brushed it with his lips.

"*Enchanté, mademoiselle.*" He'd worked many hours

to master his few words of French. Might as well work them in at every opportunity.

He treated her to *the look*—an expression he'd perfected over the years to assure a woman that she was one of the most beautiful he'd ever laid eyes on.

"You might say I've come to enjoy the *scenery*." His look and intonation were meant to leave no doubt that the lady herself was worth a long journey to gaze upon. Though Morse aped the upper-class drawl of a much-loathed officer he'd served under in India, the flattery was all his own.

For the past six weeks he'd manfully refrained from using his charm on Leonora. Their present exercise in make-believe freed him to say all the things he'd been hoarding within himself.

If he worried she might take issue with that, her trill of tittering laughter reassured him—even as it set his teeth on edge.

"Oh, Captain!" She raised her hand as if to shield a blushing face. "You are too gallant."

"Not at all, Miss Husbandhunter." Morse watched Leonora try to stifle a giggle at the name he'd invented for her. "The fact is, I came here with friends. Sir Hugo Peverill—perhaps you've heard of him? He thought the waters of Bath might do my game leg some good."

"Your leg. Oh dear. Were you wounded in action?"

"Alas, yes. My fighting days are over. I've recovered sufficiently to walk…and dance, though slowly. But I'll never be up to the rigors of campaigning again."

"What a pity! My brother is with Colonel Ebbett's regiment. Which did you serve in?"

"The Fourth Somerset Rifles." No one who heard his tone of pride could have doubted Morse on that score.

"A Rifleman—how dashing!" Some glint of a spring twilight in Leonora's eyes told Morse she was not counterfeiting. "I have relations all over Somerset. What part of the county do you hail from?"

"My mother's people were from Somerset, but I grew up in India where my father was on the governor's staff. But, really, I'm not the least interesting. You must tell me all about yourself, Miss Husbandhunter." He took her hand in his. "Do you come to Bath often? Where is *your* home? Whereabouts in Portugal is your brother's regiment, now?"

"That isn't fair, Morse...I mean, Maurice," Leonora pulled her fingers from his grasp. "How can I drill you in your cover story when you turn the tables like that?"

Morse sprawled back on the chaise. "Because that's what I'll *do*, Leonora. If some wet goose sets to quizzing me like you just did, I'll simply set her talking about herself. That's what most people want to talk about, anyway."

"I suppose you're right." She softened her words with a grin. "Thank heavens you can think on your feet, Morse. I doubt we'll meet anyone in Bath clever enough to trip you up."

A strange warmth blossomed within Morse and spread through him, as though he'd just imbibed some intoxicating potion.

"A Rifleman has to be ready to take the initiative." He shrugged off her compliment by quoting the precepts of Sir John Moore. "Never you worry now, Leonora. I'll win you this wager, whatever it takes."

Somehow, his hand got tangled up with hers. He squeezed it—for reassurance.

To his surprise, she did not pull back this time. Instead, she brought her other hand to cover his.

"I believe you will, Morse." An aura of vague sadness shadowed the confidence of her words and her touch. "If I'd had any notion of how much work it would entail, I'd have been less cocksure about accepting Uncle's wager, I can tell you. I doubt anyone else could have brought it off. I see now why Cousin Wes placed such faith in you.''

If she had fastened a medal to his chest, or placed a crown of laurels on his brow, Morse could not have been more edified. If she had gutted him with a saber, he could not have been more stricken.

He turned his face from Leonora, not wanting her to witness the unmanly evidence of his regret. ''Perhaps he shouldn't have placed so much trust in me. I wasn't able to save him.''

Though he wanted to say more, Morse feared the thickness in his voice would betray him.

Another woman might have retreated from the grim spectacle of his distress, but not Leonora.

The next thing Morse knew, she had one hand on either side of his face, turning it inexorably toward her.

''You listen to me, Morse Archer.'' Her tone resonated with bone-deep conviction. ''You are *not* responsible for Wesley's death. Uncle has his connections in the War Ministry and we know what happened. There is blame enough to go around, by all accounts. But none of it extends to you.''

He could not bring himself to meet her gaze, though he felt it boring into him. All the same, her words wrapped themselves around him.

''If Wesley were here—'' The catch in her voice enticed Morse to glance up.

A fine mist glistened in her eyes like the pearly daybreak fog on a green summer morning.

Leonora was not ashamed of her grief. She did not let the rising tears daunt her. ''If Wesley were here, he would be the first to dun it into your proud head. You have nothing to reproach yourself for.''

Since that day at Bucaso, it had seemed to Morse Archer as though a band of iron encased his chest. Never tight enough to crush him, but never allowing him the luxury of an easy breath, either.

Now a blacksmith had struck the lock holding that band in place. His heart could beat as hard as it pleased without restraint. He could laugh or cry with all the passion that was in him.

And he could breathe freely again.

Suddenly, Morse noticed Leonora's face coming nearer his own. Was she pulling him toward her, or was he approaching in spite of her?

Morse could scarcely tell.

He only knew that his gratitude and a hundred other jumbled but powerful feelings for this woman could find no better means of expression than in the homage of his lips.

It was not until they had made contact—moist, hot, sweet contact—and his arms had locked around her that misgivings assailed Morse.

Would Leonora push him away, as she had before? Would she mistake his kiss for another selfish bid to manipulate her?

Her hands had not released their hold on his face—that heartened Morse. In fact, they exerted a gentle pressure to tilt his head. The tentative flutter of her lips and tongue roused him more than the artful preludes to seduction of other women he'd known.

Morse did not stop to consider what it meant. He only knew that he wanted this woman. And he did not want to let her go—ever.

Emboldened by her innocent ardor, he kissed her harder, bringing one hand up to stroke her hair and caress her neck. The other, he gave rein to rove over her body, charting the gentle curves and tempting clefts.

Perhaps a knock of warning sounded. The blood was

pounding too thunderously in Morse's ears for him to have heard it.

But he was not so far lost to desire that he could ignore Elsie Taylor throwing wide the door and exclaiming, "Excuse me, miss, I thought I might have left my sewing basket in—"

Morse and Leonora flew apart, hands fumbling to adjust their clothes, looking anywhere but at each other.

"I believe it's on the window seat," squeaked Leonora, jumping from the chaise. "Here, let me help you look for it."

Morse glared murder at Miss Taylor. What on earth could she want with a sewing basket at this hour?

To his astonishment, she glared back, leaving Morse in no doubt that she'd interrupted them on purpose.

He tried to quell his craving for Leonora long enough to marshal his thoughts. He would have some explaining to do once Elsie Taylor fetched her benighted sewing gear out of there—an apology might be in order, too.

"Why look at the time!" Leonora shadowed Elsie as the girl collected her basket. "I must get to bed. We want to be well rested for Uncle's party, after all."

She followed Elsie out the door, without once glancing up at him. "Good night, Captain Archibald. Don't stay awake too late."

As the door swung shut behind the women, Morse leaped up and kicked the chaise.

"Ow!" He cursed the throbbing pain in his toes. At least it distracted him from a more intimate ache ignited by Leonora's kiss.

At length he subdued the emotions rampaging within him. At least enough that he was able to go off in search of Algie and the brandy decanter. An hour of Blenkinsop's cheerful, undemanding chatter and a generous snifter of Sir Hugo's brandy might secure him a few hours' untroubled slumber.

But Morse heartily doubted it.

Chapter Eleven

Well rested for the party?

Leonora might have laughed at the notion had she not been so thoroughly wrought up. Rolling over in bed, she pounded her pillow, wishing for all the world it could transform into Morse Archer.

So she could pound him—or so he could share her bed? Leonora was not certain. A little of both, perhaps.

What might have happened in the sitting room if Elsie Taylor had not interrupted? Leonora's belly boiled with panic at the very thought. At the same time, her lower regions simmered with carnal curiosity. She could not decide whether she wanted to raise Elsie's wages or to dismiss the girl without a reference.

What must Morse Archer think of her now? After she had taken advantage of his distress to entrap him into a moment of intimacy? After the way she had thrown herself at his head, he must despise her for a pathetic, desperate, man-starved spinster.

And would he be so far wrong?

Leonora cringed at the memory of how easily she'd fallen for his pretended lovemaking. This time *she'd* initiated their kiss—driven to it by the physical yearning for him she'd struggled to suppress ever since.

Not that he'd pushed her away.

Her body still smarted with remembered heat where his ravenous touch had scorched her. If she gave herself up to the memory of those intense but fleeting moments, her flesh and blood pulsed with a raw hunger she scarcely dared guess how to satisfy.

With a moan of frustration, Leonora bolted out of bed and lit a candle. Tearing off her nightgown, she poured cold water into her washbasin. With a cloth soaked in the frigid water, she scoured her body until gooseflesh rose and her skin took on the blue-white caste of skim milk.

If only Morse Archer had not been thrust into her life, making her question the direction of her safely mapped future. Longing for things that had no place in that future.

Things like desire. And love.

Yet, when she tried to picture a life in which she had never met him, its colors seemed faded and dull. Its spaces empty. And herself but an insignificant speck in one corner.

A great carbuncle on the face of Laurelwood—that's what he'd be!

With Sir Hugo's party about to start, Morse asked Dickon to retie his stock in an effort to loosen his high formal shirt collar. True, he looked the part of a gentleman. But he had come to realize there was more to that role than outward appearance.

Morse felt the lack within himself.

For the longest time he'd despised their ilk, determined to diminish those who would lord over him. But he'd been wrong. That type were not gentlemen at all, for all their wealth and impressive pedigrees.

The true mark of a gentleman was his code of honor

and his philosophy of living. Wesley Peverill had been an authentic gentleman. For all his bumbling and guileless good cheer, Algie Blenkinsop was one, too. Morse was not certain he could define the quality, let alone hope to emulate it.

He had a sinking sensation in the pit of his stomach that even the petty gentry of rural Wiltshire would see through his flimsy ruse in a minute.

If only he could have talked to Leonora. Somehow Morse knew she would have found the right words to hearten and steady him. But after their aborted encounter of the previous night, she had taken pains to avoid being alone in his company all day.

He longed to explain himself. To discover how she felt about what had happened. Was she angry with him? With herself? Did it mean anything to her, or was it a rash impulse born of the potent emotions of the moment?

Unwisely indulged. Immediately regretted.

Hearing a discreet tap on the door, he wheeled away from Dickon, who had finished with his stock and was now giving his coat a final brush.

"Oh, it's you Algie. Come in."

"Well, don't you look smart." Algie ambled over to Morse's shaving table, eyeing him from head to toe. "Wish I had a figure like yours, old fellow, instead of being the cursed beanpole I am. The most expensive tailor on Bond Street couldn't make me cut a dash like you will tonight."

Morse marveled at how the fellow could admit such a thing without the least hint of mean envy. As though he accepted his own shortcomings with good cheer and only a trace of regret, meanwhile exulting in another's good fortune.

For all that, Algie and Leonora were not meant to be husband and wife.

Morse wondered if his conviction might be born of self-interest. But when he looked deep into his heart, he was pleased to discover otherwise.

"Ta, Algie." Morse inserted a finger between his neck and his collar as he tried to coax a smile. "I don't *feel* very dashing, I can tell you. I doubt I'll make the right impression on any of Sir Hugo's guests tonight. Let alone all the swells at Bath."

"Nonsense!" Algie tucked the fillets of Morse's stock into the breast of his waistcoat. "I'll bet my month's allowance you'll be the *beau of the ball.*"

Braying with laughter at his own jest, he threw a lanky arm over Morse's shoulder. "Not if you skulk up in your room all night, though. Come along, and let's help Sir Hugo welcome his guests. If you find yourself cornered by some disagreeable female, tonight, just catch my eye and I'll come rescue you by asking her to dance."

Fortunately for Algie, Morse did not take his wager of a month's allowance. For Captain Archibald's fledgling flight in society turned out a proper triumph.

Perhaps it was the warmth of Algie's reassurance. Or the fact that the ladies outnumbered the gentlemen by a wide margin. Or it might have been his determination to not let Leonora down.

Whatever the reason, Morse soon found himself surrounded by admirers. Charming these well-born ladies with slightly more polished versions of the gestures and flattery he'd used with such finesse upon barmaids and camp followers.

Prompted by some broad hints, he squired several of Sir Hugo's female guests on the dance floor despite an agony of nerves over his performance. As it turned out, he needn't have worried. His partners were quick to attribute any misstep to his unfortunate leg injury or his long absence from polite society while in the Rifles.

The greater his success, the more his ease and confidence grew. The more confident his manner, the more Sir Hugo's guests flocked to him. By the time the party had been in progress an hour, Morse began to think Algie's prediction would be amply fulfilled.

More than once he tried to catch Leonora's eye for a smile or a look that would commend his achievement. But she did not once glance in his direction. Instead, she seemed occupied with a clutch of female guests whom Morse finally recognized as girls from the village who attended her evening classes.

He tried to ignore his own childish stab of disappointment. It was not as though he needed her seal of approval before he could take pleasure in his own triumph.

Yet that was how it felt.

Only when he overheard the remark of a pasty-faced stripling guest—a remark he felt certain was *meant* to be overheard—did Morse understand why Leonora hovered around her charges.

"What *can* old Peverill have been thinking?" sneered the young fellow who affected a languid slouch. "Why, one of those girls is the daughter of our gardener. Picture me asking *that* to dance—me, the nephew of a baronet."

Some of the girls might not have heard him, but Elsie Taylor certainly had, and perhaps one other—the butt of the young monster's mockery. The way their cheeks reddened and their eyes found the floor left Morse in no doubt.

His hands itched to close around the pompous puppy's throat and throttle him, but Morse took a deep breath and restrained himself for Leonora's sake.

Instead, he disengaged himself from the elder of Colonel Morrison's nieces and approached Leonora's pupils. He could not quite bring himself to forgive Elsie Taylor for barging into the sitting room the night before, so instead he offered his arm to the gardener's blushing daughter.

"Miss...Yates?" Morse prayed he hadn't mistaken the name from their brief introduction.

She glanced up at him with the eyes of a suffering wild creature caught in a snare.

"May I request the honor of this dance? I fear you'll have to go slowly and excuse my awkwardness on account of my lame leg."

The ghost of a smile hovered on her lips, and she cast the pasty-faced youth a look of disdain that made Morse long to applaud. "Thank you, Captain Archibald." She spoke the words as correctly as any dowager duchess. "I should be very pleased to accept your invitation."

With a toss of her curls and a proud tilt of her chin, she took the floor on Morse's arm where she acquitted herself most gracefully.

Out of the corner of his eye, Morse saw Algie approach Miss Taylor and offer his arm.

During the next half hour the pair of them saw to it that each of Leonora's pupils got at least one dance. Several other gentlemen followed suit, and a number of the ladies helped the girls to punch and cultivated conversations with them.

The baronet's obnoxious nephew, by comparison, had several of his dance invitations politely refused on one pretext or another.

By the time Morse felt his duty dispatched, his leg was crying out for respite. A whispered word in Dickon's ear produced a more potent cup of punch than the rest of the company was enjoying. Morse limped over to a chair in a dim corner alcove of the hall and flung himself down, propping his aching leg up on a handy footstool.

He took several deep drafts from his cup and closed his eyes, waiting for the spirits to numb his pain. Though he heard the faint rustle of a woman's skirt and breathed a subtle floral scent he could not identify, Morse kept his eyes shut. He did not need some tittering female hovering around him just now.

"Thank you, Morse." Warm with approval, Leonora's voice washed over him, blotting out the worst of his pain.

Opening his eyes, he drank in the sight of her. She wore a gown the rich color of claret wine. It brightened her complexion and warmed the dark hue of her hair. The bodice was modestly cut, for the fashion of the times. Yet the soft fabric draped around her with seductive elegance.

He wanted her in a different way than he'd ever wanted any other woman—save one. Morse wasn't certain whether the notion tempted or terrified him.

"You must mean *Maurice*," he whispered. "I'm not acquainted with anyone named Morse."

She glanced toward the rest of the company, as if judging their risk of being overheard above the convivial hubbub. Then she knelt beside his chair and leaned close.

"Well, *I* know someone named Morse," she murmured. "And a good fellow he is. I can't tell you how proud I am of him tonight."

Perhaps the strong spirits in his cup had begun to work on Morse. Certainly the next words out of his lips took him by surprise.

"I want to do you proud, Leonora. More than I want that plantation in the colonies. More than I've ever wanted anything."

Morse sensed his last words were not entirely true. There was something else he might want more, if only he dared let himself acknowledge it.

Oh, this man! He did have a knack for saying exactly what she wanted to hear. The notion warmed Leonora even as it unsettled her. She wanted to dismiss his compliment with a self-deprecating quip. But she could not, on the off chance that he'd truly meant it.

As she plundered her mind for *something* to say, the trio of musicians Sir Hugo had engaged struck up a familiar tune.

Morse sat straight in his chair and smiled. "'Upon A Summer's Day'! We can't have practiced that so often in the past weeks only to sit it out in company."

He heaved himself up, flinching when his lame leg took weight upon it. "Will you do me the honor of this dance, Miss Freemantle?"

Much as she longed to take the floor on his arm, Leonora shook her head. "You've already had more dancing than is good for you, tonight."

He caught her hand and hoisted her up from the floor as if she had no more weight than a butterfly. "Ah, but I insist."

Leaning closer, he whispered, "I've done my *duty dances*. Surely you wouldn't deny me one purely for my own pleasure."

Leonora might have denied him. If only she could have found her voice. If only her hand did not clasp his arm with a will of its own and her feet move toward the dance floor entirely of their own accord.

They had practiced this well-known dance often, as it was often played in assembly rooms. Though it had a sprightly tune, the tempo of the dancers was not too quick. And it was performed in sets of three couples. Morse and Leonora, Algie and Miss Taylor, Dickon and the game-keeper's daughter had practiced it over and over until the six of them could almost have danced it in their sleep.

"I see you've had the same idea." A beaming Algie towed Elsie behind him.

They made a six with Sir Hugo and Colonel Morrison's widowed sister. As they led up and fell back, Leonora watched anxiously for signs that Morse's leg pained him. Perhaps the short rest or whatever he'd been drinking had eased him, for he did not so much as wince.

She relaxed a little, letting herself enjoy the warmth of his hand on hers as they led. The brush of her gown against his breeches as they turned.

Algie and Sir Hugo joined hands to create an arch, as did Elsie and Sir Hugo's partner. Morse and Leonora led down the center, then separated—him to go through the men's arch, her to go through the women's.

It struck Leonora as an apt metaphor for their future.

In the past weeks they had worked together, toward a common goal. Once they won the wager, however, they must part. Morse going off to the rough-hewn, masculine world of the colonies. She settling into a kind of feminine cloister with her school. And how she would miss him!

A lump rose in Leonora's throat.

For all their hard work and occasional bickering during the past months, she had become accustomed to Morse's presence in her life. His going would leave a void even her long-dreamed-of school might not productively fill.

The lyrics often sung to this melody were also a distressing reminder of things to come. A discourse between a young lady and her soldier beau going off to war. Leonora had always been skeptical of the outcome of that exchange—the woman declaring she would follow her lover to war, rather than die of worry and heartbreak waiting for his return. A woman of sense could not simply abandon the life she knew to follow a man.

Or could she?

As they joined hands again for the final double, Morse leaned toward her and whispered, "Come back to earth, Leonora. Where have your thoughts been? Not here on the dance floor, that's for certain."

She flashed him a brief smile of apology. "Only thinking of what's still to come. I'm sorry if I spoiled the dance for you. I didn't mean to be so preoccupied.''

He escorted her back to the alcove, his limp more pronounced. Had he been masking it before? Or was he exaggerating it now, to deflect the hopeful glances cast his way by Mrs. Bonnell and Miss Morrison the Younger?

''I can't very well blame you.'' He spoke quietly, imparting a confidence. ''I have found myself preoccupied all day. I can't stop thinking about what happened between us last evening.''

Leonora's stomach constricted and her breath fluttered high and shallow in her chest. ''The *kiss* you mean.'' She let her voice drop to a whisper on that word, almost as if she was afraid to say it.

Morse gripped her arm tightly as he eased himself back into the chair. His weight pulled Leonora forward, until she could feel the whisper of his breath against the bare flesh of her décolletage.

''The kiss,'' he murmured, ''and all that went with it.''

The husky quality of his voice sent bewildering sensations snaking through her. Almost as if he had run his hand over her body from ankle to shoulder.

''It was a mistake.'' The words choked her. Would she ever learn to admit error or weakness without feeling so terrifyingly vulnerable? ''I shouldn't have thrown myself at you like that.''

''I didn't notice any *throwing*.'' Morse chuckled. ''I think something…sparked between us just then and we hadn't any choice but to act on it.''

Leonora shook her head. ''People may not choose how they feel, but they always have choices in how they act.''

She couldn't live without that measure of control, seductive as it might be at times to slough off responsibility for those deliberate decisions. ''I wanted to kiss you, so I did. I suppose I was curious.''

Even in the shadows of the alcove, his eyes glittered perceptively. A half smile crinkled one corner of his mouth. "Is there anything else you're curious to explore, Leonora?"

She hovered over him, her back to the rest of Sir Hugo's guests. None of them could possibly see Morse reach up and swipe his fingers across the bodice of her gown. As the sensitive tips of her breasts hardened and set a moist inferno blazing between her thighs, Leonora felt the whole company must be gaping at her. Knowing every wicked thought that passed through her brain.

Pulling back from Morse, she put a safe distance of several steps between them. If he touched her like that again, she might be forced to abdicate her will. Tossed perilously on a stormy sea of impulse and indiscretion.

"I am not about to jeopardize my future simply to satisfy my curiosity."

She was a twenty-seven-year-old virgin, and unless she lost the wager with Uncle Hugo, she intended to remain one. She could hardly run her school while trying to raise an illegitimate baby. Or was Morse suggesting he would take responsibility for their choice by making an honest woman of her, if need be?

For the first time in her life, the notion of marriage and a family tempted Leonora.

"No need to jeopardize anything."

She should have known he was not advocating a course as foolish as wedding her.

"There are ways a man can bring a woman pleasure without..." He groped for the right word. "...without any bothersome consequences."

"There are?" The words squeaked out of her parchment-dry throat.

Lounging back in the chair, Morse nodded slowly. His

sinful smile and sultry gaze *suggested* what those ways might be.

At that moment Leonora understood how Eve must have felt, tempted by the serpent in the garden. Did she dare to taste the forbidden fruit Morse offered her?

"It's beginning to look as if we may win this wager with your uncle," said Morse. "If you are bent on adopting a life of *single blessedness,* I feel it's my duty to help you make an informed choice. How can you do that if you have no idea what you'll be missing?"

Oh, Rifleman Archer had the serpent beaten altogether. Leonora scraped together enough poise to observe, "You are quite the logician, sir."

His grin broadened. "I am a rogue at heart, and none of your gentlemanly polish will alter that."

If his words were meant to warn her off, they had quite the opposite effect on Leonora. She could almost feel contrary forces tugging her in two different directions.

Her head and her will pulled one way. They were strong, having ruled her life for so many years unopposed.

But perhaps they had grown somewhat lax, lost condition, from the lack of rivalry. Now her body and her heart were putting up a fight, fueled by their resentment at being so long stifled.

"What do you say?" prompted Morse. "We have a fortnight before we must leave for Bath. Shall we turn the tables for a while and let me teach you?"

"Leonora, my dear!" boomed Sir Hugo from behind her.

She could not suppress a guilty start, but she rallied her composure enough to turn and smile. "Yes, Uncle?"

"The Morrisons are leaving. You must come along to the door with me and bid them a good night."

"Of course, Uncle. They have been most congenial guests. I want to thank them for coming."

Her mind welcomed the distraction. Now it would gain time to reinforce its defenses and temper potent weapons, such as the memories of her past.

As she made to follow her uncle away, Morse called, "Well, Leonora? Don't leave me in suspense. Are you willing?"

Her mind scrambled to repulse this sneak attack, but her tongue suddenly turned traitor, siding with her heart.

"I am."

Two tiny words. But would her whole future hang on them?

Chapter Twelve

Are you willing?

The memory of his words stirred Morse, even as he cringed at his own audacity. What had possessed him last night?

Could it have been the draft he'd taken to deaden the pain in his leg? Or the heady rush of his first social triumph? Or had he been swept away by a riptide of attraction to Leonora that he'd been swimming against for weeks?

Contemplating her answer to his question roused Morse even more. Leonora had taken up the gauntlet of his challenge, daring him to follow through.

A niggling whisper in the back of his mind urged caution.

This would not be like any of the fleeting encounters with women he'd enjoyed during his years abroad. Though he'd done his best to leave his partners well satisfied, his own pleasure had always been the object. What he had proposed to Leonora was less like teaching and more like service.

He'd been well instructed in the ways of such service. Cultivated as an instrument to bring a woman pleasure. At the time he hadn't realized it, though. He'd been sufficiently naive and infatuated to believe a man and a woman were equal partners in bed, no matter what their positions in the world. And he'd been foolish enough to expect that bedroom equality could carry over into the world.

Even a decade later, the hurt of it still gnawed at his heart. Morse was no longer certain what tormented him most—Lady Pamela's betrayal, or his own humiliation.

He'd been a young footman at Granville Manor, chafing at his servitude, when he'd caught the eye of his master's young wife. While old Sir Winthrope was alive, he had managed to keep his distance from Lady Pamela, though he burned with longing for her.

After his master's death, Morse had surrendered to that longing.

It had been heady stuff for a young man's first love affair. A very beautiful woman, somewhat older than he and infinitely more experienced. The dizzying euphoria of first love mixed with the dark thrill of intrigue to compound an intoxicating elixir.

Secret encounters. Furtive couplings. Coded gestures and looks.

He had come to crave her like a drunkard craved gin. Willing to go anywhere, at any time, do anything to be with her. Believing she loved him with equal fervor, he had begun to dream of a future for the two of them.

What a simpleton!

Her money had never been his object, so the circumstances were perfect. With no children and an entailed estate, Lady Pamela would have only a small widow's jointure once her late husband's will went to probate.

Not much, but enough to buy a modest cottage and set Morse up in a respectable trade.

Some scrap of gentle sensibility had kept him from asking for her hand while her first husband was barely cold in his grave. When he finally screwed up his courage to do it, she laughed in his face.

"Oh, my darling Archer, surely you jest! Me—settle down in some dreary village as the wife of a common wagonwright or brewer?"

His whole body blushing with anger and humiliation, he still tried to persuade her. "Better a cosy little house we could call our own and go off to bed early of a night whenever we felt like it. Instead of sneaking around a great drafty mansion."

She smiled then. At least, her lips raised at the corners. "I rather like the sneaking, Archer, darling. I find it most stimulating. Now do stop talking nonsense and come kiss me."

He kissed her, with everything in him, hoping it might convince her that his love was worth more than possessions or status.

"You have to be out of Granville Manor in another month, anyway," he persisted when they paused for air. "If you have to live more humbly anyway, why not with me?"

"Because, my sweet rustic footman, I have already promised my hand to someone else. And I *won't* be living more humbly. My new husband may be somewhat beneath my last one in social standing, but the depth of his purse will more than compensate. Now go bolt the door, there's a good fellow. I plan to enjoy your company often until then."

"You can't mean it. You *can't* do it! I love you, Pamela, and I want you to be my wife."

Her countenance hardened then, and Morse knew there would be no persuading her. "You're becoming tiresome, Archer. If you can't see why wedding you is totally out of the question, there's nothing I can say to dun it into your head, I suppose."

Sidling up to him, she unbuttoned his coat, waistcoat and shirt, running her hands over his chest. Her touch did not excite him as it once had.

"You won't have to part from me, if that's what's worrying you. Mr. Hill has assured me I may retain as many of the servants from Granville Manor as I wish to bring north with me. Of course, I shall give you glowing recommendation. Nothing needs to change between us."

Morse felt as though she had slapped him hard across the cheek, her nails gouging his skin.

He understood then that he'd never been more to her than a servant. A servant with special, intimate duties, to be sure. But always at her command, never his desire. Valued no higher than the cook for her puddings or the gardener for his neatly trimmed hedges. Not on any account to be viewed as a *person* with his own needs, dreams and griefs.

His mistress pouted her lips in a wordless demand that he kiss her again.

He didn't.

Instead Morse put his lips and his hands to work on other parts of her body, until she was purring and panting. Judging her on the very brink of ecstasy, he pulled away.

To her frustrated squeal, he replied, "Go to hell, Lady Granville."

There and then, he'd quit Granville Manor and enlisted in the Rifles, vowing he would have nothing more to do with women above his station. He had kept that vow most strictly, until he'd come to Laurelwood.

Did he dare to make an exception for Leonora Freemantle?

Leonora squeezed her bloodless fingers around her coffee cup to still their trembling. Toying with her breakfast, she only half listened to Algie and Uncle Hugo's animated discussion of the party.

She'd passed a miserable night, wishing she could take back the words she'd flung at Morse. Her sleep-starved mind almost looked forward to the day when he would be gone from her life, leaving her to untroubled slumber.

Yet, at the thought of his going, a deep chasm of loneliness seemed to open at her feet, threatening to swallow her whole.

If you can't abide the notion of losing him now, her reasonable self admonished, *how much worse will you feel if you let him closer?*

But how could she let him go without satisfying her curiosity? For the rest of her life, she would think of him and wonder.

"Sorry I'm late." Morse took his place at the breakfast table, his limp more pronounced than in several weeks.

Remembering what he had done for Dorothy Yates and her other pupils at the party, Leonora's heart softened toward him.

"Not much wonder you overslept, old fellow," mumbled Algie through a mouthful of kippers and toast. "After all that dancing and punch, I slept like a top. Splendid party, Sir Hugo," he said for perhaps the tenth time that morning.

Thank heaven Morse was going to win her wager. No matter how fond she'd grown of Algie in other ways, Leonora knew she could not abide rising every morning to face his hearty good humor. A week into their honeymoon and she'd probably be hurling soft-boiled eggs at his head!

"Glad to hear you slept well." Morse tucked into the breakfast he'd been served with table manners a good deal more genteel than Algie's. "I had roughish night."

Was it her imagination, or did he venture a furtive glance her way?

"A bit too much dancing to suit my leg," Morse concluded.

"You need to build up strength in it." Algie looked to Sir Hugo for an endorsement.

"So you do," agreed the older man. "Now that the weather's got milder, you should go for a walk every day. Leonora can trot along with you and lecture, if you're worried about missing lessons."

"That sounds like a fine idea." Morse looked at her, his eyes sparkling with amusement, or perhaps challenge.

She could not bring herself to look away, but neither could she summon up an answer.

A walk—away from Laurelwood. The chance for privacy.

"Right after we finish breakfast, I'll get my coat and walking stick." Morse's eating seemed to increase in tempo.

"I…suppose." Leonora forced the words out, embarrassed by the high, tight quality of her voice. She sounded like such a coward.

Pushing her scarcely touched breakfast plate away, she excused herself from the table. "I'll fetch my cloak and bonnet and join you shortly." She could not bring herself to meet his gaze, lest she should catch him savoring her discomfort.

In the next ten minutes Leonora donned and doffed her cloak a dozen times at least.

Yes, she would walk with Morse—what harm could it do?

No, she couldn't possibly. He had come to mean too much to her already. She could not afford to care more for him.

On the other hand, he had only invited her to stroll the grounds—not tumble about on his bed.

Her conflicting inclinations batted her heart back and

forth like a shuttlecock until her thoughts spun in a dizzy rondeau.

When she descended the staircase and saw his eyes light up at the sight of her, Leonora was temporarily convinced she had chosen the right course.

He held out his arm to her. "I wondered if you had thought better of the idea."

Beneath his light, jesting tone, she sensed a note of disappointment, which her delay had provoked and her arrival had banished. His offer to instruct her in the ways of pleasure meant more to Morse Archer than he dared acknowledge. Somehow, the notion eased her own misgivings.

"I did," she admitted, unable to suppress her accustomed candor. "Then I didn't. Then I did again. Who knows but I may change my mind again before we've walked a hundred yards."

Morse laughed as they stepped out into the mild sunshine of a world on the verge of spring. "Then it will be up to me to convince you to stay. Or coax you not to leave, at any rate."

He crooked his elbow tighter, imparting a gentle squeeze to her hand. That simple chaste gesture of fondness flooded Leonora with all the golden warmth and light of spring sunshine. The kind that caressed the frozen earth each year, luring it to thaw and flower once again.

Yet it frightened her, too. For with softness came vulnerability. She was not in control of this situation. On the contrary, she was very much at its mercy. Oddly enough, this apprehension did not quell her desire for Morse Archer, only buoyed it to new heights.

Battling her own ambivalence, she increased the pressure of her fingertips on Morse's arm in reply. She knew he felt it and understood, perhaps better than she understood herself. A smile, somewhat sheepish, tugged up the corner of his bowed mouth.

"Shall I practice up my courtly manners to employ upon the heiresses at Bath?" he asked, one full brow raised in devilish fun. "Captain Archibald goes a wooing. That's what Algie will expect of me. He's already given me some pointers."

Leonora wrinkled her nose. "Not that, I pray you. Whatever the ladies of Bath may think on the subject, *I* am far more partial to Sergeant Archer than to Captain Archibald."

He said nothing for a while as they walked at a halting pace over the garden paths. Songbirds twittered from the bare tree branches, as if calling forth the first tight green buds. The clean, sterile air of winter had given way to the pungent smell of new life quickening.

At last Morse broke the companionable silence between them. "I do believe that's the kindest compliment a woman has ever paid me."

He looked around and for a moment Leonora wondered why. Then she divined it. Morse was checking to see if they might be visible from the windows of Laurelwood.

Realizing they were well screened by a cluster of amber-needled larch trees, Leonora surrendered to a fluttering, breathless sensation high in her bosom.

Morse turned to her. Still maintaining a tight grip on his walking stick, he gathered her close with his other arm and bent to kiss her.

Determined to not be completely mastered, she raised her hands to hold his face. That way, she could push him back if need be.

As his lips took gentle possession of hers, however, all thought of stopping him fled her mind. His breath whispered over her cheek, quickening in tempo, enticing hers to race likewise. The subtle movements of his lips upon hers played a concerto of delight that reverberated through her whole body.

Returning his kiss with an intensity to compensate for her lack of skill, Leonora thrust her hands around his neck and tugged the gloves from her fingers. When they were free, at last, she let them subside. One to Morse's face, where she grazed the firm smoothness of his freshly shaven cheek. The other to his crisply trimmed hair and the contrasting softness of his side-whiskers.

Ripples of doubt drowned in a frothy, crashing breaker of exultation. Leonora felt herself overcome. Lost in the warmth of the moment and the sweetness of pure sensation. A brooding hunger kindled in her. More acute in some parts of her body than others—but nowhere immune.

They clamored to share in the indulgence of her lips and hands. When Morse's hand swept down from her waist to cup deftly beneath her backside, a gasp of bliss erupted from her throat.

"Leonora?" Algie's cheerful hail scraped against her tautly wound senses like an unskilled fiddler torturing the strings of his instrument. "Morse? Hullo—where have you got to?"

They hastily detached from one another. Leonora felt as though a sticking plaster had been ripped from a green wound. One that covered her entire body.

Her tender flesh quivered and her heart threatened to hammer its way out of her chest.

"Oh, there you are!" Algie's voice and footsteps drew nearer.

As Leonora stooped to retrieve her gloves, her hands ached to box his rather prominent ears.

"Took a notion to join you, the day looked so fine." If he noted anything amiss in their guilty fumblings or embarrassed silence, Algie showed no sign of it. Likewise, he seemed impervious to their cold welcome. "Worried Morse's game leg might give him trouble. He'd need a stronger arm than yours to lean on then, Leonora."

"As a matter of fact, I did feel a twinge," said Morse.

Piqued by the husky timbre of his voice, Leonora dared a sidelong glance at him. A curious golden luster is his dark hazel eyes told her that twinge was not in his leg. She covered her lips with one regloved hand to stifle a giddy laugh.

"We had just decided to turn back," Morse added.

"Good thing I happened along, then." Algie wedged his arm beneath Morse's shoulder and ushered him back toward Laurelwood, keeping up a hearty banter that rasped on Leonora's nerves.

With no other alternative, she fell into step behind them, devouring Morse in the only way possible—with her eyes. She wondered when he would find another opportunity to be alone with her, and what new tangent their *lessons* might take.

She found herself hoping it would be soon.

Try as he might, it was three full days and three very long nights before Morse had another opportunity to hold Leonora in his arms.

Every time he tried, Algie or Sir Hugo or Miss Taylor would blunder along, poaching on their privacy. Blithely insensible to even the broadest hint that their company was unwelcome.

Morse had been forced to rely on his voice and his eyes to convey his admiration for Leonora. Likewise, he'd been thrown back on his faculties of sight and hearing to satisfy his admiration for her.

The ripple of her laughter, which came so much warmer and more readily of late, seemed to pipe a tune that set the blood dancing in his veins. The arch of her neck or the sweep of her creamy forearm as she played the pianoforte transfixed him with their unique beauty.

And if she should glance up at him unexpectedly with

those incomparable gray-green eyes, laughter still lilting from her lips, it was as though some wondrous missile, swift and sharp, had pierced him to the very core.

At night, she waltzed through his dreams. Always so achingly elusive. Yet when they met in daylight, he sensed she craved his touch with the same ravenous desire he craved to touch her. For when they managed to brush hands while reaching for a bread roll at dinner, a hot blush would flood her cheeks, and her breath would catch in her throat, as his did.

At last, when he'd begun to despair of securing another minute alone with her, Morse overheard Sir Hugo ordering the butler to fetch a particular bottle of wine for their dinner.

"I'll save you the trouble," Morse offered, knowing poor Bramshaw had his hands full preparing for their imminent departure to Bath.

He glanced around to discover Lady Fortune smiling upon him. Leonora was just descending the stairs.

"If I can prevail upon Miss Freemantle to show me the way to the wine cellar," he added.

One hand raised to pat a dark curl in place. She knew what he had in mind—intuitive creature!

The way she murmured, "It would be *my* pleasure," left him in no doubt.

After they took possession of the key, she led the way below-stairs and he followed, savoring the delicious sway of her walk. Intoxicated by the faint bouquet of lavender that rose from her hair, as he would not have been by ten bottles of her uncle's fine wine.

"Here it is."

Was it only his imagination, or did her voice carry a slight tremor? Did her fingers fumble as she turned the key in the lock?

"Do you recall what vintage Uncle asked for?" She

held the candle high as she stepped through the low door frame.

Morse pushed the door shut behind them and plucked the candle from her hand, setting it on a high shelf within arm's reach.

"I don't recall the vintage."

He would have pulled her into his embrace, but there was no need, for she pivoted and hurled herself at him.

"I'm lucky to recall my own name," he gasped as their lips found each other.

It was true. In the past few days all concern of wagers, social status and inconstant women had fled his mind. He'd been preoccupied with Leonora and how much he wanted her.

The force of her impact against him propelled Morse backward. Fortunately a low cask broke his fall. His leg protested as he sat down hard, but the rest of his body rejoiced as Leonora pitched into his lap.

Morse forgot that he was supposed to be doing her a favor, initiating her into the mysteries of sensual pleasure. Modern, rational, nineteenth-century thought deserted his mind entirely, ousted by a host of feral instincts as old as the stone circles of Salisbury Plain.

He wanted to take possession of this woman, and to be possessed by her in turn. He wanted to drink her in until he sated his senses upon her. He wanted to feel her alternately melt and stiffen in response to his touch.

With fierce abandon he kissed her, but she did not cower from it. Instead she countered his desire, flame for flame, fueling his ardor until it threatened to consume them both.

He broke from their kiss, anxious to acquaint himself with more than her lips. Grazing her cheek on the way to her neck, he nuzzled the spot just below her ear and slowly quested his way down to her shoulder. She responded by arching toward him, a sigh of pleasure mingled with a moan of further yearning.

He brushed his hand against the brief bodice of her dress and felt the hard straining of her response that echoed his own. His lips strayed lower, to press against the soft flesh of her bosom. With his other hand, he fumbled at the hem of her skirt, tugging the cloth up over her calves and thighs.

In the cool dampness of the wine cellar, the lone candle cast bewitching shadows upon the dusty, shelved bottles. The earthy odor of the underground chamber fused with the must of ripe grapes and the subtle tincture of a man and woman roused. Stone walls echoed the rapid rasp of their breath, the soft sounds of pleasure given and received. The muted whimper of urging.

The heavy fall of footsteps and the bray of Algie's voice drowned out those faint intimate sounds.

"D'you suppose they might have got locked in? Hullo, Morse, Leonora! Where's that wine, eh?"

As Leonora jumped from his lap, Morse heard a squeal deep in her throat, the remnant of a stifled shriek. Somehow, it made his own frustration more bearable, knowing how deeply she shared it.

Algie grappled with the latch, throwing the door open just as Morse rescued their candle.

"I say, what's taking the pair of you so long? At the rate you're going, we'll have to drink our wine with breakfast. Ha, ha!"

"We couldn't recall what sort of wine Uncle had asked for." Leonora's tone was hard as flint. If Algie didn't watch it, she might break one of these bottles over his head. "Morse and I got to arguing about it."

Algie reached past her to pluck a dusty bottle from its shelf. "And here it was under your noses all the time.

Well, do come along before dinner gets any colder or Sir Hugo's temper gets any warmer.''

As Morse followed Algie, with leaden feet, Leonora clasped his hand and gave it a quick squeeze. The trifling gesture communicated so much—trust, affection...regret. His heart constricted in his chest as though it, too, had been squeezed.

Soon they would be departing Laurelwood. A month at Bath—two at most—and he'd be parting from Leonora. Parting forever.

That alarming prospect took the stomach out of Morse. Yet somewhere deep inside him, a spark of desperate hope flickered. But did he want to act upon it?

Did he *dare* to act upon it?

Chapter Thirteen

Bath.

Leonora's throat constricted as their barouche crested Widcombe Hill and the stately spa town came into view.

She had been planning and working toward this moment for weeks, yet now that it had arrived she wanted nothing so much as to turn tail and bolt back to the rustic security of Laurelwood. Gazing down at the tiers of elegantly proportioned town houses of golden stone nestled among the trees, she tried to quell her misgivings with a dose of cool logic.

It was only natural that she should feel some apprehension about their visit to Bath. So much rode on Morse's social success here, after all. If he could rise to the occasion, her future would be assured. She tried in vain to banish thoughts of her destiny—and his, if Morse should fail.

As if nudged by her worries, Sir Hugo stirred from his doze on the seat beside her. Tipping his tall beaver hat back off his forehead, he blinked his deep-set eyes and yawned. "There already, are we? Bless my soul." He cast a doting smile at his three young friends. "This is the only way to come to Bath—bring one's own company, don't you know. Leonora wouldn't come with me last spring and I had a perfectly miserable time. Mind you, those foul-tasting waters did wonders for my gout.''

Algie pulled a wry face. "No waters for me. Grandmama used to bring me here every spring when I was a child and dose me liberally with the stuff. She reckoned the tonic might fatten me up, but it never did a scrap of good that I could see. Quite spoilt my appetite, as a matter of fact.''

He turned to Morse, who sat silent and uncommonly solemn beside him. "The baths might do your leg good, though, old fellow. If you can spare the time from your heiress-hunting project, that is.''

Morse acknowledged Algie with a vacant nod. Was it the overcast day, or did he look rather pale? Leonora noted the tightness in his jaw muscles and his brow. Could the soldier who had risked his own life to pull her cousin from a sea of French bayonets be frightened of the poky, respectable gentry who flocked to Bath?

Somehow the notion endeared him to her even more. She wanted to squeeze his hand and reassure him that all would be well. She longed to embrace him in gratitude for how hard he'd worked on her behalf. She yearned to linger in his arms and soak up the sensation of it—a memory to treasure through the long celibate years ahead.

Her eyes began to sting just then, much to Leonora's chagrin. What cause had she for tears, after all, with her wager all but won? She would be able to lead a productive, independent life. A secure life, well within her control.

And if she had begun to suspect there might be something missing from such a life—something as vital as meat or drink or air—she must quell such traitorous notions. And take care to do nothing that might jeopardize her plans for the future.

* * *

His nerves stretched so taut he feared they would snap, Morse struggled with his unmanageable neck linen. Dickon had made a dreadful botch of tying it this evening. The fault lay with himself, too, Morse acknowledged with a rueful shake of his head. He simply hadn't been able to stand still. Shifting from foot to foot. Fidgeting with his watch fob and the buttons of his waistcoat. It was a wonder Dickon hadn't been overcome by an impulse to strangle him with the troublesome cravat.

Giving it one last desperate pull, Morse abandoned the project and began to pace the Persian carpet of their rented establishment in fashionable Laura Place. After a few days' grace to settle in and receive a number of complimentary welcome calls, tonight would be their first foray into Bath Society. Morse had never been this agitated on the eve of a battle.

His hands felt clammy. His heart raced as though he had run a mile. His stomach churned and a hundred thoughts chased one another in giddy succession through his head. For twopence, he'd have turned tail and scampered back to Laurelwood in disgrace.

The sitting room door eased open and Leonora entered. For a long moment Morse's fears fled his mind as he drank in the sight of her. He recalled their first meeting at the military hospital and how little she'd appealed to him then.

Had she changed so much in the meantime?

In some ways, perhaps. She wore her hair in looser, softer styles these days. Tonight, for instance, it crowned her head in a froth of fine dark curls, adorned only by a simple riband of silver-gray to match her evening dress.

Ah, the dress! Whatever the antipathy between he and Miss Taylor, Morse had to admit the young woman was a fine seamstress. Rather than concealing Leonora's charms, the cut of her gowns now emphasized her lithe grace. Their colors brightened her complexion or, as in this case, complimented her peerless eyes.

But these were only the superficial changes. The greatest alteration had been in her stance and manner. She no longer held herself so rigid and erect, as if expecting or daring some attack from the world. In the past weeks Leonora had become approachable, and Morse found himself taking every convenient opportunity to approach her.

Even some deucedly inconvenient ones.

"You're ready early, Captain Archibald." She grinned with a compound of warmth and mischief once foreign to her. "For all men complain of women taking too long to dress, I have found it quite the contrary. Algie and Uncle will both be ages, yet."

She swept an appraising glance over him, which froze when it landed on his stock. Her brow puckered. "It's not like Dickon to be so ham-handed. Bend down and let me see if I can repair the damage. We don't want you making your Bath debut looking less than your best."

Morse stepped toward her and tilted his neck, as bidden. Somehow her presence calmed him—if only by offering a distraction from his misgivings. His pulse slowed and the tightness in his chest eased.

"It's my own fault about the stock," he confessed as she untied it. "I couldn't manage to stand still for poor Dickon."

She froze for a moment, the fillets of linen in her hands. "Morse Archer, you aren't anxious about tonight, are you?"

When he flashed a sheepish grin and dodged her gaze, she chuckled. "Well, put it out of your head this instant. I'm rather glad Uncle insisted on dragging Algie along with us. Stick close to him and you're sure to sound every bit the *gentleman of information* by comparison."

As she spoke those reassuring words, she retied his linen

with steady hands. Something within Morse warmed to the domestic intimacy of the moment.

It seemed proper and natural that the two of them should spend a few close, quiet moments, preparing to venture out into society. Like soldiers, cleaning their rifles and passing a bottle over a bivouac campfire before battle. If he could always sally forth with a capable ally like Leonora by his side, Morse felt certain he'd be equal to anything life might deal him.

"Be on your guard with the men," she continued. "You're as sharp-witted a fellow as ever I've met, so keep those wits about you. No overindulging at the punch bowl."

Morse pulled a mock salute. "Aye, General Freemantle. Any other orders, Sir?"

"No. Only a suggestion." She surveyed her handiwork and gave the front of his stock a final smoothing touch. "Stick with the ladies as much as you can. After a couple of your engaging compliments, I doubt they'll care whether they're talking to a dustman or the Archbishop of Canterbury."

Before he realized what he meant to say, Morse opened his mouth and blurted, "Marry me, Leonora?"

Her eyes widened and her hands fell to her sides. "I b-beg your pardon?"

"Will you marry me?" Morse repeated in a light, jesting tone, though he could scarcely tell if he was in jest or in earnest. "Once we've won the wager, I mean. I'll be coming into a fine plantation in the colonies and you'll be independent, too. I know you have your heart set on starting a school, but they must need schools abroad as much as they need them here in England. Perhaps more."

Her lips parted, but no words came out. She gazed at him, a hundred unguessable emotions reflected in her eyes.

Suddenly, Morse realized how badly he wanted her to

say yes. How much he wanted to build a future with her. How dreadfully he feared losing her from his life. His heart shrank from wanting anything so much. It left him exposed and defenseless.

"I...I... Let me...think on it."

At least she hadn't refused him outright. Morse summoned every logical, persuasive reason why she should accept, ready to pepper her with them like so much ammunition. Before he could fire off even a single volley, the sitting room door swung open.

"Bless my soul!" boomed Sir Hugo. "You do look quite the gent, Archer...Archibald, I mean."

"Indeed," chimed in Algie, looking rather well himself in a cunningly tailored coat. "You shall have the pick of the heiresses, old fellow, upon my word."

Morse only grinned in reply, venturing a self-conscious glance at Leonora. There might be more beautiful women in the world, at least on some objective scale. But none more appealing to *him*.

He warmed to the thought that no other man could appreciate all her fine qualities as he did. Her keen intellect. Her strength of will and character. Her deep compassion that knew no bounds of birth or station. Not a heiress in Bath could tempt him as she did. Not the lot of them put together.

After a few more minutes of chat, their party set off for a Wednesday night concert in the Upper Assembly Rooms. Uncertain whether to be encouraged or disheartened by Leonora's preoccupied silence, Morse vowed to charm his way into Bath Society.

Let her see what a worthy consort he would make.

Try as she might, Leonora could not keep her attention fixed on the musical program. All the notes flowed together in her mind as an accompaniment to Morse's lyrics.

Marry me, Leonora? Marry me, Leonora? Over and over the words echoed in her thoughts like a bewildering ballad.

Could he mean it? For so vital a question as a proposal of marriage, he had tossed it out in a rather cavalier fashion. What had compelled him to raise the subject—now, of all times?

As deeply as Morse's motives perplexed her, her own reaction baffled Leonora more. Her first response had been a pleasant sense of astonishment that Morse had come to care for her so much. The thrilling aborted encounters during their final days at Laurelwood deluged her memory.

A searing blush crept into her cheeks.

Imagine having complete license to indulge her desire for him. And to learn all the delightful secrets he'd pledged to teach her. Such sanguine thoughts had lasted for the entire carriage drive.

Once they reached the Upper Assembly Rooms, however, and Morse had entered the fictitious "Captain Maurice Archibald" in the subscription books, Leonora's musings took a decidedly negative turn. For handsome "Captain Archibald" became an immediate favorite with the ladies. Leonora found herself physically pushed aside as they flocked to him.

Beautiful women. Wealthy women. Titled women. Why should he want her when he could obviously have his pick of them?

Leonora had never witnessed a group of women so smitten. They hung on his words and vied with one another for his smiles. And Morse was not miserly in dispensing, either. Rather too profligate, if anything.

A whispered aside, behind the cover of an admirer's fan. A gust of sincere-sounding laughter in response to another's dull quip. A gaze caught and held, accompanied by the seductive rise of a brow and the hint of a secret smile.

No matter how often she assured herself he was only doing what she'd trained him to do—what she needed him to do—Leonora could not dismiss the uneasy conviction that he reminded her of someone.

The last and worst of her mother's husbands.

By the time they returned home, shortly before midnight, she was nursing a vicious headache, which did nothing to help her sort out her feelings. While the men indulged in a celebratory brandy, she slipped off to her bedchamber before Morse could corner her to demand an answer to his proposal.

"You didn't look as though you enjoyed the concert much, miss." Elsie Taylor passed Leonora's nightgown over the dressing screen.

Leonora exchanged it for her evening dress and tossed a woolen wrap around her shoulders. Taking a seat at her dressing table, she began to brush out her hair. Each stroke made her headache worse, but she did not care.

"The concert was very pleasant, Elsie." She hesitated. "At least...I believe it was." Her brush-wielding hand fell to her lap. "To tell the truth, I don't recall a single piece they played."

Elsie hung the evening dress in Leonora's wardrobe. "Is there anything wrong then, miss? You look to have something weighing on your mind—and not a good something, either."

Leonora tried to hold her tongue. She felt so rudderless and confused, however, that she *had* to confide in someone. And Elsie Taylor was such a discreet, sensible creature.

"Sergeant Archer has asked me to marry him, Elsie. I don't know how I should reply."

The girl disappeared behind the screen to retrieve Leonora's shift and stockings. "I'd tell him to go jump off a bridge," she muttered.

In spite of herself, Leonora choked with laughter. "Elsie Taylor! Such a thing to say!"

"I'm sorry, miss." The girl kept her eyes downcast as she folded the undergarments. "You didn't ask for my opinion and I shouldn't have given it unasked."

"But that *is* your opinion?" Somehow, Elsie's quip had restored a measure of her composure. "You've never liked Sergeant Archer from the start, have you? He hasn't done anything to harm or frighten you…has he?"

"No, nothing like that, miss."

As she let out a long breath, Leonora realized she'd been holding it.

"He's never paid me much mind at all," continued Elsie. "But he wouldn't, then, would he? Seeing as he's supposed to be on the lookout for a rich wife. I can't fathom why you and Sir Hugo and Mr. Blenkinsop think so well of a man who's no more than a contemptible fortune hunter."

The words spewed out of her, almost defiantly, as though they'd been bottled up for a great while and allowed to ferment until they'd blown their cork.

"You don't think Sergeant Archer is after me for my money, do you?" demanded Leonora. The notion was almost as preposterous as Elsie's misplaced spite against poor Morse. "Why, I've hardly a farthing in the world to call my own."

She would have, though, once she and Morse won their wager. A sufficient endowment to build a school and allow her to live independently. Try as she might to banish the suspicion, it would not go away.

"He may not realize you have nothing in your own account, miss. I'm sure I never guessed. Don't you have expectations from your uncle?"

Leonora shook her head. "None to speak of." At least none apart from the wager. Which Morse knew all about. "Really, Elsie, I don't know why I'm bothering to argue this with you. The whole notion is quite ridiculous."

"Just as you say, miss." Elsie bobbed a curtsy, her face ashen. "I shouldn't have spoken out of turn."

Leonora relented. How could she blame her maid for entertaining doubts that she herself could not keep at bay? "You didn't speak out of turn. I asked your opinion and you gave it, with my best interest at heart."

"I'm sure I only want to see you happy, miss. What with all you've done for me and for the other girls." Her young friend looked so sweetly earnest. As though only her regard for Leonora would have prompted her to speak in so candid a fashion. "I don't believe you would be happy with…him. Not in the long run, anyway. You deserve a husband who loves you for yourself."

"I don't want any other husband." Her reply came almost by rote, from years of practice.

It was true. No other man had ever tempted her to matrimony. Only Morse Archer.

Elsie nodded. "I'm sure you'll mull it over well, miss, and decide what's best for you. Only, do think on what I've said. When a woman has a hankering for a man, it can make it hard for her to see his true character." She glanced around the room. "Is there anything else you need before I go off to bed?"

Leonora waved her away with a smile of gratitude for her candor and concern. Once Elsie had closed the door behind her, Leonora turned to the woman in the mirror with a sigh. "What *will* I tell him?"

Her thoughts swarmed back to the concert and to the attention heaped upon Morse. So many beautiful women throwing themselves at his head. Why on earth should he propose marriage to a plain, bossy, bookish creature like *her?*

Unless...?

She detested herself for thinking ill of Morse. More than anyone, she knew the fine qualities he possessed. But she was not alone in entertaining suspicions. Neither could she deny that he had duped her once already, by playing on her partiality for him. With so much more at stake, she could not afford to let her feelings for him blind her. No matter how potent those feelings might be.

Long ago she had sworn never to repeat her mother's mistakes with men. Now she found herself on the brink of doing precisely that.

Was there some way to verify that his intentions were honorable and his feelings for her genuine?

Then it came to her—the perfect test to determine if Morse wanted her for herself, or only as a means to Uncle Hugo's fortune. Leonora scarcely slept a wink that night, riddled by anticipation and dread.

If only she could be certain Morse would pass the test.

He'd passed his first test with flying colors.

Morse heaved a sigh of satisfaction as he waited in the sitting room for Leonora. The success of his first outing boded well for the Season and for their wager. Provided he kept his wits about him and didn't yield to false complacency, he might soon realize the unavailing dream of a lifetime.

The chance to make something of himself. To prove his true worth. With a woman by his side who already recognized it.

That last thought gave Morse a moment's pause. Leonora would accept him—wouldn't she? After the effort he'd made to save her from a marriage to Algie Blenkinsop. After the way he'd let her get close to him—breaching defenses he'd spent years fortifying.

He hoped the thwarted introduction to lovemaking he'd given her in their last days at Laurelwood might help overcome her aversion to marriage.

Morse had no idea what had prompted him to blurt out his proposal. Now that he'd done it, though, he wanted desperately for Leonora to accept.

A faint rattle of the doorknob brought him to his feet.

When Leonora cast him a tentative but hopeful smile as she let herself in, he could not restrain the urge to cross the room and take her in his arms.

There was nothing tentative in the way she met his kiss. But much that was hopeful.

They'd kissed often enough that the movements had become familiar as a favorite dance. He must stoop so far and she must poise on her toes to meet him. His head must tilt just so. Hers the other way. Their lips must part slightly, merging with subtle but vital mobility.

Morse sensed the blood in his veins pulsing faster and hotter. His body strained taut with desire for the woman in his arms. He could hardly wait for this tiresome idyll at Bath to be over so they could embark upon their life together. Then he could complete her initiation into the rites of love. Might there be more still for him to learn as they explored together?

Nothing could have prompted Morse to stir from that kiss. Except the longing to hear Leonora utter the words that would commit her to him. Reluctantly he pulled back and drank in the dear perfection of her face.

He'd knocked her spectacles slightly askew with his impatient ardor. He'd mussed her hair and brought a bright flush to her cheeks. And she looked all the more appealing for these traces of disarray.

Morse could not contain himself. "You *have* decided to

marry me, haven't you, Leonora? Dear heaven, lass, you've made me the happiest man in the world.''

"I will go with you, Morse." She straightened her spectacles. "If you'll have me."

If? His mouth spread into a gloating grin so broad, Morse wondered that his face could compass it.

"I'll share your home…and your bed." Her gaze faltered before his and she blushed furiously.

He could scarcely contain himself from hoisting her into his arms and whisking her off to his bed that very moment.

Leonora took a deep breath and looked back into his eyes with a gaze at once defiant and…beseeching? "But I will not take vows or sign a marriage bond with you, Morse. I have always aimed never to wed and my feelings for you have not changed that."

Though he willed himself to not flinch, Morse felt as though he'd taken the butt end of a rifle in the belly.

Perhaps Leonora did not perceive his shock and distress, for she continued, almost eagerly, "If we win the wager with Uncle Hugo, and if you are willing to take me on my terms, then I am yours, Morse Archer."

Morse tried to master his vocal organs to reply. He feared his voice would crack like that of a green boy—for so he felt. In his heart he was once again a callow youth offering his hand and his name to a woman who disdained both, even as she fancied his body and his service. How could he have been such a fool as to hope for more?

By instinct, Morse sheathed the great sucking wound in his chest with the protective armor of icy wrath. The muscles of his face, so supple and easy only moments ago, froze into a mask of rigid antagonism.

Leonora must have sensed the change, for she caught his hand and flashed him an anxious smile that beseeched a reassuring one from him. "Come, Morse. Kiss me and say it's all right."

Words from his parting encounter with Pamela Granville echoed in Morse's mind. *Stop talking nonsense and come kiss me.*

He had a vague intuition there was a difference between Lady Granville's rebuff of his marriage proposal and Leonora's. But he was too hurt, too humiliated and too furious with his own folly to consider such a subtle distinction.

So he pushed past her to the door.

"Go to hell, Miss Freemantle." Only with the most intense effort was he able to discharge the words from his constricted throat.

Chapter Fourteen

For several minutes after Morse shut the sitting room door with such restrained ferocity, Leonora stood where he had left her. Empty. Aching. Betrayed.

She had thought him a man of honor, different from so many of the men she'd known. But with his own words and his own decision, he had proven himself just another charming, grasping scoundrel.

If he cared for her—sincerely, as he claimed to, and not with any consideration of property—he would have accepted her counterproposal in the blink of an eye. Happy to have her by his side on any terms. Instead he had rejected her. Without legal rights to her fortune, Leonora, the woman, meant nothing to him.

A sob rose in her throat, but she strangled it unuttered. She had behaved like a perfect idiot over Morse Archer. Damned if she would shed one more tear on his unworthy account!

Yet when a soft knock sounded on the sitting room door, Leonora's heart bounded from her toes back up into her chest, pounding at thrice its normal speed. Had Morse reconsidered? Had he come back to apologize?

She flew to the door and wrenched it open.

"Callers, Miss Freemantle." The butler thrust out a silver tray, bearing several engraved calling cards.

As her heart sluiced back deep into her toes, Leonora picked up one of the cards and pretended to read it. She willed her hand not to tremble.

Though her battered spirit yearned for peace and solitude to recover itself, another part of her groped in vain for anything to occupy her mind. To distract her from the pain.

"Show them up, Bramshaw, with my compliments. And bring us some refreshments, if you would be so kind."

"Certainly, miss. Shall I summon Mr. Blenkinsop and…er…Captain Archibald? From the way the young ladies were speaking, I gather they are keen to renew his acquaintance after last evening."

"By all means, call them both," Leonora heard herself say.

The only fit punishment for her folly would be to watch Morse in action with other women. A severe penalty, to be sure, but one guaranteed to cure her of any imprudent yearning for him that might linger in her gullible heart.

"Captain Archibald?" The butler's voice sounded faintly over his knock on Morse's bedroom door.

"Go to hell!" bellowed Morse. That's what he had told Leonora Freemantle. Now he wanted to consign everyone else in the world to its flames—where his heart roasted on a spit.

Bramshaw persisted. "Miss Freemantle asked me to summon you to the sitting room, sir—"

Despite his firmest resolution to not stir a step, Morse strode to the door and threw it open before the man could finish speaking.

The butler started at this impassioned reception, but soon regained this composure. "Some ladies have come

calling and Miss Freemantle wishes you and Mr. Blenkinsop to join them.''

Whatever Morse had been expecting to hear—and he
was by no means certain, himself—this was not it. He
checked a powerful impulse to bid Sir Hugo's poor butler
to perdition, once again, along with all the household and
guests.

Bramshaw raised his eyebrows in a subtle but significant
look. ''Unless I'm quite mistaken, the ladies have come to
see *you,* sir.''

''Have they, indeed?'' Their fawning attention might be
the perfect antidote for Leonora's rejection.

Besides, he had the wager to win—on his own account
now. More than ever he wanted to go abroad, where a man
might be valued for his accomplishments rather than the
fortunate accident of his birth. He would prove to everyone, Miss Leonora Hypocrite Freemantle included, that he
was the equal of any beau in Bath.

''I mustn't disappoint the ladies, then, must I? Tell them
I will be down at once.''

''Very good, sir.'' The butler marched off, presumably
to summon Algie.

As Morse changed his coat, he strove to erase from his
features any sign that might betray his recent distress. Then
he manufactured a suave, flattering smile and fixed it in
place. A few deep breaths and he was ready for his performance.

He met up with Algie on the stairs.

''Didn't I say the ladies would swarm around you?''
Algie rolled his very round eyes and waggled his brows
in a droll expression that made Morse laugh in spite of
himself.

His fellow feeling for Algie increased tenfold. After all,
they now both belonged to the fraternity of men Leonora

Freemantle did not wish to wed. The only difference was
Morse knew of his membership.

Leonora ushered them into the sitting room with imper-
turbable poise. From the mirrored candle sconces on the
walls to the intimate grouping of scroll-armed settee and
chairs, the room looked just as it had when Morse stormed
out of it. His violent exit had not so much as tipped a
picture. Who would guess that scarcely half an hour ago,
in this very room, Leonora had refused his offer of marriage. Instead she'd proposed an arrangement that would
have scandalized their guests quite speechless, had they
known of it.

"Mr. Blenkinsop, Captain Archibald, I'm certain you
remember these ladies from last night's concert at the Assembly Rooms." She gestured to each of their guests in
turn. "Miss Osgoode, Miss Compton, Miss Hill and her
sister Lady Fitzwarren, Miss Ditterage and Madame Par-
mier. They have not forgotten you, Captain, by all accounts."

"No indeed," vowed the chitty-faced Miss Ditterage.
"I cannot think when we have had such an agreeable new
arrival in Bath. It is too bad of General Wellington to have
dragged all the handsomest young officers away to the
Peninsula." She thrust out her lower lip in a pout that
made her look more than ever like an overgrown infant.

It was on the tip of Morse's tongue to inform this vacuous ninny that the general had far more urgent matters
on his mind than depriving Bath debutantes of dancing
partners.

As the other guests exclaimed in sympathy with Miss
Ditterage, Algie bent close to Morse and muttered, "Her
aunt is a dowager marchioness. She's expected to come
into several thousand a year when the old lady breathes
her last."

It would take every guinea melted down to gild such an

odious pill, thought Morse. But he managed to rein in his tongue.

"I fear I am a poor replacement for my brothers in arms, Miss Ditterage." He tapped his lame leg. "The Frenchies have already had their way with me."

"Of course. Your...wound."

The other ladies broke into a flurry of twittering conversation among themselves.

"If it isn't too painful to recount," piped up the most attractive of their guests, Miss Hill—at least Morse thought that was her name. "Do tell us how you came to be injured. It's sure to be a thrilling tale."

In spite of himself, Morse glanced toward Leonora. There'd been nothing thrilling about the slaughter at Bucaso. Nothing heroic. She had understood that, as these frivolous creatures never would. She was the only person in whom he'd ever confided his shame and regret.

"It was nothing," he insisted gruffly. "A bayonet. A bullet. Cannon fire. What difference does it make? Men are wounded every day in battle. My injury is of no more consequence than any other."

Miss Hill would not be dissuaded. "A bayonet? How awful! Come have a seat beside me—you should not be standing."

Algie pushed Morse toward the settee, but not before muttering, "That one's the richest heiress in Bath. She and her sister will split thirty thousand a year at least."

As Morse lurched onto the settee beside the young lady, Algie spoke up for the benefit of their guests. "My friend is too modest by half. I shan't embarrass him by recounting the details, but I will tell you this. He'd never have been wounded if he hadn't rushed to the aid of his men. If you ask me, he should have been awarded a medal for his heroic action."

Their guests murmured zealous agreement on the matter

while Morse cast Algie an exasperated look. Desperate to escape the subject of the war and his injury, he asked how they all had enjoyed the concert.

"I can't say I paid the music much mind." Miss Hill raised gloved fingers to her lips to button up a giggle. "It all sounds the same to me—especially the Italian. Did *you* have a favorite, Captain?"

"Indeed." One he recognized, at least, from Leonora's short course in music appreciation. "I thought the Viotti adagio very well done."

"Just so," agreed the pale, plump Miss Osgoode. "That was the slow one, wasn't it?"

Morse only nodded. He feared if he tried to speak, he might give himself away with a burst of wild laughter.

The ladies hastened to endorse Morse's opinion and to commend his cultured taste in music. He glanced at Leonora and received a curt nod of approval.

Turning his attention to Miss Hill, Morse lavished upon her the smile that had charmed scores of less wealthy women. "I'll admit, I was hard-pressed to keep my mind on the music with so many engaging distractions at every turn."

"Distractions?" Clearly, the compliment was too subtle for her.

He wagged his finger. "You must not pretend to miss my meaning. Even if I hadn't been so long away in the army, the beauty of the ladies of Bath would still prove a powerful distraction." He met the eyes of each one in turn, to include her in his flummery.

They blushed and smiled and preened in reply, while Leonora looked on in stony severity. Let her play the gorgon, then! He was only doing what he'd been engaged to do. If it vexed her, so much the better. Let her see there were plenty of other women who coveted what she had spurned.

A streak of rustic common sense within Morse protested. Bath's vapid debutantes admired the fictitious Captain Maurice Archibald and his shallow facade of gentility. Not plain Rifleman Archer, the son of a poor tenant farmer.

Leonora, for all she'd misused him, had come to care for the real Morse. But not enough to wed him—damn it!

To think she had seriously entertained a notion to marry that rogue, Archer. In a relatively quiet corner of the Upper Assembly Rooms, Leonora shuddered.

She spied Morse some distance away. Mobbed by his admirers, as usual. The viper clearly took pleasure in flaunting his social triumphs under her nose. Now and then he would glance her way, his gloating grin unmistakable.

If only she could take to her bed and sleep away the time until Bath residents departed back to their country estates for the summer. Barring some unforeseen disaster, the success of their wager was assured. Must she torture herself daily with the evidence that Morse had cared for her no more than he cared for any other unwed heiress?

Indeed she must.

As punishment for her folly in caring for him and as a painful but necessary lesson, should she ever be tempted to err in that fashion again.

"I say, Leonora." From out of nowhere, Algie appeared at her elbow. "What are you doing skulking over here in the corner? Come have a dance with me. I promise not to tread on your toes—much."

"Very well, Algie." She tried to stifle a sigh, remembering what a jolly time they'd had in the great parlor at Laurelwood practicing for events like this ball.

Algie nodded in Morse's direction. "You've done wonders with him, Leonora. Why, at this rate we'll have him married off by the end of the Season to a lady of income."

"By the looks of things, he'll have several to choose

from.'' She could not keep the bitterness from her voice. It was no good even trying. Fortunately, Algie was not apt to notice. "We may have to auction him off to the highest bidder.''

"Ha, ha! Auction him off. You have such a ready wit, my dear. Between you and Morse, the pair of you keep my poor belly in stitches.''

Algie's mild words hit her like a solid clout to the jaw. Memories she had worked so hard to evict came storming back into her mind, more potent than ever. Of the many times she and Morse had goaded poor Algie into helpless fits of laughter, even when the jest had been at his expense. Why, she had laughed more in the past three months than in all her life before.

And cried more, too. Leonora could not deny it. Before Morse's advent, her emotions had been well under control. Disciplined to avoid excess. Never too happy but never too sad, either. Calm. Seldom ruffled.

Not fully alive.

Leonora tried to quench that thought, but failed when she beheld Morse approaching the dance floor with an extravagantly bejeweled young lady. Was she one of those who had come calling on the morning after the concert?

"Come join our set, Arch-ibald,'' Algie hailed him. "It'll be like old times at Laurelwood.''

By valiant self-control, Leonora managed to refrain from striking Algie with her fan.

After a hasty exchange with his dance partner, Morse approached them with obvious reluctance. Though his limp was not very pronounced, Leonora wondered if his injured leg might be bothering him. He appeared tense and very much out of temper.

Well, he needn't pretend to feel slighted over her refusal, she thought as they began to dance four hands up.

Now he had his pick of a much wider and richer field of prospective brides.

She strove to keep her attention fixed on the dance steps and to ignore the annoying flash of heat that blazed through her body every time her hand came in contact with Morse's. While Algie kept up a lively banter and Morse's partner offered a few prosaic remarks about the ball and the weather, Morse and Leonora remained mute and wooden.

As the last notes of "The Indian Queen" died away, Leonora tread on Algie's toes, not entirely by accident. Even that was not sufficient to relieve the overwrought feelings she struggled to suppress.

She was so intent on getting as far away from Morse as possible, that she scarcely noticed the gentleman who approached his partner to request the next dance. Too late she recognized the young man's voice. He must be that tiresome nephew of Lord Pewsey who'd made every effort to spoil their farewell party at Laurelwood. The intervening weeks had not taught the odious creature any better manners.

When the young woman declined his invitation, he hissed, "Fatigued yourself with a single dance, have you, Miss Hill? I'd have thought the offspring of Yorkshire peasants might have a more robust constitution."

Miss Hill let out a squeak of dismay and brought her fluttering fan up to hide her face.

Before the obnoxious youth could savor his triumph, Morse stepped in front of him, toe-to-toe. "I'd have thought the nephew of a baronet might have better manners." He did not raise his voice much above a whisper, but his words had an edge of fierce contempt. "Apologize to the lady at once, or I will *teach* you courtesy."

The young boor took a step back, but thrust out his chin in a show of belligerence as he glared up at Morse. "*Cap tain Archibald,* is it? I've been making inquiries about you since we met in Wiltshire, Archibald. No one of my acquaintance has ever heard of your family, your school or you.''

Leonora's pulse pounded in her ears. Her dreams for the future shattered around her like fine crystal beneath a stampede of livestock.

Holding her gorge, she stepped between the two men, lofting a glare at Morse that warned him to keep his mouth shut and his temper in check. ''Mr. Nettlecombe, isn't it? What a pleasant surprise to see you again so soon. Can I prevail upon you to fetch me a cup of punch? Dancing is thirsty—''

A pair of familiar hands grasped her upper arms and moved her out of the way. Before she could utter a peep of protest, Morse struck the drawling dandy a token blow with his glove.

''You have insulted my honor, sir, and the honor of a lady. I demand satisfaction.''

A gasp went up from those within earshot.

Turning his back on the fellow he had just challenged to a duel, Morse held out his arm to the young lady. ''May I have the privilege of escorting you home, Miss Hill?''

With a dumb nod, she latched on to him and they marched off with heads held high.

''Drat and blast!'' muttered Algie as the company broke into a storm of feverish tattle. ''This won't do at all. Dueling's been outlawed in Bath since the days of Old Nash. If Morse doesn't wind up dead, it'll still bring him all the wrong sort of attention.''

A hundred conflicting emotions erupted within Leonora at once. Shades of rage and despair. Even a foolish flicker of admiration, which she quashed the instant it reared its head.

"Algie, will you be a good fellow and call for our carriage? I can't stay here another minute."

By the time she got through with Morse Archer, he would be in no condition to duel with that contemptible lump of a Nettlecombe. Or anyone else, for that matter.

Morse stole into Sir Hugo's house at Laura Place as late as he dared. After seeing Miss Hill home, he had sought out a drinking establishment of rather unsavory reputation near the Cross Bath. Might as well spend some time where he belonged, Morse decided. Thanks to his touchy temper and preposterous pride, he'd be back among his own kind soon enough, never to rise again.

Prying off his shoes, he held them in one hand and began to pad up the stairs in his stockinged feet, his gait weaving ever so slightly. Behind him, he heard the sitting room door open on squealing hinges.

"Not so fast, Morse Archer." Though spoken softly, Leonora's words thundered in the stillness of the sleeping house. "I'd like a word with you."

Squaring his shoulders, he turned and descended the stairs, again. He'd sooner have stormed a nest of French artillery in full fire than walk into that quiet, dimly lit room.

He had barely closed the door behind him when Leonora vented her fury. "How could you, Morse? By calling out that young ass Nettlecombe, you've as good as thrown the wager. The vicar of St. Michael's might as well publish wedding banns for Algie and me on Sunday next."

"What do you want me to say?" Morse flared. "That I'm sorry? Well, I'm not. Nettlecombe had it coming after the way he insulted Miss Hill. What else *could* I have done?"

"You *could* have kept your mouth shut and let someone else deal with him. Besides, he didn't say anything untrue.

Miss Hill would be no one of consequence if her father didn't have a vulgar amount of money. Admit it, you did this on purpose to spite me for refusing your proposal. How could I have been such a fool as to trust a blackguard like you?''

Morse had stood for all the abuse he was prepared to tolerate. That he'd been reckless and stupid in challenging young Nettlecombe, he was prepared to own and take his lumps for. As for the other...

''That's a load of rubbish, and you know it, Leonora Freemantle.'' He took a step toward her. Whether to menace or simply out of a foolish yearning to be close to her, Morse was not certain. ''I worked hard to put on the trappings of a gentleman and win your wager. But if that means standing by while some highborn lout insults a respectable young lady on account of her grandfolks were honest working people, I'll tell you now—I haven't the stomach for it.''

He looked into her eyes, red-rimmed with dusky hollows beneath, and he saw the hurt. A raw, corrupted wound, whose cause he could only guess and whose remedy he had forfeited. Deeply as he resented her accusation, he could not deny his responsibility for wrecking her future.

Casting his pride aside, he took her hand. ''I didn't do this to hurt you. You must believe that, Leonora. In spite of...everything, I don't want to see you lose your school.''

She stared down at their clasped hands, refusing to meet his eyes. ''In spite of everything, I want to believe you.''

After a moment of awkward silence between them, Leonora eased her hand from his grasp and walked away.

At the door, she paused for a moment. ''You did right, Morse, of course. I shouldn't have let my own interests and prejudices in the matter blind me to that.''

Before he could choke out a reply, she added, ''We must

both try to get some rest. Whatever tomorrow brings, we'll need as many of our wits about us as we can muster.''

Though he knew sleep would surely elude him, Morse made his way to bed a few minutes later, just as Leonora had bidden him. For a wonder, the ale he'd drunk eased him to sleep before he knew it. Though it might have been better if he'd lain awake.

Dreams came to torment him with vivid images of his approaching disgrace. What a juicy feast of gossip he'd make for the idle pleasure-seekers of Bath. Again and again, he pictured Nettlecombe's bacon face pulled into a gloating grimace of triumph.

But the nightmare that plagued him worst of all put him in a great church with a vicar pronouncing his blessing on the marriage of Mr. and Mrs. Blenkinsop. When Morse tried to intervene, Sir Hugo held him back, saying over and over, ''Fair's fair now, Archer. You lost the wager.''

Morse sat bolt-upright in bed, sweat beading his brow and his heart tripping like a snare drum.

Was there nothing he could do to salvage the situation? If he groveled enough to Nettlecombe and withdrew his challenge, might the fellow retract his insinuations about Captain Archibald's identity?

Not likely, but it was worth a try at least.

Morse dressed with fastidious care for the interview, rehearsing his apology again and again in his mind. As befit his role of penance, he did not summon a carriage, but made his way to the Pump Room on foot.

He had no idea where Nettlecombe's lodgings might be, but someone there would be sure to know. More likely still, he would find Nettlecombe in attendance, for Bath visitors tended to congregate in the Pump Room during the morning hours.

It took every ounce of will for Morse to put one foot before the other as he entered Bath's *holy of holies*. The high-vaulted ceiling and imposing pillars made him feel more insignificant than ever. Was it his imagination, or did all talk cease in his wake? The room grew quieter with his every step, until even the musicians in the gallery fell silent.

The statue of Beau Nash seemed to glower down at him and demand an account of why he had seen fit to trespass on the decades-old prohibition against vulgar dueling. Only the long-case Tompion clock continued its ticking, oblivious to the scene unfolding below.

Morse cleared his throat. "Can anyone tell me—" his voice exploded in the breathless hush of the Pump Room "—where I might find the lodgings of a Mr. Nettlecombe?"

An ominous stillness met his question. The pungent stench of sulphur and bismuth from Bath's famed waters made Morse's stomach churn.

Then a man stepped forward, his quizzing glass raised. "Captain Archibald? I am Phineas Blount, Mr. Nettlecombe's second. He instructed me to convey to you and to the young lady his most humble apology for any insult you took from his remarks last night."

A wave of relief almost toppled Morse onto his backside. He was too overcome to reply.

Young Blount hastened to counter his silence. "Imagine Mr. Nettlecombe's chagrin when he discovered his own uncle was once an intimate of your father's. He deeply regrets the misunderstanding and hopes his apology will satisfy you."

How like the contemptible coward to back down when challenged. Lacking even the mettle to deliver his apology in person. Though he was tempted to demand it, Morse restrained himself. He had pushed his luck quite far enough for one day.

He bowed to Nettlecombe's second. "I was too hasty

in taking offense and most uncivil in proposing a duel. I can only plead my long term in His Majesty's service for making me prone to settle disagreements with force of arms. I offer my humble apology to the memory of Beau Nash and to the good citizens of Bath.''

The hum of approving comment that greeted his words emboldened Morse.

''*Errare humanum est*,'' he declared. *To err is human.* Who had better cause to know it than he?

His Latin flourish met with a smattering of applause. After a final bow, Morse withdrew. He was halfway back to Laura Place before his knees quit knocking.

Chapter Fifteen

"**B**y Jove, Leonora, have you heard?" Sir Hugo burst into the sitting room with the force of a North Atlantic gale. "Why, all Bath's agog!"

The blood in her veins congealed into ice—or so it felt. "Tell me, Uncle. Is it Morse? Has he been hurt?"

How could she have been so self-centered? Thinking only of how this duel would affect *her* future. Never considering that it might cost Morse his life.

"Hurt?" Sir Hugo looked at her as though she'd sprouted a beard or a third eye. "What nonsense are you talking, girl? Damn me for a fishmonger if that insolent Nettlecombe whelp hasn't run off whining with his tail between his legs."

The ice in her veins began to thaw, but slowly. "Now who's talking nonsense? I can't make head or tail of what you mean."

"Didn't you hear me?" Sir Hugo exhaled a wheezy chuckle and wiped his face with his handkerchief. "Nettlecombe's backed down—apologized. By proxy, mind you, but apologized none the less. In front of the whole Pump Room. Went so far as to claim his uncle was an intimate acquaintance of *Captain Archibald's* father. There isn't a soul in Bath who'll dare to question Morse's identity now.''

So her wager was not forfeit, after all? She wouldn't be doomed to wed Algie and give up her books and her teaching?

''Why, may I ask, does the news put you in such fine fettle, Uncle Hugo? I vow, I never heard a man sound so overjoyed at the prospect of losing a bet.''

''Losing?'' Sir Hugo blustered. ''What do you mean—losing? I've lost nothing yet, and you'd do well to not get complacent just because Morse has cleared this hurdle.''

He trundled over to the side table and poured himself a generous measure of port from the decanter. ''The truth is, I've come to find this whole game quite amusing and I didn't care for the thought of its being over before it had properly begun.''

Try as she might, Leonora could not let his remark pass. ''So you're like the cat who wants to toy with the mouse before he gobbles it up?''

The flush in her uncle's cheeks faded and he collapsed into the nearest armchair. ''Now, my dear, don't be too harsh in your opinion of an old man who has never meant you any harm.''

Instantly Leonora relented. No matter how she tried, she could not stay angry with him. Until Morse Archer had barged into her life, she'd never met another man who had the same vexing effect upon her.

Perching on one arm of Sir Hugo's chair, she clasped his hand. ''I'm sorry, Uncle. I know you want what's best for me.''

If only he could trust her to decide what that might be.

Sir Hugo squeezed her fingers. ''Promise me you'll remember that—no matter what happens with this wager?''

Now that her future prospects looked rosy once again, Leonora was able to nod her agreement.

The sitting room door opened hesitantly to the width of a sliver, then began to close.

"Morse, is that you?" Sir Hugo called. "No need to slink about, boy. Come in and regale us with tales of your triumph!"

The door's movement froze for a beat, then it swung fully open. Morse entered as Sir Hugo had bidden him, though, to Leonora's eyes, he looked anything but triumphant.

"Shall we drink a toast to your success?" Sir Hugo hefted his glass of port. "I heard you put young Nettlecombe in his place without so much as having to draw a blade or fire a shot."

Morse's wide mouth curled up at one corner. Was it a smug grin of victory or a self-mocking grimace? "That was a piece of undeserved luck. I'm grateful for it just the same."

Grateful on whose account? Leonora wondered.

Sir Hugo would not let Morse escape so lightly. "Luck be blasted! Men of action make their own luck, as you made yours. You knew a bullying little worm like Nettlecombe would slither off the moment someone threatened to bring him to account."

Morse shot Leonora a look. If it had been just the two men alone, he might have swaggered a little. Clearly he knew better than to try fooling her. "I knew no such thing, Sir Hugo. I threw the dice and Fate smiled. *Alea iacta est.*"

His gaze found Leonora's and she sensed that his next words were addressed more to her than to her uncle. "Sometimes there's nothing else to do when you're backed into a tight corner."

Was he referring to the Upper Assembly Rooms at Bath, she wondered, or a rearguard skirmish in Portugal? Did he regret either—or both?

The door swung open again, with no discernable hesitation this time. Algie breezed in, beaming more broadly than usual, if that were possible. He strode to the hearth and clapped an arm around Morse's shoulders. "Well done, old fellow! You're the toast of the town."

Sir Hugo held up his glass and gave it a waggle, before tossing back the last drop of port. He and Algie laughed. Morse quietly suffered Algie's forceful expressions of goodwill. He must realize it was futile to protest his unmerited luck.

"Thought I'd never get home." Algie chuckled. "For all the people stopping me in the street to go on about you. I had no notion old Pewsey's nephew had made himself quite *this* unpopular about town. You're being hailed a hero for putting the boots to him, and a true gentleman for apologizing in front of the whole Pump Room. No sending a deputy to grovel for you, eh, Morse?"

Morse shrugged, reddened and stammered something dismissive.

Leonora rose from the arm of Sir Hugo's chair. "Apologized? To whom? What are you on about, Algie?"

"Didn't he tell you? You're too modest, my friend." Algie thumped Morse on the back again. "He begged pardon from the people of Bath and from the ghost of old Nash for calling Nettlecombe out. Not that anyone held it against him. Made a great show of higher sentiment, though. And finishing up with that Latin quote—stroke of genius!"

He had curbed his pride to that extent? Leonora tried to summon the words to commend Morse. Before she could speak, another thought struck her. What had he been doing in the Pump Room in the first place?

"Oh, I almost forgot." Algie plundered his coat pocket and produced a sealed note, which he handed to Morse with a flourish.

Leonora could smell the scent of rose water on it from halfway across the room. Had the paper been fermented in perfume?

"I was asked to deliver it." Algie looked gratified by his commission. "From Miss Hill," he added for the benefit of Sir Hugo and Leonora—as if she couldn't have guessed.

Morse glanced over the note. "Her sister and brother-in-law are giving a supper party in my honor at the end of the week. Miss Hill asks me to call on her at my earliest convenience so she may express her thanks in person."

"Capital!" cried Algie. "Leave it to you, Morse, to fall in a pigsty and land in a bed of roses."

The overpowering odor of roses from Miss Hill's note made Leonora queasy.

"The young lady was far from indifferent to you before." Algie prattled on. "But now that you've championed her against Nettlecombe and won so smoothly, there's not a beau in Bath who'll stand a chance against you."

He launched into a tiresome litany of Miss Hill's virtues as a prospective bride. All of them financial. Morse did not appear to pay any heed. Instead he looked up from the note, his gaze boring straight into Leonora's.

She could not read the meaning of his look. Might it be a plea—or a challenge? Had Morse gone to the Pump Room looking for Nettlecombe in an effort to make peace for her sake? If she recanted her refusal to wed him, might he put aside the notion of Frederica Hill and the heiress's lavish expectations? Mistrust of men and her overwhelming self-doubt locked Leonora's lips from any rash commitment. Her gaze wavered before Morse's.

He might have taken that for some kind of answer. Or perhaps he never intended a question. As Algie's raptures over Miss Hill's future income petered out, Morse tucked the scented note into his pocket.

"If you will excuse me." He looked from Sir Hugo to Algie, ignoring Leonora altogether. "I've a rather urgent call to pay."

"By all means." Algie all but pushed him out the door. "Strike while the iron's hot!"

Sir Hugo chimed in with some similar hearty banality as Morse took his leave. Their heavy aura of smugness on Morse's behalf threatened to suffocate Leonora.

"I must go lie down." She bolted for the door. "I've got a terrible headache."

Her final glance at Sir Hugo and Algie found the pair of them not the least bothered by her indisposition. If anything, they looked even more pleased with themselves.

Leonora gave the door a forceful jerk shut. Really, men were the most heartless creatures!

Did the woman have a heart in her bosom? Morse fumed as he stormed off to the very elegant Camden Place, where Miss Hill's family had taken a house for the Season.

Whether by his own actions or by luck, he had managed to salvage their wager. Now, their chances of success looked better than ever. He'd been willing to prostrate himself before that odious spawn of the nobility for Leonora's sake, and she hadn't spared a single word or soft look to thank him.

Very well, then! He was done with looking out for her. From now on his own interests would take precedence.

Morse found his progress to Camden Place frequently interrupted by passersby. Complete strangers took the liberty of calling to him from their carriages. Merest acquaintances stopped him in the street to shake his hand. Little by little, his bruised self-esteem began to recover.

By the time he reached the elaborately decorated front

parlor of the Hill establishment, he was in a more temperate humor than when he had quit Sir Hugo's house. The reception he received from Miss Hill soothed him further. She greeted his arrival with raptures, towing him over to a chair by the window. Glancing out at the magnificent view of the town below, Morse could understand why rent in Bath became dearer the higher up hill one went.

Lady Fitzwarren, a thinner, paler, less vivacious version of her sister, Miss Hill, made only a token show of chaperoning.

"Truly, Captain, you were like a knight errant in a story I once read." From her chair opposite him, Frederica Hill fixed Morse with an admiring gaze, clear blue eyes fringed by pale lashes. "If that awful man had struck me with a sword, I could not have been more dismayed. I know certain superior people in Bath *think* such things about me and my family. No one has been so insolent as to say them in public, until last evening."

Lady Fitzwarren chimed in. "If my Eustace had been within earshot, he would have demanded satisfaction, you may be sure." Her tone betrayed less certainty than her words.

Having been introduced to the listless patrician, Morse had his own doubts.

"To think Mr. Nettlecombe had the impertinence to extend his insult to you, Captain Archibald." Miss Hill looked more shocked on his behalf than her own. "You cannot be as used to such slights as Henrietta and I have become over the years. Coming from such a fine family, I mean."

Morse choked back a bitter chuckle. "Short of being the king, I expect most of us suffer people who fancy themselves superior. And are more than willing to let us know it, too."

He nibbled on one of the tea sandwiches Lady Fitzwarren had pressed on him.

"So you *do* understand, Captain. I felt certain of your sympathy. Tell me more about your home and family. Miss Freemantle said you come from the north. We are Yorkshire people, ourselves, though Father sent Henrietta and I to school in London after Mother died."

After an uneasy night and the reversals of the day, Morse did not feel up to reciting the painstakingly memorized biography of Captain Maurice Archibald. Instead he noted the puckering of Miss Hill's brow as she spoke of her schooldays.

"With lots of *superior* little girls?" he asked, turning their conversation onto the safer topic of *her* past.

She nodded readily. "Some very superior. And the teachers, too. One day they'll be sorry they snubbed me."

"Why did you not ask your father to send you somewhere else?" Morse felt his sympathy rising higher. Unbidden came the thought of Leonora's school—how much warmer and more encouraging a place it would be than the pretentious establishment Miss Hill and her sister had suffered.

The young lady grew pensive. "We begged him to, but he'd have none of it. Said his daughters must attend the best school and cultivate the right friends so we could take our places in society one day."

Heaving an almost tearful sigh, she made an obvious effort to recover her spirits. "Thanks to your gallantry, Captain, we have been invited into company that was quietly barred to us, up until now. Father will be so pleased when he and Stepmother come next month." Her tone suggested he was not easily pleased.

At Morse's urging, she talked of the family's summer home in the Yorkshire dales. Of travels she had taken abroad with her sister. The excitement of Henrietta's wed-ing to Sir Eustace Fitzwarren. Miss Hill was not the most stimulating company in the world, Morse had to admit. Instead she had rather a soothing effect on him, which proved a pleasant change from… Resolutely he pulled his thoughts back from that path and tried to concentrate on Miss Hill's plans for the party in his honor.

"Of course we must invite your particular friends, Mr. Blenkinsop, Miss Freemantle and her uncle."

Morse nodded. It was futile to hope Miss Hill's transparent admiration might provoke Leonora to jealousy.

He looked forward to the party—hoping, just the same.

Leonora had dreaded this party since the moment she heard about it. Now that the evening had arrived, she found the experience no better than she'd expected.

"By Jove, don't they make a handsome couple?" Sir Hugo gazed the length of the Camden Place dining table where Morse and Frederica Hill sat side by side.

"Most agreeable." Leonora nibbled at her poached salmon. She might deny it, but what would be the use? Anyone with eyes and even a pinch of aesthetic taste could see how well Morse's bold, dark aspect contrasted with Miss Hill's fair, bland beauty.

"Got to admit it, my dear," Sir Hugo lowered his voice. "I'm becoming anxious about the outcome of this wager." Despite his words, her uncle did not *look* much distressed.

"What took you so long?" Leaning toward Sir Hugo, Leonora spoke softly. "Three months of my tuition and Morse Archer is the equal of any beau in Bath."

Her whispered words resonated with pride. *She* had worked this transformation. From a penniless soldier in disgrace, she had fashioned a sought-after gentleman officer, able to take his place in the town's most fashionable company.

Sought-after, indeed. The notion soured Leonora's sense

of accomplishment. Ever since Morse had come to Miss
Hill's defense, the young lady had set her cap for him i
the most blatant manner. Either he was too dull-witted t
realize it, or he was actively encouraging her. Leonor
knew better than to think Morse dull-witted.

"Glorying in your success, old girl?" asked Algie. He
too, nodded in the direction of Morse and Miss Hill.

Leonora uttered a vaguely affirmative noise, unable t
make herself smile, nod or say *yes*. She was beginning t
feel like a sinner in hell with grinning demons on eithe
side who took turns poking her with hot, sharp objects.

"You set about to make him heiress bait and hasn't h
gone and hooked the most eligible catch in Bath."

Leonora raised her glass again in mockery of a toast t
herself. "A female Pygmalion, I am, Algie." She bolte
a mouthful of wine—anything to raise her spirits, eve
temporarily.

"Come now, I think you're every bit as pretty as Mis
Hill, in your way."

Leonora just managed to raise the napkin to her fac
before wine came sputtering indecorously out her nose
"Pygmalion, Algie!" It felt good to laugh—even at her
self. "You must have studied him in Classics. The myth
ical Greek sculptor who created a statue of the perfec
woman."

"Oh, Pyg*ma*-lion, of course!" Algie nodded vigorously
"Refresh my memory. What became of this sculptor cha
and his pretty statue?"

Against her will, Leonora's gaze strayed back to Morse
"The poor fool fell in love with his stone woman."

Algie clucked his tongue. "Hard luck."

"Oh, that wasn't the end of it. Conveniently for Pyg
malion, the gods took pity on him and turned his belove
statue into flesh and blood."

"Well, that's all right then. I do like it when everything works out at last."

Leonora nodded absently. She knew better than to expect such a miracle for herself. Life was not some morality play where everyone got what she deserved just by wishing for it. With books as her sculpting tools, she had fashioned Morse Archer into the outward semblance of her ideal man. Like Pygmalion, she had come to care for the image—forgetting that beneath his appealing facade lay the flint heart of a fortune hunter.

For the first time Leonora's faith in her philosophy faltered. Perhaps it was *not* enough to elevate a person's intellect with knowledge. Not enough to cultivate proper dress, speech and manners, if the soul remained unenlightened.

Some chance remark by Miss Hill's brother-in-law made Morse laugh. Leonora watched his emphatic features contort with unforced merriment and golden glints of glee flicker in his compelling hazel eyes. Her heart strained in her bosom, as though trying to pull her physically closer to him.

Like an obstinate sunbeam forcing its way into a tightly sealed chamber, memories of Morse's good qualities penetrated her thoughts. The diligence with which he'd applied himself to his studies once he understood what the wager meant to her. His kindness to her pupils during their farewell party. Even his hotheaded defense of Miss Hill, which might have cost him the means to better his lot in life.

The more she mulled it over, the more obvious it became. Morse Archer was not beyond redemption. If only he could recognize the error of his mercenary ways—the unfairness of using his power over women to secure his own selfish ends.

Leave well enough alone! her common sense warned

her. Morse's attachment to an heiress like Miss Hill woul
go a great way toward winning her wager. Uncle Hug
had as much as admitted it himself. Besides, if Morse ha
his cap set for Miss Hill, he might resent any meddling. I
he suddenly refused to cooperate, her wager would be los
beyond recovery.

Ignoring the ache of her wounded heart, as she'd sper
most of her life doing, Leonora allowed cool, reliable rea
son to reassert itself. At the first opportunity, she followe
Miss Hill to the retiring room and regaled the heiress wit
an account of all Captain Archibald's virtues.

Chapter Sixteen

'Come along to Cross Bath, Morse?" Algie asked as he pair of them breakfasted alone. "Sir Hugo and I are oing to make a morning of it."

Morse pulled a face. He'd smelled Bath's pungent waters often enough. He felt no inclination to drink the stuff, et alone immerse himself in it. "Not today, Algie. I promised Frederica I'd go along with her to Milsome Street this norning."

Now it was Algie's turn to make mouths. "Hope I never ve to see the day I traipse behind a woman while she's hopping. What kind of occupation is that for any self-especting man? Toting all her purchases like the lowest egree of footman—without even a tip for your trouble."

Morse grinned ruefully. He had good reason to know lgie was not exaggerating. This would not be his first uch excursion with Frederica. His youthful training as a ootman had stood him in good stead.

"Come with you and risk putting the richest heiress in ath out of temper?" he asked. "This is strange advice rom a fellow who's been nudging me in Miss Hill's diection practically from the moment we landed in Bath."

Algie spread a hot roll liberally with butter. "What fool

ever told you the way to win a woman is by scurrying all
over town at her beck and call? You've got her well and
truly hooked, but you may lose the catch if you let your
line go slack. Nobody wants what they can get too easily,
and I daresay that goes double for rich women.''

Since Leonora was not around to lecture them on deportment, Morse picked up a bread roll and pitched it at
Algie's head. ''Who says I have any intention of *landing*
this catch? Really Algie, you make Miss Hill sound like a
fine fat brook trout!''

Snatching the bread roll, Algie looked ready to lob it
back until Morse's jest sobered him. ''Do you mean you
don't plan to ask for Miss Hill's hand? That would make
quite a scandal after you've let things get this far. I'm sure
the lady is expecting a proposal soon, and the *quality* of
Bath certainly are. I wouldn't have the nerve to disappoint
either of them.''

Had he *let things get this far?* Morse mused as he finished his breakfast coffee and pretended to read the newspaper. On reflection, he supposed he had. After Leonora
had turned down his proposal, some nagging insecurity
within him had responded to Frederica's transparent admiration. She'd invented reason after reason to keep him
in her company, until it had become a matter of course.
Who, Morse asked himself, was landing whom?

''Really, you ought to come with us,'' Algie persisted.
''Miss Hill or no Miss Hill. The baths might do your leg
good.''

To his surprise, Morse heard himself agreeing to accompany them. Before he could change his mind again, Algie
dispatched a servant boy to Camden Place with a message
for Frederica.

The bells of Bath Abbey were chiming the hour of ten
when Morse, Algie and Sir Hugo crossed Pulteney Bridge

n their sedan chairs. Though heavily overcast, the day felt even milder than usual. A good thing, too, reflected Morse when he discovered they were to make the trip clad in their dressing gowns.

The novel experience proved much more pleasurable than he had anticipated. His sedan chair conveyed him directly into the slips at Cross Bath where he donned a bathing costume of canvas waistcoat and drawers. Easing into the hot, pungent water, he waded over to join Algie and Sir Hugo.

Wisps of vapor rose from the surface of the water, where bathers' heads bobbed, as if disembodied. A few voices echoed off the walls of the chamber, but not many. Morse could understand why. The hot bath quickly sapped a person of energy, even for conversation.

"Glad you could join us, my boy," Sir Hugo greeted Morse. It would take more than Bath's famous waters to still his voluble tongue for long. "I like to see a man not too tightly tied to his mistress's apron strings."

"Keep your voice down, Sir Hugo! Miss Hill is *not* my mistress!" In fact, the notion of bedding the young lady held little appeal for him. Morse was blasted if he could think why, for she was pretty and agreeable.

"Planning to make an honest woman of her, are you?" If anything, Sir Hugo's voice rumbled louder than before. His deep chuckle rolled out over the steaming water.

"Yes," blurted Morse. "I mean…no. That is, I haven't given the matter much thought until this morning."

"You really had better think on it." Algie harped back to their talk at breakfast. "You can't squire an eligible heiress around the Parade Grounds, escort her to concerts at the Assembly Rooms and sit in her family's box at the Theatre Royal without asking for her hand in due course. Besides, wasn't that the very object of your coming to

Bath? You mustn't let your enjoyment of the chase distrac
you from the necessity of the kill.''

"It's not much wonder you're still a bachelor, Algie,"
Morse snapped. "Talking about marriage as if it was a fo:
hunt or an afternoon's angling.''

If Algie was put out, he gave no sign of it, but lapse
into giddy laughter at Morse's quip.

Eyes closed, face serenely relaxed, Sir Hugo weighe
back in with less than his usual vigor. "Algie may not pu
it very delicately, but he's right all the same, my boy. I
you love this Miss Knoll…''

"Miss *Hill*, Sir Hugo. Miss Frederica Hill.''

"Hill, of course. Did I not say that? If you love Mis
Hill, you'd better ask for her hand. And if you don't, you'
better push off and let some serious suitor have a go.''

Their conversation ebbed into languorous silence for th
rest of the hour. While Morse's body relaxed, his min
churned. Did he love Frederica Hill? Then why had he le
himself with no choice but to ask for her hand?

When his hour's soak was up, an attendant remove
Morse's bathing costume, dried him off and manhandle
him back into his dressing gown. He sagged into the seda
chair, his flesh as warm and flaccid as rising bread dough
Algie had been right about his leg wound, though. It ha
never given him less pain. He resolved to visit the bath
frequently for the rest of his stay.

Returning to Sir Hugo's establishment, Morse dressed
then set off for Frederica's house. He needed to discove
for himself if the girl was expecting a marriage proposal

He found the house at Camden Place in some confusion
with luggage being toted to and fro. A ripple of relie
washed over him as he wondered if Miss Hill and he
family might be quitting Bath. Then he realized the trunk
and cases were all going *into* the house from a massiv
barouche parked by the curb.

"Captain Archibald, how kind of you to call...at last."
A harried Lady Fitzwarren did not look especially pleased
by his arrival. "Father and Stepmother will be joining us
next week," she added, gesturing around at the bustle.

"I beg your pardon for calling at an inconvenient time."
Morse bowed and backed away, bumping into a perspiring
footman laden with luggage. After more apologies to Lady
Fitzwarren, and to the servant whose toes he'd trodden on,
Morse added. "I'll return when your household is more
settled."

"Do stay." Miss Hill's sister looked ready to seize the
breast of his coat and detain him by force if necessary. "It
will do Frederica good to see you. She and Eustace are
lunching in the small parlor. You must join them."

Seeing it was no use to resist, Morse picked his way
through the entry hall, strewn with boxes and parcels. He
found Frederica by herself in the parlor, nibbling on a
sandwich.

"Your sister insisted I must join you and Sir Eustace
for luncheon...but..." Dining alone with a young lady,
even on a sliver of bread and watercress, suggested a level
of familiarity that suddenly made him uneasy.

"Eustace does not feel equal to food at present," she
said, as if to explain her brother-in-law's absence.

He could not have faced luncheon, either, thought
Morse, if he'd drunk quite as much brandy as Eustace
Fitzwarren had on the previous evening.

"Then perhaps I should come back at a more convenient
time." He attempted another strategic retreat.

Frederica Hill looked up with red-rimmed eyes, loosing
a barrage of guilt at Morse. "Do stay. I'm certain Henrietta
will join us presently."

"If you insist." Morse perched on the edge of a chair
and accepted the cup of tea she poured him.

A cumbersome silence settled over the parlor like an

invisible dust cover. Morse drank his tea and made a determined effort to avoid Frederica's gently reproachful gaze. Each second of quiet seemed to chide him, and he hated it.

If Leonora had been angry with him, she would have made him aware of her displeasure in no uncertain terms. They'd have a jolly set-to. Attacking, defending and counterattacking in passionate ringing tones, stirring his blood, until one delivered the victory blow. Then they would put it behind them, all the better friends for a good open quarrel.

"Did you make satisfactory purchases at Milsome Street?" he ventured. Might as well get it over with.

"I decided against going." Frederica sighed. "Shopping is never so enjoyable without company."

Morse sucked in a deep breath. To surrender without a fight felt so craven. Yet he could no more combat this passive censure of Frederica's than he could grapple with a shadow.

"Look here. I'm sorry I wasn't able to come with you as I promised." He looked into her liquid blue eyes and discovered an apology would not be sufficient. Her wounded but expectant gaze demanded a good excuse for his actions.

"My leg was paining me." Not an outright lie, but hardly the truth, either. "I paid a visit to Cross Bath to see if the waters might ease it."

"Your wound, of course." She looked vastly relieved. "It helped you, I hope."

"Tolerably."

"Good."

Silence fell again. Morse could hear the servants still moving about. Had Mr. Hill dismantled his entire house in Sheffield and sent it ahead to be reconstituted for the arrival of he and his wife?

Frederica cleared her throat. Morse glanced up to discover a bright blush staining her cheeks.

"I thought perhaps…that is…I worried you might have…well, Eustace said you must be squiring some other lady and hadn't time for me." Her words tumbled out faster and faster. "He can be perfectly beastly when he's…er, out of sorts."

Though wary of where it might lead their conversation, Morse offered vague reassurance. "Then you mustn't pay him any mind."

"That's easier said than done." She reached behind her and pulled out a much-crumpled handkerchief. By the thickness in her voice and the plaintive downturn of her eyebrows, Morse could tell she would soon need it.

"Eustace has such a horrid way of divining the most hurtful thing one can possibly hear." Sure enough, her tears began to spill. "Why, he insisted you are in love with Sir Hugo Peverill's niece. Imagine, claiming you would prefer a poky, bluestocking tabby like Miss Freemantle to me!"

"I'll thank you to not speak slightingly of Leonora in my hearing." The words were out before Morse could restrain them. "She's shown me great kindness while I've been Sir Hugo's guest."

"Then it *is* true!" Frederica wailed. "Eustace said you love her and you're only dallying with me to make her jealous."

What could he say to that? Morse sat stunned by the verbal ambush. Fitzwarren's cup-shot malice hit far too near the mark.

"F-f-father's coming next week," Frederica blubbered into the sodden scrap of linen. "And he'll be expecting me to have a s-suitable suitor…"

The rest was impossibly muffled by her sniffling and the handkerchief, but Morse needed to hear no more. Algie had been right. Miss Hill was expecting a proposal—and more to the point, so was her father.

He opened his mouth, not certain what might come out. Half afraid to discover.

A noise at the door heralded the arrival of two footmen, who struggled into the parlor bearing a large picture swathed in canvas.

"Sorry, miss," said one. "We was told to bring this 'round here and see it hung up straightaway."

So grateful was Morse for the interruption, he longed to treat the men to a frothing pint at the nearest alehouse.

Frederica Hill appeared to welcome the distraction, too. She leaped from the chaise and pretended to look out the window.

"Bring it in, then," she ordered over her shoulder. "We dare not leave it down and risk its getting damaged."

Morse eyed the footmen's burden. "Does your father always take his pictures along when he travels?"

"Only this one." Though still muffled from earlier weeping, her voice conveyed an edge of bitterness. "He paid a great sum to have Mr. Lawrence paint a portrait of my stepmother. It must always hang in the parlor when they are in residence."

Two ladders were brought and the landscape hanging above the mantel was taken down to make room for Mrs. Hill's portrait.

"She must be a very decorative creature, your stepmother," quipped Morse, mentally rehearsing his excuse to leave.

"She was the widow of a viscount, Captain Archibald. Her picture is a sort of trophy for my father."

The servants removed Mrs. Hill's portrait from the wrappings, and it began a lurching ascent to its place of honor.

Morse's mouth fell open.

He hoped Frederica would not suddenly turn back from the window, for he had no hope of disguising the look of dismay that gripped his features. There could be no mistaking the insolent beauty that stared back at him from the portrait.

Not trusting himself to speak, Morse bolted.

From her window seat overlooking Laura Place, Leonora glanced out for the tenth time that hour. The low-hanging clouds had been menacing all day. If they meant to douse Bath in rain, she wished they would get on with it and be done! She could weather the inevitable deluge, but she hated waiting for it.

Just then Morse limped into view, making his way from Pulteney Bridge. From what Leonora could tell, he appeared to lean upon his walking stick more heavily than he had in some time. A shame his visit to the baths with Algie had not improved his mobility. With a guilty start Leonora realized her shallow pretext of checking the weather had only been an excuse to watch for Morse.

Closer and closer he came, and Leonora could not take her eyes off him. No use telling herself she had made her choice. The only safe, rational choice she could make. Her heart still yearned for Morse Archer. Irrationally. Dangerously.

But what was this?

As she watched, he passed the entrance of Sir Hugo's premises and kept right on walking through Laura Place and up Great Pulteney Street. Where could he be going?

Before she had time to convince herself the matter was no concern of hers, Leonora had thrown a shawl around her shoulders, seized an umbrella and dashed out of the house after him. She managed to stay at a discreet distance while still keeping him in sight, until he reached Sydney Gardens.

The hexagonal expanse of lawns, groves and vistas was Leonora's favorite spot in all of Bath. A day seldom passed without she and Elsie coming here for a stroll. She liked it best on days like this, when unsettled weather left the park free of fashionable ladies and gentlemen out parading their finery.

Indeed, Leonora found the pleasure garden all but deserted. For a moment she almost forgot her pursuit of Morse, captivated by Sydney Gardens at the height of its springtime charm. The wholesome sweetness of flowering fruit trees distilled in the mild, moist air. The varied, vivid greens of grass and leaf would have taxed an artist's palette.

She soon overtook Morse, sitting on a low stone bench beside one of the footpaths, staring down Bathwick slope toward the River Avon. Leonora approached and retreated several times before she strayed close enough to catch his eye.

"Oh, hello." He smiled, but absently, as though his thoughts were on something...or someone far away. Then he glanced behind her. "Miss Taylor not with you?"

Even that slight degree of awareness seemed to tax his concentration.

"No." What use was it pretending she had just happened upon him during one of her strolls in the park? Even as unconventional a creature as she did not usually roam Sydney Gardens unchaperoned. "I saw you wander past the house. I wondered if something might be wrong."

Since Morse appeared too preoccupied to offer her a seat, Leonora claimed one for herself, beside him on the bench. "Well, is there? Have you challenged someone else to a duel? Or has Miss Hill thrown you over for a suitor of more exalted pedigree?"

Morse answered with a slow shake of his head that told her nothing at all.

A fat, cold raindrop struck Leonora on the nose. Others followed. Opening her umbrella, she shifted closer to Morse, holding it up to shield them both from the rain. "We should get back to Laura Place. The sky has been threatening this rain all day. It's likely to keep up for some time."

His vacant gaze met hers. "Did you say something?"

Leonora's curiosity gave way to alarm. "There *is* something wrong, isn't there, Morse? Come now, you must tell me. Perhaps I can help."

He stared back out over the vale, where a swath of mist had gathered above the river. His lips did not appear to move. Perhaps the words issued straight from his heart. "It was her."

"It was *she*." Schoolmistress reflex made Leonora say it before she could think to stop herself.

Morse's head whipped around, the better for him to glare at her. "Her. She. What does it matter? It was my Pamela in that picture!"

The words slammed into Leonora, stunning her into silence. She half expected Morse to leap from the bench and hobble off.

But he didn't.

Instead, as if drained by his outburst, he slumped forward until his elbows rested upon his knees and his head nestled in his hands. Leonora was suddenly conscious of the contact between them—from hip to knee. Her hand holding the umbrella began to tremble.

"It's been so long." Morse's voice sounded oddly hushed and again his mouth scarcely seemed to move.

Leonora fought the uncanny notion that she might be hearing his unspoken thoughts.

"So long. All the army years between then and now. But when I looked at her picture, it might have been yesterday."

Word by word it poured out, with no attempt to explain or interpret for her sake. Some instinct forbade Leonora to question. Yet, piece by piece it came clear at last.

How it had been between Lady Pamela Granville and young Archer, the footman. He spoke of their intimacy, with no thought of censoring it for Leonora's ears. A smarting heat radiated from her leg where it pressed against Morse's. An answering fervor smoldered in her heart—a combustible compound of passionate arousal and primal jealousy.

He had done things with another woman that would make her writhe and whimper in her empty bed, wanting him. When he described—or relived their final interview, Leonora scarcely heeded the bitter pain in his voice, so consumed was she by the image of Morse provoking the lust of his highborn mistress. The passions within her had reached their flash point when Morse struck tinder.

His own agitation had eased with the gradual seepage of memories, until at last he was able to expel a slow breath—part wistful sigh, part derisive chuckle. "To think our lives would collide again after all this time, and in such a way. It would serve Lady Pamela right if I *did* wed her stepdaughter."

Leonora could contain herself no longer. Surging up from the bench, she let the umbrella fall forward until it loomed between them like a shield. Or a weapon.

"What manner of warped creature are you, Morse Archer? To casually speculate on wedding this young woman only to revenge yourself on her stepmother. Whatever made me think I could turn *you* into a gentleman? I'm sorry I ever set eyes on you!"

Her charge struck Morse like a load of grapeshot to the bowels. Putrid shame gushed from the wound.

No sense protesting that he hadn't meant it *that* way. Perhaps, in some coarse, petty corner of his soul he had.

But blast him to hell if he'd bow to Leonora Freemantle's self-righteous judgment.

Pulling himself erect, though his leg throbbed worse than it had since Bucaso, he covered his weakness by going on the attack. "No sorrier than I am, madam. I'm so sick of your hypocrisy, I could gag."

Thunder rumbled in the distance and the rain pelted down upon them. Morse raised his voice to be heard above the storm. "Quit pretending such lofty scruples. I can see through them well enough. Too good to wed me yourself, but you can't abide the notion of my being happy with some other woman. You're nothing more than a dog in the manger!"

She raised a hand to wipe the sodden hair from her forehead, but made no move to hoist her umbrella. "That's the most ridiculous—"

"I'm not finished! You're no better than Pamela Granville. At least she didn't pretend to care for anything but rank and fortune. No fine-sounding cant about education and equality." He strode past her in the downpour, marching back toward Great Pulteney Street with his best parade ground swagger.

His leg wound revenged itself upon him with every step and threatened further reprisals in the days to come. Morse's pride refused to submit. He would not give Leonora Freemantle the satisfaction of watching him falter.

Oh, they were cut from the same cloth, these two well-born ladies who provoked his desire as intensely as they mutilated his pride. It would serve them *both* right if he wed the most eligible heiress in Bath!

Chapter Seventeen

Leonora did not even watch Morse go.

For a few moments after he stalked off, she continued to stand there with the sky weeping spring rain upon her. Too stunned and indignant for action—even the slight effort of lifting her umbrella.

A dog in the manger. How dare he accuse her of such pettiness?

Her own steady, dispassionate reason suddenly turned traitor, asking if she truly wished to see him happy with another woman. It seemed pointless to lie to herself.

No, she acknowledged with a shuddering sigh. She did not want to see him with another woman. Did not want to think of him with another woman. Could not even stand to hear of his past encounters with another woman.

Morse was wrong about the rest, though.

He'd claimed she didn't want him, and *that* was not true. She did resent Frederica Hill's place in his life and Pamela Hill's former place in his arms. But only because she wanted so badly to be there in their stead.

In the throes of anguish too hot for any amount of rain to quench, Leonora turned and ran back through Sydney Gardens and down Great Pulteney Street.

* * *

Afterward, Morse scarcely remembered wending his way to Camden Place in the pouring rain, his heart smoldering in his chest like a white-hot coal. In his mind, Leonora Freemantle and Pamela Granville melded into one. Provoking him to desire and love. Then turning on him to demand the former and disdain the latter.

If he'd had his wits about him, he would never have turned up at Frederica's door soaked to the bone and hardly able to stagger another step. What had drawn him there, he could not guess. By this hour she and the Fitzwarrens must be out to a concert at the Assembly Rooms or some private party.

The servants knew him well enough by sight, though. Out of pity they might show him to a chair by the kitchen hearth until he could muster the nerve to return to Laura Place.

Morse knocked.

The door opened about halfway and the butler eyed him with suspicion. "Tradesmen to the kitchen do— Dear me, is that *you*, Captain Archibald? Come in, sir, before you drown."

"Too late." Morse managed a wry grin as he stepped into the entry hall. Strangely, he felt his own cold and wetness to a greater degree in contrast to the warmth and dryness around him.

He was about to apologize to the butler for turning up during the family's absence, when Frederica called from the head of the stairs. "Hardy, who's come calling at this hour and on such an evening?"

Before the butler could answer, Morse did. "I thought you'd be out. May I stay a few minutes to get myself dry?"

"Maurice?" She came flying down the stairs in her dressing gown. "Henrietta and Eustace went out to a party, but I didn't feel— Gracious! We must get you into dry clothes at once.''

"Really, that won't be nec—"

"Go fetch a dressing gown of Lord Fitzwarren's," she ordered the butler. "Nothing else would be big enough."

Though Morse tried to protest, she peeled off his coat and made him sit down to pry off his boots. Before he could gain his feet again, she plucked off his hat.

Then, perhaps realizing it would be improper for her to disrobe him further, she blushed a very becoming shade of pink. "Perhaps you had better go change clothes in Eustace's dressing room. In the meantime I'll see if Cook has a little mulled wine on hand. She often does on a rainy night."

"Please, don't go to any trouble."

His protests fell on deaf ears. "Come down to the drawing room once you've put on dry clothes. The fire's better there than in the parlor."

The news did not disappoint Morse. Rather than sit in the same room with Lady Pamela's portrait, he would have walked back out into the storm—coatless, hatless and barefoot.

When he limped into the drawing room a quarter of an hour later, Morse smelled the mellow spicy aroma of mulled wine and the faint smoke of a well-stoked coal fire. He shrugged his shoulders, trying to get comfortable in the borrowed dressing gown. A fine, warm garment, it must have hung loose on Fitzwarren's whippet frame. It clung to Morse like a luxurious strait waistcoat.

"Come sit by the fire and dry out." Frederica perched on a footstool beside the massive wing chair she'd tugged in front of the hearth.

Sinking into the chair gratefully, Morse closed his eyes for a moment to rest them. And to avoid Frederica's searching gaze. He could not stop his ears to her questions, though.

"Whatever were you doing out in such weather?"

"Walking." His hoarseness made the answer sound gruff, which he instantly regretted.

She fell silent for a time. Morse occupied himself with drinking his toddy. A few sips sent a ripple of warmth coursing through him.

"You left here so abruptly." Her words held a question.

"I remembered a piece of urgent business."

Her voice took on a tentative, wary note. "I wondered if I'd frightened you off with my talk of matches and suitors."

Morse squirmed in his physically comfortable seat. Just then he felt like an accused criminal in the docket.

What could he answer? *Yes* would brand him a coward and a cad. *No* might suggest he welcomed such overtures.

"Business," he croaked again. "Urgent business."

"At least you came back here." She seemed determined to find reassurance. If not in his words, then in his actions.

When Morse made no reply, she abruptly changed the subject. "Have you heard Colonel Maxwell is coming to Bath?"

"No, I hadn't. What brings him, do you suppose?"

"The same thing that brought you, perhaps. An effort to recover his health."

Having received grievous wounds during his service under Wellington, Colonel Sir Geoffery Maxwell was esteemed only a degree below the great general himself. His coming would set Bath society atwitter. Morse knew he would have to keep a safe distance from his idol and former commander, for Colonel Maxwell could expose his true identity in the blink of an eye.

"Let's hope the colonel has more sense than to go walking in the rain." Morse laughed giddily at his feeble quip.

Both the tension in his body and the turmoil in his thoughts began to ease. The mulled wine must be more potent than he'd realized.

"There's to be a grand ball in Colonel Maxwell's honor at the Guildhall," said Frederica. "Father and Stepmother will be in town by then. That should put father in a good temper—he admires the colonel so."

She talked on about the ball. What she would wear. The music. The refreshments. How Morse's presence would open all the right social doors for her and her family. Her conversation washed over Morse, bubbling around him and buoying him up. Like the hot spring water of Bath—soothing and relaxing him.

Perhaps this was what he needed from a woman.

The notion formed in his mind as if planted there by some outside agency. It found fertile ground, though, tilled by the day's disturbing events and the wine he'd consumed far too quickly. Perhaps this *was* what he needed from a woman. Not challenge and zest, but ease and tranquility. If nothing else, a woman prepared to greet his marriage proposal with an enthusiastic *yes*.

Frederica's chatter trailed off little by little as he added no fresh fuel to the conversation. Yet she did not chide him for failing to speak or interrogate him about the privacy of his thoughts. By degrees she subsided against him until her head rested lightly against his knee.

Almost of its own accord, his hand reached out and stroked her hair. She excited not an ounce of desire in him, but perhaps that was no bad thing. Having been scorched by the heat of passion in the past, more tepid feelings now appealed to him.

"Your father expects you to make a good match this season?" His hoarseness now sounded husky and tender.

Frederica held still. Her head continued to rest against

his knee as she stared toward the hearth. "He may not say it in so many words. But I know he does."

"Would I suit him, do you suppose?"

"Suit him?" She whispered the words on an intake of breath.

"As a son-in-law, I mean," Morse persisted. "Or perhaps what I should ask is, will I suit you?"

She sat up and turned to stare at him. "Are you asking for my hand, Captain?"

"I suppose I am." His own voice sounded as surprised as hers. "Shall I be disappointed?"

"Yes!" She lunged at him, throwing her arms around his neck. Morse wondered if her excitement stemmed more from relief than affection. "I mean—no. No, you shall not be disappointed. Yes, I will accept."

Morse recalled the sensation of his body after emerging from Cross Bath—limp and boneless. He felt something akin to that now in his mind and his heart. Had he just crowned a life full of mistakes with the most grievous mistake of all? If he tried to back out now, Leonora's wager would be lost.

Uncle did not look well. The folds of his craggy face hung flaccid, as though someone had just clubbed him senseless with a poker. He held the open newspaper before him, but his eyes did not scan the page. Rather they fixed on one spot and gazed into a distance far beyond it.

"Whatever is the matter, Uncle Hugo?" Leonora dropped to her knees beside his chair. "Shall I summon the doctor?"

He shook his head, and his spirit seemed to return to his body from its wayfaring. "No doctors. I'm plenty fit with all that vile mineral water I've been drinking."

Leonora had scarcely expelled a breath of relief when Sir Hugo folded up his newspaper and announced in a most accusatory tone, "I suppose you've been party to all this."

"Party to what? I promise I've been behaving myself."

"Are you saying you had nothing to do with this engagement nonsense Morse has taken into his head?"

Sir Hugo's words bludgeoned her.

"Engagement?" she squeaked. "To Miss Hill?"

"Who else do you think? He came to me this morning as bold as brass and asked if he might borrow a sum of money against his expectations of winning the wager— cocky cub! Said he needed it to purchase a ring for his intended. I suppose if he marries into a rich family he won't need to make a fresh start abroad."

Leonora rose and took several steps away so Sir Hugo would not detect the subtle signs of her distress. "Did you give him the money?"

"What else could I do? This wager of yours is as good as won—has been ever since Morse called out young Nettlecombe. By Jove, I had no idea he'd serious designs on his heiress creature. I suppose you egged him on."

"I did not." No, indeed. She'd been too busy playing dog in the manger.

"Well, I won't pretend to approve." Rising from his chair, Sir Hugo shook his newspaper at her.

Did he seriously think she'd pushed Morse into this alliance? Then again, perhaps she had.

Sir Hugo stalked off, muttering to himself. "What's this creature got to recommend her besides her fortune? Why, in my day, folks didn't go 'round wedding to improve their..." His grumbling trailed off down the corridor.

Like an autumn leaf falling to earth on a breathless day, Leonora settled into the chair her uncle had vacated.

So Morse had gone and done it, after all. He'd proposed to another woman and she had pushed him to it with both hands. Goaded by her own frustrated desire, she had lashed out at him—flinging accusations she had no right to utter. Her own motives were far from honorable, after all.

Restless and fighting for composure, she sprang from the chair and paced to the window. Outside, May's golden sunshine warmed the honey-colored buildings of Laura Place. A carriage trundled past, its matched team shaking their chestnut manes in the breeze. Even a young barrow boy pushed his cart with a jaunty step and cried his wares in a cheerful singsong. All of Bath contrived to mock Leonora's dark, tempestuous spirits.

She heard the door open behind her and Morse's voice. "Sir Hugo, would you care to see…"

Schooling her face to counterfeit serenity, she turned to face him.

"Oh, Leonora. Excuse the intrusion." He pocketed a small box and beat a retreat from the sitting room. "I was told I would find your uncle here."

"He was here reading his paper until a few moments ago." She chose not to mention that Sir Hugo had departed ranting against the folly of Morse's engagement. "Please don't leave."

Morse stepped inside and shut the door behind him. Chagrin and defiance warred for control of his too candid features. Clearly he expected her to erupt in fury.

"You've heard, then?" he asked. Her show of composure must not be good enough.

"Uncle told me." She fixed a smile on her lips, sincere in wishing him well if nothing else. "Congratulations. I hope you and Miss Hill will be very happy together."

Morse appeared to be weighing her words for mockery. "It isn't the money, you know."

How Leonora wished she could believe that. Could Morse be so blind to his own motives?

"And it isn't revenge," he added with bitter assurance.

"Of course not. I should never have said so." Another

thought ambushed her. If Morse was prompted to wed for wealth, did it matter so much, provided he was true to his wife—treating her with kindness and respect?

"You weren't the only one whose tongue ran away with you." He flashed her a fleeting, wry grin. As near as he could come to an apology, she guessed. Like her, he must still believe the pith of his accusation.

"Uncle told me he advanced you the price of a ring."

Morse nodded. "This is as good as an admission he's lost the wager. That must make you happy."

"It does." At least, it should have.

"Would you like to see it?" He pulled the tiny box back out of his pocket.

Leonora nodded, feeling like a criminal about to receive her sentence. Harsh, but just.

As Morse held the ring out for her inspection, she stared at it, nestled in velvet. At least she would feel no envy of Miss Hill sporting this gaudy piece of jewelry upon her finger.

Morse appeared to read her thoughts. "Not the most modest expression of the jeweler's art, is it?"

"It's very…" She searched for an inoffensive truth. "…large."

"It's what Frederica wants. She pointed it out to me the last time we passed the jeweler's on Milsome Street."

Leonora backed away. "That's good, then."

"Well, I should go find Sir Hugo and show it to him."

"I'm not sure that would be wise, just now."

"Oh?"

"He seems put out about your engagement." She shrugged. "I can't think why, except that it shows he's lost the wager."

Pocketing the ring again, Morse brightened. "Algie, then."

Leonora nodded. "He's sure to be excited about it."

With a brief wave of parting, Morse quit the sitting room. He was back again before Leonora had time to slump. "I could use your help."

She raised an eyebrow, afraid her voice might betray her.

"I still need to ask Mr. Hill for his permission, and I'd just as soon not run into his wife before it's all settled."

"You'll have to run into her sooner or later, Morse, if you mean to marry her stepdaughter."

"I know that. But I plan to steer clear of her as much as possible. At least until after Frederica and I are married and you've won your wager."

"Oh, dear. I hadn't thought of that." If Pamela Hill recognized Morse and broadcast the news, her good-as-won wager would be forfeit. "How can I help, Morse? You and I have worked too hard to see it all come to naught this late in the game."

His features thawed into a genuine comradely smile. "I knew I could count on you, Leonora. If we put our heads together, I reckon we can come up with some way to save the situation."

He fairly radiated trust in her. If only…

Leonora tried to force the thought from her mind, but it would not accept banishment.

If only she had been able to trust him as he so obviously trusted her.

"Good luck with your mission, old girl." Morse treated his co-conspirator to a sardonic salute. "I'll be watching for your signal."

It felt good to be on the same side again. Though he could think of few worthier opponents than Leonora, Morse vastly preferred being allies. Still, he could not subdue a wish that they might have been the closest of allies. Always and forever.

She cast an anxious glance at the Hill abode, third from the end of this prestigious row of houses. "What if something goes wrong? Suppose I can't keep the ladies occupied? Suppose Mr. Hill decides to join us?"

"Take a deep breath." He reached out to pat her shoulder, then pulled back his hand at the last minute. "You made a tolerable gentleman out of a rough-and-ready soldier, remember? You're equal to whatever life pitches at you, Leonora Freemantle. Don't ever forget that. Once you signal from the parlor window, I'll slip in and speak to Mr. Hill."

"Right." She sucked in a deep draft of air, then blew it out again, not very steadily. "We'll meet back here, afterward."

"I'll be waiting."

He should have waited for her. The conviction buffeted Morse as he watched Leonora approach the Hill's town house. In time she might have come around. Once he'd proved his gentlemanly veneer ran deeper. He'd let his too sensitive pride and his volatile temper get the better of his good sense. Now he must salvage as much as possible from the situation—Leonora's school and her independence.

He watched the parlor window, his uneasiness swelling by the minute. All Leonora's *supposings* of possible disaster stalked his thoughts, along with a few perverse imaginings of his own.

Then he saw Leonora silhouetted in the parlor window, pretending to admire the expensive view Camden Place afforded Bath's wealthiest visitors. She had accomplished her mission. Now his turn had come.

The butler answered his quiet knock. "Come to call on Miss Frederica, have you sir?"

"No." The word exploded from Morse. "Don't disturb

her on any account, will you, Hardy? It's *Mr.* Hill I've come to see.''

He pulled the ring box far enough out of his coat pocket to proclaim the nature of his errand.

The butler's tufted eyebrows shot up. ''Mr. Hill will be delighted to receive you, I'm sure.'' His voice fell to a confidential whisper. ''You certain about this, Captain Archibald?''

Though his hackles rose with a Rifleman's instinct for trouble, Morse pretended to chuckle off the warning. ''Come now, Hardy. You should be telling me I'll be a lucky chap to win the hand of such an estimable young lady.''

''Aye, sir. You're right, of course.'' The little man's face drained of color. ''I meant no slight on Miss Frederica. Pardon me for speaking out of turn.''

''No offense taken, Hardy. I know how confirmed bachelors hate to see any defection from the ranks. Many's the time I've counseled prudence to some besotted fellow.''

''You do understand then, sir.'' Hardy worked up a shaky smile. ''A man gets more than his lady when he weds into a rich family. You've always seemed like a good fellow, sir, and…''

Whatever the butler meant to say, he did not get the opportunity.

At that moment, the library door swung open and Mr. Herbert Hill strode out. Though less than average height, he was stout through the chest, as though accustomed to thrusting it forward in pride or belligerence. His coat boasted the most expensive tailoring money could buy, but the garish pattern of his waistcoat suggested more gold than good taste. His sharp-featured countenance was weather-beaten and his hands betrayed a history of manual labor.

He advanced with his hand outthrust. "You must be the Captain Archibald I've heard such a great deal about."

With a grin and a shrug Morse shook the older man's hand. "I suppose I must."

Mr. Hill glowered at the butler. "What took you so long showing Captain Archibald in? Flapping your jaws, I suppose. The captain's an important man. He doesn't have time to be remarking on the state of the weather with a servant who's too bloody familiar for his own good."

The butler bowed his head before this abuse. "Yes, Mr. Hill. Very good, sir." If his employer had emptied a bucket of slops on top of him, poor Hardy could not have looked more thoroughly humiliated.

"You mustn't blame your man for *my* eagerness to talk, Mr. Hill," Morse insisted with forced heartiness. "The fact is, I couldn't help boasting of my errand." He patted his bulging coat pocket. "Might I have a private word with you, sir?"

Mr. Hill's foul humor with the butler passed like the sun emerging from behind a thunderhead. "That you may, Captain Archibald. Come right this way, sir."

He ushered Morse into the library.

"I hope you won't take it amiss, if I say I've been expecting this interview, Captain Archibald. Our Frederica's been filling my ears with your praises ever since the wife and me arrived from Sheffield."

What if Mr. Hill should refuse his consent? This faint ray of hope suddenly tantalized Morse. Unlike jilting Frederica, Mr. Hill's veto would not create a scandal that might spell doom for Leonora's wager.

"Your daughter is very kind and perhaps too partial." Morse took a seat. "Given your position, I should understand entirely if a prudent father frowned on the match."

Mr. Hill held up the brandy decanter. When Morse shook his head, Frederica's father poured himself a small glass. "What makes you think I'll be disposed to deny you, when my young lass has her heart set on you?"

Morse scrambled to frame his argument. Whatever others had reported about him, he did not want to lie outright. "Well, sir, while I would do my utmost to provide for your daughter, I'm little more than a crippled soldier without prospects."

"Don't worry your head about money, son." Mr. Hill plumped himself down in a chair opposite Morse. "By and by, Frederica will have more than enough to keep you both. And if you do your duty and present me with a litter of fine strapping grandsons, I may well settle the bulk of my fortune on you. Any fool can make money. What I want is to see my kin sitting in the Lords, or commanding His Majesty's Guards."

In rising from obscurity to make his fortune, hadn't Herbert Hill proven himself the equal in merit of any peer? Not to his own satisfaction, apparently.

"Though I take pride in my family," Morse measured his words, "we are not as wellborn as your present son-in-law."

"Useless Eustace, you mean?" Mr. Hill sneered. "What good's a title without a son to carry it on? Besides, you're being too modest. Modesty is a singular fault in a gentleman if you ask me. I'll hear no more of it. As far as I'm concerned, you and my daughter are engaged to be wed."

He thrust out one meaty hand. "Welcome to the family—son. Let's go find the ladies and drink a toast."

Morse shot to his feet. "I can't…just now, sir. I have urgent business elsewhere, but I couldn't delay speaking to you. You've made me a very…happy man. I assure you I'll do my best to make Frederica happy, as well."

Feeling like a hobbled stallion who'd just been purchased for stud, Morse escaped from Camden Place and waited for his rendezvous with Leonora. His one shard of hope lay crushed beneath the heel of Frederica's forceful father.

Chapter Eighteen

If Morse did not appear soon, Leonora feared she would wear a furrow in the Hill's carpet from their parlor chaise to the window. Once she knew for certain he'd cleared the house, she'd be free to conclude her call upon Miss Hill, her sister and stepmother.

Leonora racked her brains to invent a novel excuse for looking outside yet again. No good rhapsodizing over the view. She'd done that often enough to justify Mr. Hill's expense in renting these costly premises. Checking the weather had grown stale, too. Bath's climate could be fickle enough, but today there was scarcely a cloud in the sky to warrant concern.

What was taking Morse so long?

"*More* tea, Miss Freemantle?" asked Frederica. Ill-disguised impatience with the length of Leonora's stay sharpened her question.

Leonora pretended to not notice. "Just a drop, if you'd be so kind. What a lovely portrait!" She rose and walked to the mantel for a closer look. Her route there and back would take her past the window twice. "The work of Mr. Lawrence, isn't it?"

Mrs. Hill did not bother to suppress a yawn. "My husband commissioned the painting shortly before we were married. The way he carts it along when we travel, he scarcely needs to bring me in the flesh. I'm heartily sick of the sight of it.''

It could not be very agreeable to face this constant reminder of her passing youth and beauty, Leonora realized. Lady Pamela's most partial admirers would now call her *handsome* or *striking* rather than beautiful. The blame lay less with time than with her perpetual expression of haughty ill-humor and an intemperate campaign to stave off age with powder and paint.

While the sight of young Lady Pamela stirred the flames of her tightly suppressed jealousy, Leonora could not help pity the woman a little for having made the wrong choice. She'd been a fool to refuse Morse's love in favor of a mercenary marriage. And she had clearly reaped the bitter harvest of her folly.

Picture yourself at her age, urged an insidious little voice deep within Leonora's own mind. *Will you be as ill content with the bargain you've made?*

"Perhaps you'd rather have remained behind in Sheffield, Stepmother?'' The peevish tone of Lady Fitzwarren's question roused Leonora from her unwelcome musings.

"I'd rather have gone to London or Brighton, or somewhere fashionable,'' snapped Mrs. Hill. "Bath has fallen from its past brilliance. It gets more poky and provincial with every Season.''

"Clearly you and the town have much in common.'' Miss Hill fired the broadside to cap her sister's setup.

Leonora sensed this was but a minor skirmish in a long campaign of domestic warfare. If they engaged in such cordial hostility before company, she wondered what pitched battles must be fought over the privacy of their dinner table. She did not envy Morse having to find out.

"Have you so much in common with your precious

Captain Archibald, my dear?'' Clearly, Mrs. Hill could hold her ground against her stepdaughters. ''Our Frederica has hopes of your friend, the captain. Did you know that, Miss Freemantle? No doubt he has *expectations* of her, as well.''

''Look at the time!'' Catching sight of Morse making his way to their meeting place, Leonora could not wait another moment to make her escape. ''I have several more calls to pay and I've trespassed upon your hospitality—''

Before she could dash off, Mr. Hill burst into the parlor. ''Let the wine flow. We have good news to celebrate!''

He caught sight of Leonora. ''Begging your pardon, ma'am. I'd no notion my ladies had company.''

''Don't delay your celebration on my account. I must be on my way.'' She managed to withdraw, though they urged her to stay.

Hurrying across the street, she slipped behind the hedge where Morse waited. ''I've never been so glad to get out of a house in my life!''

Giddy with relief over her escape and the success of their plan, she clasped him in a brief, triumphant embrace. At least she meant it to be brief.

When she made a token effort to pull back, he held on to her.

''Morse.'' Her intended protest emerged more like a plea.

She had no opportunity to correct it, for he gave her lips a far more pleasant occupation. Surely cool reason would soon assert itself and extricate her from Morse's arms.

Wrong again.

A kiss unfolded between them. Gentle, laden with regret, but all the sweeter for that. They had kissed often enough in the past that Leonora experienced an overwhelming sense of homecoming. The circle of his arms had been tailored to her precise fit. The subtle interplay of their lips progressed like a dance—practiced to perfection, keenly enjoyed.

"I'm sorry, Leonora." Abruptly he backed away, breaking all contact with her. "I shouldn't have done that. It isn't fair to Frederica and it isn't fair to you. I have a positive talent for doing the wrong thing."

Not daring to look into his eyes, lest she see genuine regret, Leonora patted her hair and adjusted her spectacles. Surely the sweet storm of emotion that had raged through her must have left her appearance as disheveled as her heart.

"We must get home." She spoke in a breathless rush. "I believe we are engaged to dine with Algie's aunt this evening."

They spoke not a word on the walk back to Laura Place. And whenever their eyes met in a tentative sidelong glance, both quickly looked away.

Why had Morse kissed her? Leonora puzzled all the way home and as she dressed for the evening. It could have nothing to do with her small fortune, since he had now secured the hand of a truly wealthy heiress. If they had been discovered in their embrace, it might have cost Morse his advantageous match, and perhaps their wager, as well.

Why, then?

Not her beauty. That much was certain. While she could not ignore the improvement in her appearance the past months had wrought, Frederica Hill was much closer to the contemporary ideal of feminine perfection.

Leonora's logical mind could not ignore the obvious conclusion. With his engagement to the rich and comely Miss Hill secure, Morse Archer could have no motive for holding and kissing another woman.

Unless, perhaps, he had genuine feelings for her?

The thought continued to haunt Leonora as they dined with Algie's aunt—a querulous old dowager, far too sharp-witted for the good of their wager. Lady Jerrod's interrogation of Morse about his invented pedigree gave Leonora several moments of serious alarm. Fortunately, Morse's charm carried the day. He soon had the old girl fawning over him like some wet goose making her Society debut.

Was she just as silly? Leonora wondered. Dreaming up wishful nonsense on the basis of a kiss that had probably meant no more to him than the shallow compliments he heaped upon Algie's old aunt. After all, if Morse truly cared for her, why had he rejected her offer of a relationship outside marriage? Rejected it with such a show of indignant anger.

Like a thunderbolt, the truth struck her. Leonora's sorbet spoon slipped from her slack fingers and dropped onto the saucer with an explosive jangle. They all turned to stare at her.

"Something the matter?" asked Algie.

"It's nothing. Please excuse my clumsiness."

"Perhaps you *are* unwell, Miss Freemantle." Lady Jerrod looked down her patrician nose with frosty disapproval. "You've been very backward in conversation this evening."

"Be fair, milady," Morse cajoled their hostess. "I'll take the blame for monopolizing our table talk, but you must share the responsibility. If you did not have such a fascinating history, I'd be less compelled to pester you with questions and let no one else get a word in. Can you blame Miss Freemantle for hanging on your every word until she forgot herself and dropped her spoon? Now, pray continue what you were saying. How can you be certain Mr. Sheridan modeled the character of Lady Teasel upon you?"

Jollied back into good humor, Lady Jerrod kept them entertained with story after story, never again questioning Leonora's silence.

Though she dropped no more silver and went through the proper motions of a dinner guest, Leonora could not govern her thoughts as easily as her actions. Like messenger pigeons, they flocked back to Morse at every opportunity.

She recollected all he'd told her of his illicit romance with Lady Pamela Granville—this time concentrating on Morse's feelings instead of her own foolish jealousy. When he'd accused her of playing dog in the manger, hadn't he also said she considered herself too good to marry him?

Did Morse think she'd refused to wed him because of his birth? Try as she might to deny the possibility, reason led Leonora back to it again and again. Her own proposition, meant only to test his motives, must have echoed the humiliating offer with which Pamela Granville had broken his heart.

You have managed to avoid your mother's mistakes, life seemed to mock Leonora. *Gullibility was poor Clarissa's downfall. Carefully cultivated suspicion may have been yours.*

"Morse, what's wrong?" Leonora's words broke in on his anxious preoccupation. Lowering her voice to a whisper, she added, "Did Mrs. Hill recognize you?"

Returning home from separate social engagements, he had just got in and removed his coat when she arrived with Algie. If he had not grown so fond of him in the past months, Morse might have envied Algie bitterly for sharing an evening with Leonora. Too few evenings stretched between now and the time they must part. Morse grudged every one spent without her.

Shaking his head in mute answer to her question, he glanced toward the sitting room door, hoping she would understand that he must talk to her.

As soon as Algie had toddled off to bed, she hurried to join Morse. "There *is* something amiss. I knew it."

With a curt nod, he bolted back a drink of his brandy. "I've managed to keep out of Pamela's way, though it hasn't been easy. Fortunately, Frederica isn't a suspicious creature."

"Very fortunate," replied Leonora, though she looked as if he had struck her.

Morse hadn't time to ferret out what was wrong with her. "I'll be in for double the trouble, soon. Nothing will do for Frederica's father but we announce our engagement on the evening of the fete for Colonel Maxwell. Of course, Pamela will be on hand for that. I'm not certain Maurice Archibald can pass muster with one person who's met Morse Archer, let alone two."

"Oh, my."

"What will we do?" Morse wasn't certain what had rattled him so. He hated feeling all churning belly and clammy palms, like some raw recruit getting his first taste of enemy fire.

Leonora laid her hand on his. "Buck up, Sergeant. You've been in worse straits than this and managed to turn things around. Let's approach it as a battle to be won, and plan our tactics accordingly."

Twisting his hand so it met hers, palm to palm, Morse gripped her fingers. "I can't say it often enough. You'd make a fine general, Leonora Freemantle."

Without question, she had conquered his heart. No matter who he wed or did not wed, it would belong to her. He could bear the situation easier if she was free and celibate. As much his as any man's. For that reason, more than any consideration of fortune or material advantage, Morse was doubly determined to win the wedding wager.

"Don't you worry, Morse. We'll win this wager, yet." As Leonora cast an approving eye over him, her heart seemed to wrench within her breast. Privately, she blessed Uncle Hugo for suggesting they walk the short distance from Laura Place to the Guildhall. Anything for a few minutes alone with Morse.

She savored the look in his eye. Clement sunshine of admiration that had enticed the blighted bud of her confidence to blossom. Like a banked fire, the heat of her longing for him had kindled her womanly desires. If she was not careful, she might melt into a useless puddle of sentiment. Neither of them could afford that now.

"You're not still worried, are you?" She tried to suffuse her tone with confidence and faith in his abilities. "Tell me, how did you used to calm your nerves before battle?"

He blinked rapidly, as if her question had suddenly drawn his thoughts from someplace deep within him. "Concentrate on being prepared for action, I suppose. Make certain your powder's dry. Review the lay of the terrain." He thought for a moment. "Trust that your comrades will watch your back."

Thinking of a military action in the Guildhall banquet room made Leonora chuckle, though her heart felt leaden. "I'll watch your back, Morse, I promise. You keep your pretty fiancée on the dance floor and I'll keep Mrs. Hill away from the pair of you, by hook or by crook."

"Didn't I tell you?" Sir Hugo called back as they crossed Pulteney Bridge. "We're better off to walk on such a fine evening. Carriage traffic is so thick, it's at a standstill. We'll be there far earlier than the fools who drive."

"Congratulations on your very wise idea, Uncle." Leonora could not resist baiting him a little. "Though you needn't talk as if you had to haul us down Pulteney Street kicking and screaming. Algie, Morse and I have enough sense to recognize a good idea when we hear one."

She let her voice drop to a whisper. "Being early to the

all will give us an opportunity to scout the terrain for the dvantage of position, will it not, Sergeant Archer?''

"Uh-uh.'' He cast her a sidelong smile that made her vant to sing and cry at the same time. "That's *Captain \rchibald.* Let's not get careless so close to victory.''

Leonora stifled a sigh. She did not feel victorious in the east.

As they joined the throng of guests entering the mag- ificent Guildhall, she snapped open her fan like a soldier ocking his rifle. Behind cover of it she whispered to Morse, "Make your way to the other end of the banquet oom and find some gentlemen to engage in conversation. 'll keep a lookout for the Hills and let you know when ey've arrived.''

With an intense gaze that called a blush to her cheeks, Morse discharged a nod that looked strangely like a salute. 'I'm yours to command, General Freemantle.''

Quickly she turned away, so he would not see the rogue ear that escaped her eye. If only she dared command him s she wished. If only Uncle Hugo's innocently enticing ager had not snared them both in its sticky web. If only he'd had the courage to accept Morse Archer when he roposed to her.

Overhead the magnificent chandeliers glittered brilliant andlelight on the gathering. The soft floral hues of the dies' gowns and the mingled perfume of rose and vender water put Leonora in mind of a spring garden. A oisy garden, where the songbirds of the orchestra com- eted against a chorus of gossiping ravens!

Just then, Leonora spied the Hills, none of whom looked a very festive mood. Mr. Hill scowled. Mrs. Hill plied er fan languidly, as if already bored beyond bearing. rederica Hill gnawed her lower lip, while Lady Fitzwar- en looked daggers at her husband and stepmother. As for

Sir Eustace, Leonora had never seen anyone who appeare
so desperately in need of a drink.

Perhaps their carriage had gotten delayed in the traffi
and they had fallen to quarreling amongst themselves
Having suffered the ordeal of an uncongenial family, Leo
nora hated the thought of sentencing Morse to such a thing
But what choice did she have?

Squelching her reservations, she threaded her wa
through the crowd and greeted Frederica Hill warmly. "
believe you'll find your fiancé in the far corner, entertair
ing the beaux of Bath with more war stories," she whis
pered.

"Trust you to know where he is every moment of th
day," snapped Frederica.

Jolted by her ungracious reply, Leonora watched as th
heiress made her way through the company in search c
Morse.

Taking Mrs. Hill by the arm, Leonora steered her in th
opposite direction. "What a great pleasure to see yo
again, ma'am! Shall we go in search of some punch?
declare, every visitor in Bath must be here tonight."

Pamela Hill cast her a look brimming with jaded amuse
ment. "Good evening to you, Miss Freemantle. Yes, d
let us get out of this press of humanity and find som
refreshment. We had better slip away quickly before m
husband takes it into his head to drag me around the roo
for introductions—his captive dowager viscountess. I de
clare, if I predecease him, Herbert is likely to have m
stuffed and mounted like a prize Highland stag he ca
show off to visitors."

Behind a forced smile, Leonora bit her tongue. *Yo
should have thought of that when you married Mr. Hill fo
his money.*

They found a somewhat less crowded spot in the cavern

ous room and managed to commandeer two glasses of
punch from the tray of a circulating waiter.

After several caustic remarks about some other members
of the company and a scrap of salacious gossip, Mrs. Hill
swept Leonora a glance from head to toe. "Your costume
this evening is very becoming, Miss Freemantle. I'm surprised not to find you surrounded by a bevy of swains. Are
you aware that my stepdaughter is insanely jealous of your
friendship with her fiancé? I hope she has good reason to
be."

Before Leonora could protest, she added, "You must
keep an eye out for this mysterious Captain Archibald and
introduce him to me. I believe Frederica is intentionally
trying keep him from me, and that will never do."

Just then Sir Eustace passed close to them. Mrs. Hill
handed her punch glass to Leonora and caught the young
man's arm. "Make yourself useful, my son, and squire
your dear mother-in-law for a turn on the dance floor."

Though he turned a shade of red that clashed furiously
with his ginger hair, Fitzwarren did as he'd been bidden.
Catching sight of Lady Fitzwarren's ashen face in the
crowd, Leonora guessed why Frederica might have become their unwitting accomplice in protecting Morse from
meeting her stepmother.

After passing the empty punch cups off to a waiter, Leonora hurried toward the ballroom. As the music concluded,
she approached Morse and Frederica. "So you were able
to find the captain, after all, Miss Hill. Dancing is such
thirsty work. Why don't the pair of you come back to the
banquet room with me and take a cup of punch?"

Frederica clutched Morse's arm tighter. "Thank you for
your concern, Miss Freemantle, but I am resolved to enjoy
one more turn on the dance floor before *we* stop to take
refreshments."

"In that case—" Morse glanced around "—perhaps I

can find Algie Blenkinsop to deputize for me. Much as wish to oblige you, Frederica, my leg is beginning to pro test the exertion.''

"Your leg? Oh, dear, of course! I should have remem bered, but you have been so light of step, this evening Maurice. Do let us go find you a place to sit and rest.' Turning pointedly away from Leonora, the heiress towe her fiancé off to safety.

Algie's voice piped up from nearby. "Dare to ventur a turn 'round the dance floor with me, Leonora?''

Trying to stifle a pang of longing as she watched Mors and Miss Hill retreat to the banquet room, Leonora too Algie's arm. All the better to keep a watchful eye on Mrs Hill.

"Did I overhear you telling Morse that you're ac quainted with Sir Eustace Fitzwarren?'' she asked.

"Knew him from school,'' replied Algie as the musi cians struck up a leisurely tune. "Play cards with him no and again since we've been at Bath. He used to be n such a bad fellow in the old days, but he's got a bit sou since. Drinks rather more than he should.''

They managed the entire minuet without him once tread ing on her toes.

"Will you do me a favor, Algie?'' Leonora trained he gaze on Mrs. Hill. "The next time you're talking to Fit warren, could you find out how he gets on with his wife' family?''

"I suppose so, but why on earth…''

Leonora wandered off before he could finish.

For the next two hours she managed to keep Morse an Mrs. Hill apart. Sometimes more by good fortune than b dedicated application. Once or twice her concentratio lapsed dangerously as she became caught up in watchin him. Or spinning fruitless fantasies of how magical this eve ning might have been, if only she, not Frederica Hill, had attended as Morse's bride-to-be.

Were those blunders truly accidental? Leonora chided herself as she foisted Algie upon Mrs. Hill for the next dance. Or was she trying to sabotage her whole future—and Morse's?

From somewhere in the crowd, she heard him laugh. For an instant it warmed her. Then she shivered to think how soon she might never hear his laughter again.

When Leonora looked up to survey the dancers, she could not see Algie and Mrs. Hill anywhere in the ballroom. The music played on, but they had clearly left the floor. Slipping through the crowd, she looked this way and that for Algie's head topping those around him.

Suddenly the throng parted before her, like the Red Sea before an astonished Moses. She saw Algie leading Mrs. Hill directly to Morse and Frederica.

"There's the fellow, now." Algie's voice rang out heartily. "Archibald, old chap, there's someone here frightfully keen to meet you."

Morse glanced up, then froze for a moment. Leonora froze, too. Unable to look away as disaster bore down upon them in the shape of Pamela Granville Hill.

Chapter Nineteen

"I say, Archibald, old fellow. Here's someone frightfully keen to meet you."

Morse heard the words—loud, slow and slurred, as if he and Algie were fathoms deep under water. His thought and limbs moved sluggishly, too. Staggering to shore under the weight of sodden clothing and his own exhaustion. He'd been desperately treading water for so long, he almost wanted to drown and be done with it. Except that would pull Leonora down with him.

At the thought of Leonora, all Morse's training came flooding back, together with a reckless aplomb born of having nothing left to lose. He fixed his former mistress with a pleasant but vacant smile, as if he'd never laid eyes on her before this moment.

"Mrs. Hill," proclaimed Algie. "It gives me great pleasure to present my dear friend Captain Maurice Archibald. I feel certain he'll make Miss Frederica a devoted husband."

Pamela Hill assessed Morse with her eyes. Eyes still seductive after all these years. Her look implied the hope that he would not prove *too* devoted to her stepdaughter. Though time had given her a face more in keeping with her character, she was still an alluring creature. Particularly in a scarlet gown with the briefest bodice modesty allowed, and an exotic-looking turban of scarlet and gold.

As he stared, overwhelmed by still-potent memories, an unasked question furrowed her brow. Had she perhaps seen him somewhere before?

Trying to recover his composure, Morse bowed low over her hand, so she might not get too long a look at his face. His voice had deepened since the old days and he deliberately deepened it further still. "Mrs. Hill, this is a pleasure, indeed. We have missed each other so often, I wondered if someone might be trying to keep us from meeting."

She gasped.

Fearing the worst, Morse glanced up. Then he heard the glass shatter. Leonora had come to his rescue, nudging one of the waiters to spill the whole content of his tray on Pamela Hill's provocative red gown. Some splashed on Frederica, too.

Morse knew there was no love lost between his fiancée and her stepmother. But in common calamity they put aside their differences and fled together toward the ladies' retiring room.

He and Leonora fled in the opposite direction. Once they'd gotten far enough away, their laughter exploded like shaken champagne. "When you mount a counterattack, you don't go in for half measures do you, General?"

"Not very subtle." She flashed him a wry smile. "But effective enough. It was my fault Mrs. Hill caught up with you. I should have known better than to leave her with Algie. You handled it well—do you think she recognized you?"

Morse shook his head. "A mild suspicion that she's seen me before, perhaps. Since you gave her no opportunity to pursue it, I think I'm safe for the moment. I'll be more careful to keep clear of her until the wager's won.''

Was he relieved or insulted that his former mistress had failed to recognize him? Morse wondered.

Relieved, he decided at last. In more ways than one. After so many years wasted trying to forget Lady Pamela Granville, he had come face-to-face with her again. Only to discover she had lost all power over him. He had been a fool comparing Leonora to such a vain, shallow creature.

''Captain Archibald *is* a well-spoken fellow.'' Leonora's voice held a note of banter, but her eyes glowed with absolute sincerity. ''When all's said and done, though, I still prefer Sergeant Archer.''

They had found a relatively quiet corner in the convivial hubbub of the Guildhall banquet room. Now Morse maneuvered himself to shield Leonora from the rest of the company, creating a tiny bubble of privacy in this very public place. He reached for her hand and held it with gentle but implacable pressure, as if he could not bear to let it go. Ever.

''If you prefer Morse Archer, why did you refuse him?''

With a gallant tilt of her chin, she looked him in the eye. Try as she might, she could not mask the pain and uncertainty that clouded her gaze. ''Do the reasons matter, now?''

''They matter a great deal to Sergeant Archer.''

She sighed. ''Then perhaps I will tell him, one day. But for now, it would serve no good purpose.''

Or because she could not bear to speak of her reasons?

He'd been so occupied with *his* hurts and griefs, foolishly supposing those of higher station must not suffer such things. Now he knew better.

The pressure of her hand on his increased and her gaze intensified. ''It is important that you know what my reasons were *not*.''

His puzzlement must have been comical to behold, for Leonora smiled briefly. "Besides, you seem to forget, I did not refuse you. You refused me—in rather vehement terms as I recall. I've come to understand why, and I regret with all my heart answering your proposal with so grievous an insult."

What *had* made her do it? He should have known Leonora Freemantle was not the kind of woman to offer herself to a man without benefit of clergy. But he'd been too absorbed in his own cares to ask himself, or her, why she resisted matrimony so strenuously.

"You must believe me." Her hand grasped his tighter as if to compel his assurance. "I swear upon everything I hold dear—I did not decline your offer of marriage on consideration of your birth or because..." she hesitated "...I did not care for you enough to be your wife."

Morse sensed what it cost her to admit this.

Her lower lip trembled and her eyes begged his forgiveness. He had never imagined his indomitable little general could look so vulnerable. Or so invitingly beautiful. Forgetting where they were. Forgetting how Sir Hugo's wager now loomed between them. Forgetting everything but how she had taken possession of his heart, Morse leaned forward to kiss her.

A forceful hand clutched at his coat sleeve and an insistent voice barked, "Captain Archibald!"

It brought him crashing back to earth. Reluctantly he dropped Leonora's hand, the kiss he longed to bestow still aching on his lips.

He turned to face Herbert Hill.

"Don't go skulking in the corner, lad. This is to be your night. Come, I've someone who's anxious to meet you."

Morse understood how this man had managed to wrest so large a fortune into his control. The force of his personality was almost impossible to resist. As Morse stam-

mered excuses and tried to dig in his heels, Mr. Hill
dragged him forward, until they stood in the presence of
Sir Geoffrey Maxwell.

One look into the colonel's sound eye and Morse knew
with sickening certainty the jig was up. Unlike Lady Pamela, Morse's former commander had last seen him only
months before. Neither was the colonel afflicted with *class
blindness* that prevented him from seeing plain Sergeant
Archer beneath the fashionable trappings of Captain Archibald.

"Sir Geoffrey, I don't suppose this young fellow needs
any introduction to you, being one of your gallant lads
wounded in the service of his country. Folks forget there's
only one army in Europe has stood up to old Bonaparte
and prevailed."

Colonel Maxwell swept a look over Morse. One corner
of his mouth curled up in a suggestion of tolerant amusement. "Give the Russians their due, Mr. Hill. They've
made mince of the French legions in recent months."

"There you go, Sir Geoffrey, being too modest again,"
Herbert Hill persisted. "I'm always lecturing Captain Archibald not to underrate himself. A starved and frozen
army can't fight worth a damn, and who knows what the
outcome might have been if Bonaparte had been able to
send all his troops east, instead of needing to leave so
many back in Spain to guard his back door?"

"That I will concede you, Mr. Hill." The colonel
planted his legs wide, perhaps to balance the wooden one.
"I would be the last to slight our Peninsular army. The
tide is turning on the Continent, and England has played
her part bravely. Would you not agree, *Captain Archibald?*"

For a moment Morse could not coax his vocal organs
to frame a reply. Didn't Colonel Maxwell intend to expose
his masquerade?

"M-many fine soldiers have fought bravely in this war, Sir." Morse picked out Sir Hugo's face in the crowd clustered around Colonel Maxwell. "And many gave their lives. It was an honor to serve with them."

Colonel Maxwell held out his hand. "Good to see you again, lad—and looking so fit. You're a walking testament to the restorative powers of old Bath. I only hope the waters may do me as much good."

Morse snapped the colonel a salute, then grasped his hand. "Thank you, Sir. I hope so, too, Sir."

Herbert Hill insinuated himself between them, so puffed up with pride and felicity, his expensively tailored coat could barely contain him. "Lad's fit as a fiddle and so will you be in jig time, Sir Geoffrey. Though it's not only the waters that have worked their medicine on the young captain. I fancy the tonic of love had a bit to do with it. Where's our Frederica?"

"Here I am, Father." She squirmed through the press of admirers surrounding them. Her rose-colored gown looked none the worse for Leonora's liquid ambush. She latched onto Morse's arm with at least as much force as her father had.

Mr. Hill introduced his daughter to Colonel Maxwell. "Sir Geoffrey and Captain Archibald have just been renewing their acquaintance, my dear. What do you think of that? The colonel remembering your particular young man?"

Morse spoke up. "I expect Colonel Maxwell would remember soldiers even beneath a captain's rank. That's why the men of his command would follow him anywhere."

"I'm certain any commander would remember you, my dear Maurice." Frederica looked to Colonel Maxwell. "Captain Archibald is modesty itself when it comes to his exploits in battle. Can you tell us something of his heroic actions?"

"Please, Frederica, I'm sure the colonel would—"

Colonel Maxwell cut Morse off. "Tut-tut, my boy. We must not disappoint this charming young lady."

He proceeded to spin the most fantastic tale of Morse's heroism. To hear him tell it, one would wonder how any French troops on the Peninsula had survived. The performance sent Frederica and her father into paroxysms of reflected glory.

Morse's cheeks burned scarlet with shame. Once upon a time he would have chafed at not receiving his due. Now he squirmed with chagrin as unearned honor heaped upon him.

When Colonel Maxwell's powers of invention had exhausted themselves, Herbert Hill could contain himself no longer. "It does my heart good to hear what I suspected all along. Sir Geoffrey. Ladies and gentlemen of Bath. It is my supreme honor to announce the engagement of my youngest daughter, Miss Frederica Hill to Captain Maurice Archibald!"

He acknowledged the applause of the company as if he had contrived the courtship himself, from start to finish.

Frederica flashed her enormous engagement ring for all to see. She looked up at her fiancé, eyes brimming with adoration. Morse knew he deserved it no more than he deserved Colonel Maxwell's counterfeit accolades. He'd asked Frederica Hill to marry him in large measure because he knew she would say yes. After Leonora had turned him down, he'd needed that reassurance. Now Morse realized she had not accepted *him* at all and never would. Frederica had accepted Captain Maurice Archibald.

A man Morse Archer was growing to hate more by the minute.

From the fringe of the crowd, Leonora watched Morse transform disaster into triumph. Her heart swelled with pride.

Swelled so much, it pained her.

"I have another announcement." Mr. Hill raised his voice to be heard over the drone of congratulations. "Since Captain Archibald and my daughter met and courted here in Bath, I think it only proper that they cap off the Season by wedding here. As many of you will soon be taking yourselves back to the country for the summer months, I propose the wedding take place as soon as a Special License can be procured for the purpose. That way, Sir Geoffrey may attend the nuptials as our honored guest."

Leonora could picture it all. The ceremony in Bath Abbey. A magnificent wedding breakfast in the Lower Assembly Rooms. It would do wonders for the town's economy.

And herself?

She would find some excuse to quit Bath before then. Perhaps she'd return to Laurelwood and scout out a site for her school. Possibly begin construction for it to open in the fall. Her life would slip back into a safe, familiar groove, with the added benefit of an independent future assured. In short, everything she'd so ardently desired before fate and Uncle Hugo had flung Morse Archer into her path.

As if summoned by her thoughts, Leonora heard Sir Hugo's voice behind her. "Will you look at that, now? From a rough-mannered Rifleman facing court-martial to the toast of Bath. I wouldn't have believed it if I hadn't seen it with my own eyes."

The wonder in his voice softened to regret and he heaved a great sigh. "No question you've won the wager, my dear. I'll have my solicitor draw up all the necessary papers tomorrow."

She could not bring herself to gloat. He had gone to great trouble—engineering this wager in hopes of obliging her to do what he believed would make her happy.

"Thank you, Uncle." She was not referring to the solicitor.

As she watched the cream of Bath Society surround Morse and Miss Hill with congratulations, Leonora fought down a lump in her throat and exhorted herself to rejoice. After all, she had accomplished everything she'd set out to. Soon she'd be free to found her school and to live her life in complete independence.

Why, then, did it feel like her heart was breaking?

Morse woke in a sweat with the bedclothes twined around his body like a strait waistcoat. Never in all his years soldiering, with his life in daily jeopardy, had he been prey to such nightmares. He'd dreamed of standing in a docket while the judge signed his death warrant. Then he'd been trussed to a stake for burning. The fancy had been so vivid, Morse woke with the stench of smoke in his nostrils.

For a moment, when he realized it had only been a dream, the weight on his chest lifted and he took an easy breath. Then he remembered his *triumph* at the Guildhall, and thought ahead to his future. The weight settled upon him once again, all the heavier, for there could be no fortunate escape from what awaited him.

Wait just a minute! his reason demanded. What great terrors did his future hold? Marriage to a beautiful, congenial young woman of fortune. A life of luxury and ease. No more pressing worry than which coat to wear or how many weeks of hunting season left. Every retired Rifleman should endure such hardship.

But he would be living a lie, his conscience protested. Many lies. Pretending to be a gentleman. Pretending to love Frederica. Part of him yearned to take to his heels and reclaim his lost liberty. Let the whole benighted mess of this wager sort itself out without him!

When he heard a soft tap on his door, Morse longed to

ignore it. Force of gentlemanly habit made him call, "Come in."

In Dickon came, grinning as widely as if he had just consumed a quantity of potent hard cider. "Good morning, sir, and congratulations! I heard all about your triumph from Lord Melbury's valet. You're the talk of Bath after last night. We shall be sorry to lose you around Laurel-wood, though, sir. Perhaps you'll come for a visit now and again, what?"

"Thank you, Dickon. Perhaps so."

"Sir Hugo sends his compliments, sir, and asks if you might join him and Miss Leonora in his library in half an hour."

What could that be about?

"You've also had several messages from Miss Hill this morning." Dickon handed him the notes.

As he dressed, Morse read Frederica's messages.

He must come to Camden Place at once to consult on the wedding plans. Send word immediately to his family in case they wished to attend. On second thought, he mustn't inform his family—they could never hope to arrive in time. Before anything else, he *must* acquire the Special License that would allow them to wed without the bother of posting banns.

When he finished the last one, Morse tossed them all onto the grate. At this time of year there were no glowing coals to set the paper alight…unfortunately.

In spite of the season, Sir Hugo had a good fire going in the library when Morse joined him and Leonora there.

"That was quite a performance last night, Morse, I must say. Have a seat, lad. I won't keep you long—I know you'll be wanting to get off on your wedding errands."

The older man's words lacked their usual hearty note. In truth, everything about him seemed diminished. "Well,

I got a wedding out of this wager, though not the one I planned.''

Morse could not bring himself to look Leonora in the face as he dropped into a chair beside her. He longed to ask if she knew why they'd been summoned.

Sir Hugo did not keep them long in suspense. Taking two papers from his writing desk, he handed one to Morse and one to his niece. In his own paper, Morse recognized the promissory note he'd signed when Sir Hugo had advanced him the money for Frederica's engagement ring.

''I pride myself on being an optimist.'' Sir Hugo shook his head. ''But I can see the writing on the wall. The Season here in Bath won't be breaking up for another week or two, but I don't foresee much changing between now and then. You have won the wager, both of you.''

Morse turned the note over and over in his hand.

''Toss it on the fire, lad,'' Sir Hugo urged him. ''That ring is yours now, free and clear. By my calculations you're owed a bit besides. Might come in handy for that license—I've heard they're deuced expensive.''

With a convulsive twitch of his hand, Morse consigned his note to the flames. As he watched, it blazed and blackened into a tissue of cinders.

''Leonora,'' continued Sir Hugo. ''Your paper outlines the settlement I've made over to you. It should provide sufficient income to build and maintain your school. And to let you keep your precious independence.''

He produced a handkerchief from his pocket and blew his nose. ''I only hope you won't remove too far from Laurelwood.''

Leonora catapulted out of her chair and threw her arms around his neck. ''Of course not, Uncle. I'll look for a piece of property within walking distance and I'll visit every day.''

Morse fought down a lump in his own throat. His af-

fection for Lieutenant Peverill's father had grown with
each passing day of their acquaintance. Now came respect.

Nothing bound Sir Hugo to honor the costly terms of
this wager—as expensive to his heart as to his purse. He
could have kept Leonora dependent on him until she was
left with no choice but to wed the heir to Laurelwood. But
he'd given his word as a gentleman, and that was sacred,
no matter what the cost.

"There, there, my dear." Sir Hugo patted Leonora on
the shoulder. "You must not feel obliged to weep over my
loss. Instead, let us raise a toast to your victory."

He produced a bottle of champagne and three glasses.
The cork erupted from the bottle with a hiss. Sir Hugo
poured a measure of wine into each of their glasses and
held his in the air for them to toast. "Here's to Leonora
and Morse. May your winning bring you much happiness." Try as he might, Sir Hugo could not censor the
doubt from his voice.

"To the wager." Morse wondered if there had ever been
such a tepid toast drunk in all of history.

He could understand Sir Hugo's low spirits and his own
well enough. But what right had Leonora to look so glum?
She would have her independence and her school.

His own brief taste of education had convinced Morse
that would be the most worthwhile consequence of their
wager. He would do nothing to jeopardize it. Once he and
Frederica were married, he would set about to complete
his own education, which Leonora had begun.

Morse permitted himself one brief glance at her. Two
bright spots glowed high in her otherwise pallid cheeks
and her eyes shone with unshed tears. Yet she forced a
little smile and mouthed the words, *Thank you.*

If he had to strive the rest of his life, Morse vowed, he
would become a true gentleman to do her proud.

Chapter Twenty

Soon after Morse departed on his wedding errands, an unshaven, hollow-eyed Algie sought out Leonora.

"I've never felt so ashamed of myself!" Slumped on a chair in the sitting room, he cradled his head in his arms.

"Come now." She patted his shoulder. "It can't be as bad as all that. You haven't got a wicked bone in your body."

"Oh, I acted with the best of intentions." Fumes of stale tobacco smoke and sour brandy rose from Algie's hair and clothes. The latter looked as though they'd been slept in. "But you know what they say about good intentions and the road to hell."

Leonora struggled to keep a bubble of welcome amusement in check. "I don't think that's quite what the saying means. Now what exactly did you do? Are you certain it can't be undone?"

"I hope it can." Algie sighed—his fervor comically at odds with his dissipated appearance. "That's why I came to confess, Leonora. So you can help me figure out a scheme to put things right again. You're so awfully clever."

If she was so clever, why was the man she loved about to wed another woman?

"There are more important things than being clever, Algie." She hadn't thought so until recently. She'd prided herself on her learning and her sense. On the calm rationality that curbed a capricious heart.

"There are?"

Leonora nodded. "There's kindness. And trust. Even charm isn't a bad thing in moderation. Let's hear what you have to say for yourself. Confession's supposed to be good for the soul."

"It's Morse."

"What have you done to him?"

"Only pushed him with both hands into a marriage that's certain to make him perfectly miserable."

Poor Algie could not have pushed Morse any harder than she had. Whichever of them bore the greater responsibility, Leonora could not bear to think of him being *perfectly miserable*. From what she'd seen of his fiancée's family, she feared it might be true. Or was she just playing dog in the manger again?

"I thought you considered the match an ideal one." She tried to jolly Algie out of his black mood. Not an easy task when she'd have preferred to wallow with him in self-pity and self-blame. "Miss Hill's beautiful, agreeable, and has plenty of money. Morse is handsome, agreeable, and has none."

Algie shook his head slowly, as if afraid to agitate it. "Remember last night at the Guildhall when you asked me to chat up Eustace Fitzwarren?"

Only vaguely. "Why? What did you find out?"

"Once the ball broke up, a few of the lads went off for a private card party on Gay Street." He winced at the memory. "Fitzwarren was pretty well in his cups by then and didn't need much urging to talk about his wife's family."

"I see." Leonora was not sure she wanted to hear what Algie had to tell her. Difficult enough to get on with her own life, imagining Morse blissfully happy.

"I gather Miss Hill isn't nearly so agreeable in private as she is in public."

Leonora had seen a glimpse of that. Still, a woman's conduct with her detested stepmother could hardly indicate how she would treat her husband.

"As for the money," continued Algie, "Mr. Hill still has hopes of getting a son by his second wife, so the daughters have almost nothing in their own right. Papa keeps them on a tight rein by pulling the purse strings. As for Mrs. Hill, you'd be shocked speechless if I told you what she's got up to with her own stepdaughter's husband."

"Perhaps not as shocked as you think, Algie."

Lady Pamela had once wanted Morse at her service in Mr. Hill's household. After he and Frederica were married he could not keep his identity a secret from her stepmother for long. When she discovered it, she would have him in her power.

"It's my fault. It's all my fault," Algie moaned.

No. The fault is mine.

"Oh, don't be silly!" Was she trying to convince Algie—or herself? "Nobody forces Morse Archer to do anything he doesn't want. Once you tell him what you've told me, he'll break the engagement and that'll be the end of it."

"Give a fellow credit for a little sense." Algie cast her a withering look. "Do you think I'd have come pestering you if talking to Morse had done any good?"

The champagne in Leonora's stomach soured. "You've spoken to him already?"

"Didn't I just say so?"

"And told him everything you've told me?"

Algie squirmed in his seat. "Rather more than I told you, as a matter of fact. Being man-to-man and all that."

"What did he say?" Better than anyone, she knew how Morse loathed taking orders and being controlled. She couldn't imagine he'd go willingly into the kind of situation Algie had described.

"That's the trouble." Algie rose and began to pace the room. "He didn't say much of anything. Just heard me out then told me to get to bed and sleep it off."

"That's all?"

"My memory of the interview isn't as clear as it might be," Algie admitted. "Due to the lateness of the hour and my own vile state of intoxication. He has no intention of backing out of the match, that much I did grasp. I think he may have said something—more to himself than to me—about it not making any difference because he knew what he had to do."

"And I know what I have to do," muttered Leonora, more to herself than to Algie, as she sent him off to wash and change. She didn't really, but hammering some sense into the thick skull of a certain ex-Rifleman seemed like a positive start.

Some giant invisible blacksmith had his skull between hammer and anvil!

Morse staggered out of the open carriage in which Mr. Hill had shipped him home to Laura Place. During the drive he'd felt like a human trophy on display. Several people had called out to him as the gig passed, and he'd made an effort to acknowledge them with a forced smile and a limp wave. The afternoon's endless discussion of wedding plans had his thoughts racing in dizzying circles. And to top it all off, he'd had his first row with Frederica.

She'd been tearfully vexed by some gossip's report of his laughing and talking in private with another woman just before the announcement of their betrothal. He'd done his best to placate her, without actually lying through his teeth.

It had proven a difficult balancing act. How could he swear Leonora meant nothing to him when she was his chief reason for going ahead with this marriage? Frederica had her good qualities and he would do his best to be an attentive husband. Must she try to command a level of devotion he could not supply?

As he approached the front door of Sir Hugo's house, Leonora breezed out with Algie and Miss Taylor in her wake. If he hadn't known better, Morse would have sworn they'd been lying in wait for him.

"Morse, are you ill?" asked Leonora. "You look a fright."

He tried to make light of it. "Only a headache."

"They must be contagious." She nodded at Algie. "Your friend has one, too. Elsie and I decided a bit of fresh air before dinner might be just the cure he needed. So we're off for a stroll around Sydney Gardens. Will you join us?"

Morse doubted Sydney Gardens would do anything beneficial for his head. Unless walking aggravated his leg enough to take his mind off it. But the three of them looked so anxious for his company—even Miss Taylor. This might be the last chance for them to be together, as they had at Laurelwood. Weighed in the balance against that, even his throbbing temples came up short.

Morse shrugged his unconditional surrender. "I suppose anything's worth a try. Sydney Gardens's air is a sight more palatable than Bath mineral water."

Leonora and Miss Taylor unfurled their parasols and they all set off up Great Pulteney Street. To Morse's surprise, they had not gone far when his headache did begin to ease. The tightness in his neck and shoulder loosened, and his spirits began to rise.

May sunshine burnished the hues of nature like the great colored windows of Bath Abbey. The sky had never looked such a deep, vivid blue, nor the clouds so soft a white. The grass and the trees each seemed to possess their own unique luster of green. Morse wondered if the world would ever look so beautiful to him again. He pushed the thought away, unwilling to let it shadow this special moment.

Algie and Miss Taylor carried most of the conversation, as a gap gradually widened between them and the other two. Morse ambled along at a very easy pace—to spare his leg. Or so he told himself.

Leonora did not seem eager to catch up with their companions, either. At length Morse discovered why.

Without any preparatory throat-clearing, praise of the weather, or even turning to look at him, she spoke. "Algie told you about his talk with Sir Eustace Fitzwarren."

Morse's jaw tightened and his headache threatened to return with a vengeance. "Don't let's start on that now, please. I'd rather enjoy our time here."

She continued to stare ahead at Algie and Miss Taylor. Her voice soft and moderate, as though she did not want to call anyone's attention to what she was telling him. "It's no good, you know. When I was a child, I used to pull a bonnet over my face and think no one could see me because *I* couldn't see *them*."

"What were you hiding from inside that little bonnet, Leonora?" Part of him wanted to distract her, but another part of him sincerely wanted to know. To understand what made her think and act as she did.

"Oh, no you don't, Sergeant Archer. No feint attack with your right flank to protect your center line. You can't mean to go through with this wedding knowing what you know about Miss Hill's family.''

A squirrel dashed across the path in front of them. Some rebellious streak within Morse wanted to flee Bath and Frederica Hill and the wedding wager just as swiftly. He didn't need Leonora spooking him worse.

"What would you have me do?" He couldn't keep the bitterness from his tone. "Break off my engagement? I can guess how Mr. Hill would react. Why, he'd think nothing of calling out a brigade of Bow Street Runners to mount an assault on Captain Archibald's reputation. And when he discovered he'd been duped by a commoner who used to be his wife's footman..."

Realizing his voice had risen, Morse hesitated. Then he continued more quietly. "Let's just say my true identity would be common knowledge throughout Bath within the hour. And your wager would be lost."

"But Uncle's already conceded defeat."

If only she knew how he longed to justify his selfish actions with that same argument.

For an instant Morse wavered. Then he shook his head in the face of temptation. "Out of generosity and good faith, Sir Hugo settled his debt to us early. With the understanding that I'd continue to act the gentleman for the rest of the Season. He could have tried to wriggle out of it, for it was plain the outcome broke his heart. I can't go and throw the wager over now because circumstances no longer suit me."

"Damn your honorable hide, Morse Archer!" She seemed no longer to care who might overhear them. "I've made a gentleman of you and now you're throwing it back in my face. Do you love Miss Hill so much you refuse see what this marriage will cost you? Or perhaps you're attracted by the notion of taking up with Mrs. Hill where the pair of you left off ten years ago!"

A week earlier such an insinuation from her would have goaded him into some act of spite and proud folly. Today, Morse stopped walking and turned to look at Leonora. "Are you trying to make me so angry I'll throw the wager on purpose?"

Above a guilty grin, her eyes searched his. "Could it work?"

How he wished it might. "Sorry."

"I was afraid of that."

Slowly he lifted his hand and with the lightest touch of his forefinger caressed her chin. That indomitable little chin—always thrust out to meet the world. To convince everyone she was invulnerable. Herself, most of all.

"You know neither of those women will ever mean half to me what you do. *That* is why I'll honor the terms of this wager, Leonora. Because I have faith in your dreams and I cherish your independence. You do believe that, don't you?"

She was silent for a moment, as though looking within herself for the truth. A solid, burdensome truth, but one she owed him at all cost.

"Yes." So quietly the word escaped her that Morse might have mistaken it for a soft breeze rustling the leaves.

Yet that brief whispered word seemed to crack a flood wall of reserve. "Yes, I believe you, Morse. How arrogant of me to say I have made you a gentleman. You have always been a gentleman at heart."

Morse wrested his hand back from her face. If he let it linger, he might succumb to his longing to kiss her. Drawing in a deep breath of spring air, he made himself turn away and begin walking again.

"I'm glad we've had this talk." It had heartened him to do what he must. "Don't fret for me, lass. I'm not quite so spineless a jelly as poor Fitzwarren. You build that

school and make it a credit to us. There's only one thin
I wish I knew.''

''Oh?''

''Why you're so set against marriage? Is it because yo
think you couldn't have your school and be wed, both? C
did you think no man would ever offer, so you convince
yourself you didn't want one to?''

She walked along in silence beside him for so lon
Morse was convinced she had no intention of replying. H
wasn't even certain he'd expected an answer.

At last she spoke. ''I'll tell you, Morse, since you'v
asked. I owe you far more than that, so I'd better repa
what little I can. Only, not here. Not now.''

He was prepared to accept that. So they walked, comi
back circular fashion to the park entrance. Slowly catchi
up to Algie and Miss Taylor, who chatted away like lif
long friends.

''Not now,'' Leonora repeated in a whisper that bare
caught Morse's ear. ''But soon.''

She would have to act soon.

Soon. Before old fears paralyzed her or old aspiratio
called her with a siren song, luring her from the path s
knew was right. As they walked home from Sydney Ga
dens, Leonora steeled herself for it.

If Morse would not break his engagement, then she mu
find some means to break it for him. But what means?

Too late to throw another suitor in Frederica's way
even if one could be found to equal Morse's appe
Though she was no great admirer of Miss Hill, Leono
acknowledged the young lady's good taste in men.

Might she convince Morse's fiancée he was addicted
a number of fashionable vices? Or perhaps… She recall
something Pamela Hill had said to her at the ball for Col
nel Maxwell—about Frederica's jealousy of her particu

friendship with Morse. Could there be a way to play on that?

The problem, Leonora decided at last, was that two very strong-willed people were resolved to see Morse wed to Frederica Hill. Miss Hill herself. And her father.

Herbert Hill had his heart set on acquiring another well-born son-in-law, esteemed by the gentry. Since Captain Archibald filled the bill to perfection, Frederica's father would most likely wink at any peccadillo that might otherwise cause his daughter to throw Morse over.

Exposing Morse's identity might dampen Mr. Hill's enthusiasm for the match, but would it extinguish the young lady's ardor? Or might she decide to brave her father's reproach and make a love match in spite of him?

From what Leonora had seen of her, Miss Hill was a creature of excessive romantic sensibility. If she insisted on retaining her connection to Morse in spite of his birth and lack of fortune, he would consider himself bound to honor his proposal.

There was no help for it—Morse's identity must come out. Moreover, it must come out in such a way that Miss Hill would break the engagement herself.

"Were you able to talk some sense into him?" Algie asked, after Morse had left for the evening.

Leonora shook her head. "Didn't I tell you no one *makes* Morse Archer do anything?"

"What's to be done, then?"

"The only thing that can be done when a frontal assault looks futile, Algie. We must resort to subterfuge."

His high brow furrowed in an unasked question.

"A ruse," said Leonora. "A trick."

"Oh, a *trick!*" Algie nodded vigorously. "What kind of trick, exactly? Can I help?"

"You'll see by and by. And you can help by not breathing a word of this to Morse."

He raised his hand, as if swearing an oath. "Not a peep upon my honor."

Though her nerves fairly jangled at the thought of he desperate plan, Leonora could not help smiling at him. " knew I could count on you."

She *could* count on Algie. Though she must give up on the notion of founding a school, he might be persuaded to provide the funds for Elsie Taylor to start one. They would never have to leave Laurelwood and Uncle Hugo would be beside himself with happiness. Better she should have to wed such a kind fellow, than go on to fulfil her dreams at the expense of Morse's freedom.

Algie turned to go, but she called him back. "Coul you hunt up Elsie and tell her I must speak to her in th library?"

"My pleasure. Anything else?"

"Just one." Leonora stared down at the toes of her slip pers and tried in vain to fight back a blush. "Whateve happens tomorrow, whatever…fuss may arise, howeve bad it looks, you *will* remember it's the only way to ex tricate Morse from the Hills?"

Algie pulled a face. "You make it sound so dire, ol girl. But you mustn't worry on my account. A Blenkinso is loyal to his friends through thick and thin."

Choking on a great lump of guilt and gratitude, Leonor rose on the tips of her toes and planted a kiss upon Algie' lean cheek. "I don't know what I've done to deserve friend like you. Now go find Elsie before I lose my nerve.

Once he'd gone and she had regained something of he composure, Leonora slipped into Sir Hugo's deserted l brary. Plucking a piece of paper from one of the slots i her uncle's writing desk, she selected a pen with a reasor ably sharp nib and dashed off a brief note.

She had just signed her name at the bottom when Els arrived. "Mr. Blenkinsop said you needed me, miss."

"That's right, Elsie." Leonora waved the paper in the air to dry the ink. "I need your assistance in a very delicate matter. I know I can rely on your discretion and good sense."

"Thank you, miss. You know I'd do anything in my power to oblige you."

As she folded the note and sealed it with wax, Leonora tried to steel her scruples against the trust and respect in Elsie's eyes. This could well be the last time she'd see them.

"Early tomorrow morning, I want you to deliver this note to Camden Place and make certain Miss Hill and her stepmother receive it."

"Very good, miss." With more than a little curiosity, Elsie glanced at the paper Leonora handed her. "Anything else?"

Leonora nodded. "Once you've delivered the note, you must hurry back here and wait for them to call. Then you must show them up to my private sitting room."

Elsie's fine tawny brows arched. "But, Miss Freemantle, you haven't got a private sitting room."

"Indeed I do, Elsie. Third door on the left at the top of the stairs."

"But that's—"

"My *private* sitting room."

Elsie looked down at the note, then back up at her mistress. "I hope you know what you're doing, miss."

Though she continued to stare at Elsie steadily, Leonora did not reply until after the girl had bobbed a curtsy and left Sir Hugo's library. "I hope so, too, Elsie." She breathed in the aroma of books—perhaps for the last time. "I hope so, too."

Chapter Twenty-One

Where was he and what was he doing?

Less than half-awake, Morse rolled over and pulled the bedclothes around his neck. He'd had a late night, and something told him he needed to sleep longer. Dickon had been ordered to not rouse him until noon at the earliest.

Something else roused Morse from sleep. A warmth in his bed where none should be. The faint whisper of breath drawn in and out, at odds with the rhythm of his own. A bouquet of lavender.

Or perhaps he was dreaming. This would not have been the first time he'd dreamed of having Leonora in his bed. His body stirred in anticipation as he reached out for her.

His hand found flesh, sheathed in some fine, soft cloth. Almost as exciting to the touch as bare skin. His fingertips began a reconnaissance of this inviting landscape. The smooth plateaus. The gentle swells. The provocative clefts.

Lost in the pleasure of their quest, they called for reinforcement from his lips. Morse obliged, diving to a fragrant locale and laying claim. Part of it rose to acknowledge him. Mute, but imperious in its demand for tribute. A levy Morse was only too eager to render.

Growing impatient with the gossamer barricade between

his envoys and their conquest, he mounted an assault and sacked it. Poised for plunder, Morse hesitated. The sound of cloth tearing, a woman's gasp—this dream had become far too vivid!

He wrenched his eyes half-open.

"Leonora!" The word erupted from him in a hoarse discharge.

No question it was she. Her dark hair unbound and splayed upon his pillow. Fingers of morning sunlight coaxed glints of copper from her sable tresses. Skin like blushing apple blossoms. Eyes like a spring morning swathed in mist. And her nightgown ripped from throat to belly, gaping open around her bare breasts.

How he wanted to convince himself she wasn't real—so he could plunge back in again.

He mastered himself enough to croak, "How did you get here? What are you doing here?"

She made no attempt to pull the jagged edges of her torn shift closed. Nor did she pull up the bedsheets to cover herself.

Instead she looked into his eyes and spoke as if her presence in his bed was the most natural thing in the world. "You asked me why I was so set against marriage. I came here to tell you."

"C-couldn't it wait? For a more...proper time and place?"

She shook her head. "It is a private confidence, I have to share with you, Morse. And I could think of no more private place than here."

"Very well." Morse flopped onto his back and lifted his arms behind his head.

If he continued to stare at Leonora as she was, he would never be able to concentrate on what she had to say. Unless he pinned down his hands, he would not be able to curb his inclination to touch her again. "Say what you came to say."

"Very well." She took a deep breath. "Do you recall my telling you once that I considered the best husband in the world to be no husband at all?"

Morse grunted something vaguely affirmative. That night at Laurelwood, when he'd walked her home from the village and begged her for another chance at the wager. He'd told her how he hated to take orders because he'd been raised on a tenant farm—always at everyone's beck and call.

She'd told him something, too. Something he had trouble recalling now. About needing to give orders because she'd grown up with no regularity in her life. Why hadn't he listened then? Why hadn't he asked?

"My second stepfather gambled away almost every penny of my mother's small fortune. We were always moving residences or traveling down to the country on the spur of the moment in order to keep ahead of his creditors."

"Second stepfather? How many did you have?"

"Only three. But they were three too many. The first scarcely recall, and a good thing, perhaps. He used to bellow at mother and me over the least trifle. Then when mother would get upset and cry, he'd get angrier still and…"

Morse's arms wrestled themselves free and gathered her close to him. Was that what she'd hidden from, by pulling her bonnet over her eyes? He wished he could hurl himself into the past, to stand her protector when she'd been frightened. Now all he could do was offer her a haven against the heartache of those memories.

She did not push him away, but accepted the crumb of comfort he extended. It seemed to hearten her, for she began to speak again. "Fortunately, he let his temper ge the better of him with someone able to defend himself. My first stepfather was killed in a duel when I was seven years old.''

"And the next one gambled?" Morse prompted.

"He fell from the roof of our house one winter, trying to evade his creditors. He left mother and me with just enough money to attract her last husband.''

Leonora shuddered in Morse's arms. "I believe he may have been the most odious of the three. He used my mother's money and connections in society to go hunt richer women to keep him. I believe she died of the humiliation and a broken heart.''

"What made your mother marry such rascals?''

Morse realized he was clutching Leonora too tightly. The boundary between protection and imprisonment was a thin one—too easily crossed. He eased his hold on her.

She rested her head against his chest, as if speaking straight to his heart. "They were charming, Morse, when they chose to be. Handsome and glib. And my mother, heaven rest her, didn't believe she could live without a man.''

Now he understood. Perhaps more than she intended.

"Your mother's example convinced you of the opposite.''

The tantalizing silk of her hair whispered against his chest as she nodded. "I became persuaded that *without a man* was the only way for a sensible woman to live.''

A load of shame landed upon him. Almost as great as the one he'd carried after Lieutenant Peverill's death. Leonora had lightened that—absolved him.

Now, Morse could find no absolution. He had behaved no better than Leonora's stepfathers. Callously employing his looks and his charm to deceive her for his own purposes. A wonder she'd given his marriage proposal even passing consideration.

As if she'd read the contents of his heart, she murmured, "When you asked me to marry you, I *wanted* to say yes. I knew you could not be like those men who preyed upon my mother, only..."

"Only, I had behaved like a cad once."

"Partly that. And partly...well...I couldn't believe you'd want me, bluestocking spinster Miss Freemantle, when you could have your pick of the belles of Bath."

So that was it.

Her long-standing mistrust of men, heightened by memories of how he'd once exploited her feelings. All intensified by deep doubts about her worth as a woman.

"You gave me a chance, though, didn't you?" An opportunity to break her heart. "A chance to prove I didn't want anything but you."

"I was wrong. I should never have tested you that way. No wonder you thought me no better than..."

"Hush, now."

He lifted her close and kissed her. The sensation of her bosom pressed against his chest made the blood pound in Morse's ears until he could scarcely hear himself think. After what she'd just confessed, he wanted Leonora more than ever.

But this was no dream. This was life—with choices and consequences. He'd made too many bad choices in his life. Some out of ignorance. Some out of selfishness. And he'd resented the consequences. Now he was prepared to live with the consequences of a choice he had made out of knowledge and out of love.

Breaking from that kiss was one of the most difficult things Morse had ever done in his life. "You've told me what I asked. Now you'd better go."

She clung to him, and he was not certain he possessed the strength to push her away. "I think you know that's not the only reason I came here this morning."

"It isn't?" He forced the words from his arid throat.

"No. I came because you once offered to teach me how a man could bring a woman...pleasure."

He remembered. All too well.

"I have too many memories of them inflicting pain, and I fear it has soured my opinion of your whole sex. I would be doing my future pupils a grave disservice if I did not seek a more...balanced view."

Laughter came bubbling out of Morse until his body shook with it and tears came to his eyes. At least, he would blame the tears on his laughter.

Leonora sat up in bed, glaring at him. For the first time modesty overcame her and she clutched the bedclothes to her bosom. "Does the notion of making love to me strike you so very funny, Morse?"

"No!" he gasped. Then more laughter took him. "No," he repeated, breathless and spent as if from a seizure. He lifted his hand, resting his knuckles against her shoulder and sliding them down to her elbow. "I've heard lasses give many reasons for wanting a man to bed them. But never one like that."

"It was just an excuse, anyway," she admitted, glancing up at him through her lashes.

A good thing he was lying down. Such a look would have knocked him onto his backside if he'd been standing.

"The real reason is—I want you." There could be no mistaking it. The longing glistened in her eyes and glowed from her bare skin. "I want all of you, forever and ever, Morse. But since I can't have that, I want whatever I can get. Part of you, for a little while. A memory I can take out now and again to warm myself by."

What would a gentleman do?

"I shouldn't..." He held out his arms to her.

"Don't you want to?"

He pressed his face to the base of her throat, as if to

devour her. Kiss by ravenous kiss, his lips climbed toward hers. When they reached their goal, he drank her in and invited her to do likewise. He thrust his hips out to meet hers, that she might feel his swollen desire and know how much he wanted her.

But...

"I'm engaged to be wed." He moaned the words as if they'd been pulled from his mouth with hot pincers.

"You aren't wed yet." She wriggled in his arms, freeing herself from the wreck of her nightgown. And driving him mad with desire.

"Must...I beg you?" she whimpered between kisses. "I will."

Must he beg her to stop? He could not.

Morse touched his forehead to hers as he tried to curb his runaway passion. "You needn't beg. I'll give you what you ask for. And I won't pretend it isn't a gift for me, too."

A gift of trust. She had trusted him enough to confide her secret hurts and the secret weaknesses they had bred. Now, in spite of her reasons for mistrusting men, she trusted him enough to initiate her in the secret rites of lovers.

Bridling his own bone-deep hunger for her, Morse swore to himself that he would pour all the tenderness of a lifetime into this one bittersweet tryst with Leonora. Never again would she have cause to doubt that she was a beautiful, desirable woman.

"You will go slowly, won't you?"

Now that she had provoked and convinced Morse to make love to her, Leonora grew anxious on another account. They must not finish before her invited guests caught an eyeful.

In fact, they must not *finish* at all, if that meant Morse relieving her of her virginity. Should the events of the morning unfold as she had planned, Morse would no longer be in danger of wedding Miss Hill.

But, in all likelihood, she would be bound to wed Algie Blenkinsop. Though not the man she would have chosen for herself, she had grown fond of Algie. His loyalty to her and Morse would be severely tested. At the very least, he deserved to know that any children she might bear were his own offspring.

Could she hold to that honorable intent, though, when every inch of her flesh ached to surrender to Morse's tender siege?

With a lingering sweep, he ran his hand up her leg, over the curve of her hip, up the plane of her belly. Skimming the sensitive swell of her bosom, caressing her neck until it paused to cradle her chin.

"No need to rush," he murmured. "I am willing to take all the time you require."

"Good." Reaching down, she ran an exploring hand over his body, just as he had done to her. "As this may be my only lesson, I wish to investigate every possible area of study. I am fortunate to have so skilled and patient a teacher."

She pulled his face to hers and commenced to make its intimate acquaintance with her lips. The boldly jutting chin and nose. The cheeks with their provocative bristle of unshaven whiskers. The full, emphatic brows.

"I'm the fortunate one," he breathed, grazing her eyelids. "To have such an apt and eager pupil."

Her lips found his again. With a sigh, almost of surrender, he kissed her again. Long and wondrous, it was a kiss of discovery and homecoming. Of impudence and worship. A sweet eternity of hot, dark, liquid velvet.

She had only thought her body yearned for him, before. Now, as Morse twined his fingers in her hair and withdrew his lips from hers, Leonora felt a pull in her blood like the tides surging high for the waxing moon.

"Hands serve well to touch elsewhere." His voice sounded husky and his breath came fast. "But I have always considered lips the proper instruments for the neck and throat."

A great sigh shuddered out of her as Morse applied his instruments with exquisite skill. She'd had no idea the flesh of her neck could be so sensitive in so many places.

The spot behind her ear—she gasped as he swiped his fiery tongue over it. The area beneath her chin. As he nuzzled it, a deep purr vibrated in Morse's own throat. The mix of sound and sensation gave Leonora gooseflesh.

The hollow at the base of her throat, which he hovered above, touching it with nothing but his brooding breath until she could stand it no longer. Thrusting her fingers into his crisp, dark hair, she pressed his face close. He took her cue, parting his lips and assailing her throat with reckless abandon.

A pulsing, gnawing ache spread from her neck down into her bosom...and lower. Leonora tried to grasp the lifeline of reasons why she should make this last as long as possible.

Miss Hill. Algie. And the deep, clinging reluctance to see her time with Morse come to an end. The rope of logic slipped through her fingers, greased by the slippery moisture of need and hunger.

Just when she feared she would cry out for immediate satisfaction, Morse wrenched himself clear of her and collapsed onto his back. Even in her extremity, she could see the sheen of sweat on his brow and the arch of bedclothe mounded over his hips. Eloquent testimony to his counter need.

"First declension," he muttered to himself, punctuated by gasped breaths. *"Barba, casa, femina, lingua."*

"What are you doing?" A shaft of doubt pierced her heart. "Did I do something wrong? Don't you want me anymore?"

"Not want you?" A gust of laughter shook him—shaking the bed in turn. "If ever I had cause to doubt your innocence, Leonora—that one question would restore my faith a hundredfold."

Her complete bafflement must have broadcast itself on her features, for Morse's laughter subsided to an affectionate chuckle. "I want you too much, lass. No woman has ever taxed my control as you do. I was reciting that Latin you drummed into my head as a way to cool my ardor. It's good to know all those tiresome lessons weren't for naught."

"Oh!" The notion made her giggle like the flighty schoolgirl she had never been. "What a novel idea. Perhaps it will work for me as well. Second declension— *amicus, caseus, ventus, oculous.*"

The feverish pitch of her desire did begin to ease. As long as she could keep from dwelling on Morse's words. *No woman has ever taxed my control as you do.* Just recalling them ignited her whole body in a fierce blush.

"Third declension—*mater, nox, miles, mons.*" Together they recited the Latin nouns, beginning to regain a measure of equilibrium. "Fourth declension—*arcus, manus, tribus, portus.*"

Then Leonora heard a noise in the corridor beyond Morse's door. No one entered, but they might soon. She wanted to make certain Miss Hill viewed a most incriminating spectacle.

"*Tangere,*" she chanted. "To touch."

Reaching beneath the bedclothes, she put the word into action, running her hand over the firm length of his arousal, without a saving shred of modesty.

It brought a growl from deep in his throat. And when

Morse rolled toward her, his hazel eyes gleamed with emerald fire from their brown-velvet depths.

"*Tangere,*" she squeaked.

"Indeed I do, my wanton little schoolmistress." One dark brow and the matching corner of his mouth hoisted in perfect concert. Together with the heat of his gaze, it lent him such an air of seductive devilment that Leonora's throat tightened and her mouth went dry.

With one hand, he nudged her thighs apart and began to stroke them upward. First one, then the other—alternating. Each rising caress took him higher.

Took her higher. Ascending to bliss.

"*Comedo,*" he whispered. "To partake."

Sensing his target, she arched herself to meet his pursed lips with the pouty tip of her breast. It slipped into the snug, sultry sheath, and Leonora wondered if she could bear to take it out ever again. It fit so perfectly and so pleasurably, Morse's mouth must have been formed for this service and no other.

Likewise his fingers.

They investigated the intimate secrets of her womanhood. Researching each humid fold and dimple. Discovering the source of her pleasure and tutoring her, ever so gently, in the subject of ecstasy.

She tried to not be *too* apt a pupil. But neither the Latin conjugations nor the algebraic equations with which she attempted to divert her thoughts could distract her from Morse's enthralling lessons.

Learning to trust, at last, she had presented herself to him—an open book. He treated her with the reverence of a devoted scholar for some rare and precious manuscript. In doing so, he opened before her a whole new world of sensuality and delight.

His tongue and his fingers began to work in concert. Both urging her to scale the heights of passion. Then thrusting her off the edge of a precipice. Launching her into flight.

Thought and reason deserted her as she wafted on currents of pure sensation, wheeling and plunging. She could recall only a single word in her whole vocabulary—his name. It became the title of this potent, vibrant new experience.

"Morse!" She gasped it. Moaned it. Purred it.

Over and over it reverberated in her heart.

"Morse?" The word was right, but the tone all wrong. Strident with shock and outrage, when it should be pealed like a note from a golden bell. Or sighed like a gentle night breeze through the hedges of Laurelwood.

"Morse Archer!" Why, the voice was not even her own. And what was that unintelligible whimper in the background?

Remembering she had eyes, Leonora opened them.

Though she had planned the whole thing, the tableau of Miss Hill and her stepmother frozen in the doorway came as a shock to her. Belatedly, she snatched a sheet and pulled it up to cover herself.

"I thought I must know you from somewhere." Mrs. Hill spat the words, then turned to her blubbering jelly of a stepdaughter. "You spineless little fool! This precious Captain Archibald of yours was once my footman. Why he hasn't a drop more noble blood than a dustman."

"M-Maurice, how c-could you?" sobbed Frederica.

"I expect his distinguished military record is every bit as much a sham. He only courted you for your father's money, of course. What did you expect?" Lady Pamela could not resist rubbing the poor girl's nose in her humiliation.

Leonora wished she could have found a way to save Morse without hurting Miss Hill…and Algie.

Why had she not warned him to stay clear of the house

this morning? Upon hearing the commotion, he'd come to investigate. Now he stared pop-eyed at her and Morse while Elsie Taylor made a feeble attempt to close the door again. Perhaps naively hoping she could jam the whole scandal back into Pandora's box.

Morse's former mistress was not through spewing her bile. "No doubt he hatched the whole plot with the help of his mistress, here. They've probably been laughing at you behind your back all the while they've been..."

"Enough!" Morse bellowed. "Algie, clear them out of here."

Before Algie could oblige by helping Elsie wrestle the door shut, Miss Hill pried off her gaudy confection of an engagement ring. Wailing at the top of her lungs, she hurled it at Morse. It missed him, coming to rest on the pillow beside Leonora.

The bedroom door slammed shut and the clamor in the corridor retreated. An ominous silence fell. Assessing her chances of slinking out, unnoticed, Leonora found them feeble at best.

Morse dragged a hand down his face. "I suppose you engineered all this?"

"I can explain, Morse."

He rose from the bed and rummaged in his wardrobe for a dressing gown. "Did you only come to my bed so Frederica would find us together?"

The heightened emotion of their lovemaking and their humiliating discovery had left Leonora defenseless. Almost. "If you believe that, then you *are* a fool, Morse Archer. Have you got another robe I can put on?"

"Take this one." He stripped it off and tossed it onto the bed. Then he pulled out a shirt and began to dress.

"Couldn't leave well enough alone, could you?" He jammed one leg into his breeches, then the other. "*You* always know what's best for everyone. Never in my life have I met such an infuriating, high-handed—''

Leonora pulled on his robe, then hurled herself at Morse. ''I'm sorry if you wanted to marry Miss Hill and I've spoilt it for you. I am high-handed, and selfish. I gave myself lots of noble reasons for doing this. But in the end, it was because I couldn't bear to think of you with her. I wanted this time with you so much, I was willing to do anything to get it.''

She expected him to push her away with more angry words. Instead he wrapped her in his arms and rested his cheek on the top of her head. ''I won't pretend I'm not relieved to be free of Frederica and her family.''

''Then nothing else matters. It'll all have been worthwhile.''

''Will it?'' His arms tightened around her. ''Now *I* must watch you wed another man—one you don't love. We'd better brace ourselves, dear heart. I expect all hell's about to break loose.''

Chapter Twenty-Two

As Morse had predicted, all hell did indeed break loose.

By suppertime that evening, Herbert Hill and his family had decamped back to Sheffield. And everyone in Bath, from the exalted master of ceremonies to the lowliest bath attendant and sedan carrier knew the reason.

Captain Maurice Archibald, Miss Hill's fiancé and erstwhile toast of the Upper Assembly Rooms, had been discovered by his betrothed and her stepmother, practically on the eve of his nuptials, with another woman *in delicto flagrante*.

That was one Latin phrase no one in Bath had trouble understanding.

Even more scandalous, the handsome captain had turned out to be a fraud. A nobody named Morse Archer, who had once been in service to Mr. Hill's wife. As to the nature of that *service,* it would keep tongues awagging long after Bath's visitors had abandoned town for a summer round of hunting and house parties.

Morse received his summons to Sir Hugo's library with the brittle calm of a prisoner facing a death sentence. He tried to convince himself he was better off now than when Leonora and Sir Hugo had plucked him out of Bramleigh.

His leg had healed well enough, if he didn't tax it. He'd parted from the Rifles, but not under court-martial. And the large chip he had borne on his shoulder for so many years had been knocked off at last.

He had walked in a gentleman's boots. Dined at a gentleman's table. Slept in a gentleman's bed. In doing so, he had come to realize they were much like the rest of humanity. Some good. Some bad. Some with a fine facade and nothing to back it up. Others whose true worth one came to appreciate only with time and close acquaintance.

As Morse entered the library, he saw Algie standing somewhat apart from Sir Hugo. Leonora's uncle resembled nothing so much as a sleek tomcat who had recently tipped the contents of a cream pot, after having sampled the favors of every she-puss in the neighborhood. Morse could not find it in his heart to resent the old fellow's button-bursting felicity.

By contrast, Sir Hugo's prospective nephew-in-law appeared anxious and permanently embarrassed.

As the three men waited for Leonora to join them, Morse sidled over to Algie. "About this morning, old fellow." He couldn't bring himself to look his friend in the eye. "It wasn't as bad as it appeared, you know. Bad enough, but not *that* bad."

How did one gentleman go about telling another that he hadn't deflowered his friend's bride-to-be?

Algie made a determined effort to swallow his Adam's apple. "You're not terribly angry with me, are you, Morse? I should have guessed what Leonora was up to and warned you."

Had he heard right? He—angry with Algie?

Before Morse could ask what nonsense Algie was talking, Leonora entered. Could she be the same woman who had confronted him on the ward at Bramleigh with her preposterous wager? It scarcely seemed possible.

She wore a gauzy morning dress, the color of newly flowered lavender. Her dark hair fell in gentle waves and curls, with tendrils clustered at her temples and behind her ears. Morse wondered if he had kissed them into existence. The prim little spectacles had disappeared altogether. Perhaps she had decided she would no longer need them, since she must give up her studies. Much as Morse enjoyed an unobstructed view of her incomparable eyes, he would take the spectacles back in a minute, if it meant Leonora could keep her beloved books.

Sir Hugo cleared his throat, but before he could speak, Leonora held up her hand. "Remember, Uncle, you did concede defeat. Some people would not feel bound by the terms of the wager, thereafter."

She looked at Morse as she spoke. "I did what I did in the full understanding I would forfeit my winnings. Morse did not. He acted in good faith and would have gone on playing the gentleman, and getting away with it, until long after this Season at Bath. He should not have to suffer for my choice."

"Agreed." Sir Hugo's beaming countenance did not darken a whit. Clearly, Morse's part in the outcome of the wager, win or lose, was of little account to him.

"No." Morse pilfered his pocket for Frederica's engagement ring. "This belongs to you, now, sir. I'm prepared to make my own way in the world."

Sir Hugo shied away from the ring as if it might bite him. "Bless my soul, whatever would I do with such a thing? No, my dear boy, I believe you'd better keep it. You lived up to your part of the wager. Not your fault Leonora chose to forfeit."

"Please, Morse." Two brief words from Leonora, but they spoke volumes. Taken with her wistful tone and the plea in her eyes, they told how it would comfort her to know he hadn't been left wanting. At least not materially.

There had been a time, not so very long ago, when Morse's stiff-necked pride would not have countenanced such a notion. But if it would ease Leonora's mind in the days and years to come...

"Thank you, Sir Hugo. It's very generous of you." Besides, he had a project in mind that would please Leonora. Selling this ring would raise the necessary capital.

"Now that we've got that matter out of the way," said Sir Hugo, "the time has come for me to collect upon my wager."

Leonora's face went pale, but her chin tilted high with the indomitable spirit Morse had come to admire. And love.

"Since you were not able to pass Sergeant Archer off as a gentleman for the *entire* season at Bath, I now exercise my right, under the terms of our wager, to choose you a husband. It is my wish that you, my dear niece should wed...Sergeant Morse Archer."

Morse looked from Algie to Leonora to Sir Hugo. His ears must be playing wishful tricks on him. Algie wore a delighted grin that stretched the full width of his face. Leonora looked dumbfounded.

Sir Hugo stared at Morse expectantly, then burst into booming laughter. "Smile, at least, will you both? After the tricks you've been up to lately, I thought you'd be better pleased than this."

"I—I don't understand, Sir Hugo," Morse stammered. "Don't you want Leonora to marry Algie?"

Sir Hugo laughed harder. Algie joined him.

"You can't be serious, Morse. I love this boy like a son, but I long since gave up any notion of him making a match with Leonora. For his sake as much as hers. You have been my choice from the outset."

Two bright spots flamed in Leonora's cheeks. Morse feared she might pluck the champagne bottle from Sir

Hugo's hand and christen his balding pate like the prow
of a ship.

"Why didn't you say so, Uncle? What possessed you
to go through the motions of this ridiculous wager?"

"Harrumph! Nothing ridiculous about it," Sir Hugo
protested. "It was a brilliant plan. Let me ask you this,
missy. If I'd told you from the beginning that I wanted
you to marry Archer, would you have done it?"

"Of course...not."

Sir Hugo shook his finger at Morse. "Don't you pretend
any different, sir. Five months ago, I couldn't have bribed
you to wed her."

Morse and Leonora exchanged sheepish smiles. The
shock of Sir Hugo's announcement was wearing off. A
bubble of hope began to swell in Morse's chest.

"I knew from the moment I first clapped eyes upon you
that you were the man for Leonora." Sir Hugo's hearty
tone turned husky with emotion. "After the way you
risked your life for my Wesley, I could think of no better
reward than helping you to such a peerless bride."

"That's as may be." Leonora ignored her uncle's flattery. Clearly she was still having trouble grasping their
good fortune. "Once you saw how we'd...come to care
for one another, why didn't you tell us then and save
everyone all this upset?"

"Ha!" Sir Hugo reverted to his bluff, sardonic self.
"When could I be certain you did care for one another?
The pair of you have been up and down like a mile of bad
road. I set Algie spying on you at Laurelwood and still
never got a clear sign."

Algie piped up, "I can vouch for that."

Sir Hugo planted his hands on his substantial hips. "The
minute I'd think you were on the verge of an understanding, you'd stop speaking, or get yourselves engaged to
someone quite unsuitable. This whole business has been

plague on my nerves. From now on, I swear not to meddle in other people's lives.''

"I know you meant well, Uncle. You always do.''

"And everything's come out right in the end,'' declared Algie. "Just the way I like it.'' He looked around at the others. "I'll admit, I was more than a little smitten with Leonora before Sir Hugo dragged me down from London. Once I saw how you looked at Morse, though, I knew I hadn't a chance. Just hoped I might find a gel who thought half so highly of me.''

Unable to contain himself, he blurted the rest. "And I think I have, finally. After we barged in on you two this morning, Miss Taylor seemed to think I needed comforting. Imagine my surprise to find such a pretty, clever little creature fancied me. You might as well know, I've asked her to marry me, and I believe with a little persuasion, she may accept.''

"Oh, Algie!'' Leonora threw her arms around his neck, while Morse and Sir Hugo pumped his hands in hearty congratulations. "Of course, she'll have you. And you both shall be as happy as you deserve.''

"So shall we all, I hope.'' Algie looked as though he'd already downed the contents of several champagne bottles. "What do you say we make it a double wedding?''

"Nothing would suit me better!'' cried Sir Hugo. "I'm prepared to host a bridal breakfast for the whole county.''

Morse had grasped the situation at last. Everything he wanted was within his reach. But what of Leonora?

"Sir Hugo.'' He searched for the right words. "Please believe I appreciate your generosity.''

He sucked in a deep breath. Could he afford to throw away a *sure thing* and take one last gamble? "Your niece may be bound to your choice by the wager. But I am not.''

If Leonora had been prone to swooning, Morse's words might have melted her legs. Did he not want her, after all?

Had his prickly pride reared up at the last moment to spoil everything? If so, he would have to answer to her. Having come to recognize her own worth at last, she would demand her due from Morse Archer, if necessary!

"I have good reason to understand Leonora's distaste for marriage." Morse turned the expensive engagement ring over and over in his hand. "I won't see her compelled to wed me, simply to satisfy the terms of the wager."

He stepped toward her. "She is free to marry or not, as *she* chooses."

When Leonora tried to speak, the words could not break free of her constricted throat.

Morse took her hand and turned it palm up. "I love you with all my heart, Leonora. More than ever, knowing what you were prepared to give up to secure my freedom from Miss Hill and her family. Make no mistake, I *want* to be part of your life. More than I've ever wanted anything. But it must be on your terms. If that means without a wedding, so be it."

On her outstretched palm he laid the ring that represented his entire capital in the world. Enough to buy him a fine plantation abroad and a fresh start in life. "I want you to sell this and use the proceeds to set up your school. Whether you accept me or not."

Her eyes blurred with tears, Leonora struggled to compose herself to reply. Her hand closed over the ring—token of a gift Morse had given her. One beyond price.

"That's a noble gesture, my boy." Sir Hugo clapped a beefy arm around Morse. "Quite unnecessary, though. I have every intention of honoring the settlement I made on Leonora. She will have plenty of money for a school…and a family. And perhaps a little house not far from Laurelwood?"

A sound broke from Leonora's lips—a laugh and a sob sweetly mingled. She looked long at these three dear men.

In different ways, each had gambled with her heart. And won.

"Of course, Uncle Hugo. A little house near Laurelwood will be the very thing. But we won't need your settlement."

Morse had respected her need for independence. She could respect his pride. "All I want is to marry Morse, so we can build *our* school and raise *our* family…together."

"I'm afraid I must insist. I pride myself on always paying my gambling debts and this is no exception." After giving Morse a resounding thump on the back, Sir Hugo picked up the champagne bottle and popped its cork. "I'll admit I had my doubts at first, but you've convinced me of your radical theories about education. Besides, you've fulfilled the spirit of our wager by proving you can make a silk purse out of a sow's ear."

"I protest, Uncle!" Laughing, Leonora threw herself into Morse's waiting arms. "My fiancé was never a *sow's ear.*"

Morse kissed her then, reviving all the delicious memories of their morning tryst. How much more could they learn from each other of love and life in the years to come?

Stirring from their kiss, Morse plucked the engagement ring from Leonora's fist and placed it on her finger for safekeeping.

"I must protest, too, Sir Hugo." He laughed. "I do not fancy myself a silk purse."

"No, indeed." Leonora caressed his freshly shaven cheek. "But certainly a fine leather wallet."

> *Omnia vincit amor: et nos cedamus amori.*
> *—Virgil*
> *Love conquers all, so let us yield to love.*

* * * * *

*In October 2001, be sure to look for
Deborah's next book,*

WHITEFEATHER'S WOMAN,

*a rare and exceptional glimpse
into the world of*

MONTANA MAVERICKS

*and how it all began!
Please turn the page
for an exciting preview.*

Chapter One

May 1897
Whitehorn, Montana

A frontier saloon was just about the last place on earth Jane Harris had ever expected, or wanted, to find herself. Why, Mrs. Endicott and her Ladies' Temperance Society back in Boston would have been properly horrified. They'd have been more horrified still by the knowledge that Jane had stolen and sold a brooch of Mrs. Endicott's to get here.

The jarring notes of a tinny piano pummeled Jane's already throbbing head, and the reek of raw spirits and tobacco smoke made the flesh at the back of her throat constrict. If she'd had anything to eat in the past twenty-four hours, the stink, the noise and her own overwrought nerves might have conspired to make her violently ill.

Perhaps it was a harsh blessing she'd run out of money for food back in Omaha.

"Kin I pour ya a drink, little lady?" bellowed the man behind the bar, his voice laced with genial mockery.

Jane gasped, her heart hammering against her corset like the pistons of a runaway steam engine.

"N-no thank you, sir." She raised her voice louder than she'd ever spoken in her life to make herself heard above the *music* and the babble of voices. "I'd be most obliged if you'd point out the foreman of the Kincaid ranch to me. I was told I'd find him here."

As she turned to speak to him, the bartender flinched. Probably at the sight of her face. She'd hoped the bruises and cuts would be healed by the end of her long trip west. They must still have a ways to go if her appearance distressed a man who worked in such a rough establishment.

"Yep, ma'am. I seen him come in awhile back and he ain't left that I know of." The bartender squinted through the haze of smoke around the cavernous room, with its sinister shadows and a huge, lowering buffalo head mounted behind the bar.

Raising a gnarled finger, he pointed to one particularly murky corner. "That's John Whitefeather, over there. He don't come in here much as a rule, but when he does he's always by himself in the corner."

Jane heard nothing after the bartender spoke the name. *Whitefeather*? An Indian! Her knees commenced to tremble beneath her skirts and petticoats.

Back in Boston, Jane's sole dissipation had been reading Western dime novels from Beadle's Library, which often featured lurid accounts of Apache atrocities. Were there any of that fierce tribe this far north? Perhaps she was about to find out.

"Thank you...sir. I—I appreciate your assistance." Like a condemned prisoner appreciated a deputy's *assistance* to climb the scaffold.

Jane tried to smile at the man, but between her mounting agitation and the still healing gash on one side of her mouth, she doubted she'd made a very good job of it.

Step by halting step, she crossed the saloon floor, conscious of curious, predatory eyes following her movement.

Had Daniel felt this way walking through the lions' den? Probably not, for Daniel had been a man and he'd had the Lord on his side. With the sin of her desperate theft weighing on her conscience, Jane was certain she'd left any protection of the Almighty far behind her in New England.

The Kincaids' foreman sat at a corner table, all alone, his back to the wall, as though he knew better than to turn it on the denizens of the Double Deuce. The bartender's pointing finger must have alerted Mr. Whitefeather that she wished to speak with him, yet he did not rise or otherwise acknowledge her approach.

Reason assured Jane the man was hardly apt to pull out a tomahawk and scalp her in the middle of a crowded saloon. But her tautly stretched nerves refused to unwind for logic. Stopping before his table, she stood like a convicted felon in front of a hanging judge. Jane longed to turn and flee, but she'd been told the Kincaids lived miles outside of town. John Whitefeather might be her only means of reaching them.

For perhaps the hundredth time since stealing out of Boston, Jane wished she'd been able to spare the money for a wire to advise her new employers that she was on her way. Mrs. Kincaid might have come to the depot to meet her, or at least have sent her a less alarming escort to the ranch.

"A-are you Mr. Whitefeather, the Kincaid foreman?"

The man gave a slow nod. Jane sensed his gaze sweeping over her.

"What can I do for you, ma'am?" His voice, a soft rumble with a queer melodic inflection, was barely audible over the raucous hubbub of the saloon.

"I'm Jane Harris, Mr. Whitefeather. I've come from Boston to work for Mr. and Mrs. Kincaid, taking care of their boys."

Her words tripped all over one another in their haste,

and she had to pause frequently to gasp for breath. ''
regret that I was unable to send a wire to announce m
arrival. I'd be most obliged if you could arrange my trans
portation to the ranch.''

He muttered something to himself, but what Jane coul
hear made no sense to her. Was he speaking some India
dialect?

Draining the contents of a tall bottle, he rummaged i
his pocket and tossed several coins onto the table. The
he scooped up his hat, pushed back his chair, and stood.

Jane's last sound nerve shattered.

He was so big. John Whitefeather towered over her, hi
shoulders alarmingly broad under an enormous duster coa
that fell almost to his ankles. And his hands—Jane nearl
swooned to imagine the horrible damage they could inflic
on a woman's vulnerable face and body. Emery Endico
had been a runt compared to this giant. Before she'd ru
away to Montana, though, her fiancé had managed to bea
her badly enough to put her in hospital.

''I expect you'd better come along with me, ma'am.''

Any man who spoke so softly and with such a respectfu
tone surely wouldn't harm her. Jane didn't really believ
it, but the alternative was simply too terrible to contem
plate.

MONTANA MAVERICKS

Bestselling author

SUSAN
MALLERY

WILD WEST WIFE

THE ORIGINAL MONTANA MAVERICKS HISTORICAL NOVEL

**Jesse Kincaid had sworn off love forever.
But when the handsome rancher kidnaps
his enemy's mail-order bride to get revenge,
he ends up falling for his innocent captive!**

RETURN TO WHITEHORN, MONTANA, WITH

WILD WEST WIFE

Available July 2001

**And be sure to pick up
MONTANA MAVERICKS: BIG SKY GROOMS,
three brand-new historical stories about Montana's
most popular family, coming in August 2001.**

HARLEQUIN®
Makes any time special ®

Visit us at www.eHarlequin.com

PHWWW

Harlequin truly does make any time special.... This year we are celebrating weddings in style!

To help us celebrate, we want you to tell us how wearing the Harlequin wedding gown will make your wedding day special. As the grand prize, Harlequin will offer one lucky bride the chance to "Walk Down the Aisle" in the Harlequin wedding gown!

There's more...

For her honeymoon, she and her groom will spend five nights at the **Hyatt Regency Maui.** As part of this five-night honeymoon at the hotel renowned for its romantic attractions, the couple will enjoy a candlelit dinner for two in Swan Court, a sunset sail on the hotel's catamaran, and duet spa treatments.

Maui • Molokai • Lanai

To enter, please write, in, 250 words or less, how wearing the Harlequin wedding gown will make your wedding day special. The entry will be judged based on its emotionally compelling nature, its originality and creativity, and its sincerity. This contest is open to Canadian and U.S. residents only and to those who are 18 years of age and older. There is no purchase necessary to enter. Void where prohibited. See further contest rules attached. Please send your entry to:

Walk Down the Aisle Contest

In Canada	In U.S.A.
P.O. Box 637	P.O. Box 9076
Fort Erie, Ontario	3010 Walden Ave.
L2A 5X3	Buffalo, NY 14269-9076

You can also enter by visiting www.eHarlequin.com

Win the Harlequin wedding gown and the vacation of a lifetime!

The deadline for entries is October 1, 2001.

HARLEQUIN®
Makes any time special ®

HARLEQUIN WALK DOWN THE AISLE TO MAUI CONTEST 1197
OFFICIAL RULES
NO PURCHASE NECESSARY TO ENTER

1. To enter, follow directions published in the offer to which you are responding. Contest begins April 2, 2001, and ends on October 1, 2001. Method of entry may vary. Mailed entries must be postmarked by October 1, 2001, and received by October 8, 2001.

2. Contest entry may be, at times, presented via the Internet, but will be restricted solely to residents of certain geographic areas that are disclosed on the Web site. To enter via the Internet, if permissible, access the Harlequin Web site (www.eHarlequin.com) and follow the directions displayed online. Online entries must be received by 11:59 p.m. E.S.T. on October 1, 2001.

   In lieu of submitting an entry online, enter by mail by hand-printing (or typing) on an 8½" x 11" plain piece of paper, your name, address (including zip code), Contest number/name and in 250 words or fewer, why winning a Harlequin wedding would make your wedding day special. Mail via first-class mail to: Harlequin Walk Down the Aisle Contest 1197, (in the U P.O. Box 9076, 3010 Walden Avenue, Buffalo, NY 14269-9076, (in Canada) P.O. Box 637, Fort Erie, Ontario L2A 5X3, Can Limit one entry per person, household address and e-mail address. Online and/or mailed entries received from persons residing in geographic areas in which Internet entry is not permissible will be disqualified.

3. Contests will be judged by a panel of members of the Harlequin editorial, marketing and public relations staff based on th following criteria:

   - Originality and Creativity—50%
   - Emotionally Compelling—25%
   - Sincerity—25%

   In the event of a tie, duplicate prizes will be awarded. Decisions of the judges are final.

4. All entries become the property of Torstar Corp. and will not be returned. No responsibility is assumed for lost, late, illegib incomplete, inaccurate, nondelivered or misdirected mail or misdirected e-mail, for technical, hardware or software failure any kind, lost or unavailable network connections, or failed, incomplete, garbled or delayed computer transmission or any human error which may occur in the receipt or processing of the entries in this Contest.

5. Contest open only to residents of the U.S. (except Puerto Rico) and Canada, who are 18 years of age or older, and is void wherever prohibited by law; all applicable laws and regulations apply. Any litigation within the Province of Quebec respectii the conduct or organization of a publicity contest may be submitted to the Régie des alcools, des courses et des jeux for a ruling. Any litigation respecting the awarding of a prize may be submitted to the Régie des alcools, des courses et des jeu for the purpose of helping the parties reach a settlement. Employees and immediate family members of Torstar Corp. and D. L. Blair, Inc., their affiliates, subsidiaries and all other agencies, entities and persons connected with the use, marketing conduct of this Contest are not eligible to enter. Taxes on prizes are the sole responsibility of winners. Acceptance of any v offered constitutes permission to use winner's name, photograph or other likeness for the purposes of advertising, trade ai promotion on behalf of Torstar Corp., its affiliates and subsidiaries without further compensation to the winner, unless prohibited by law.

6. Winners will be determined no later than November 15, 2001, and will be notified by mail. Winners will be required to sig return an Affidavit of Eligibility form within 15 days after winner notification. Noncompliance within that time period may re in disqualification and an alternative winner may be selected. Winners of trip must execute a Release of Liability prior to tie and must possess required travel documents (e.g. passport, photo ID) where applicable. Trip must be completed by Nover 2002. No substitution of prize permitted by winner. Torstar Corp. and D. L. Blair, Inc., their parents, affiliates, and subsidiar are not responsible for errors in printing or electronic presentation of Contest, entries and/or game pieces. In the event of printing or other errors which may result in unintended prize values or duplication of prizes, all affected game pieces or er shall be null and void. If for any reason the Internet portion of the Contest is not capable of running as planned, including infection by computer virus, bugs, tampering, unauthorized intervention, fraud, technical failures, or any other causes bey the control of Torstar Corp. which corrupt or affect the administration, secrecy, fairness, integrity or proper conduct of the Contest, Torstar Corp. reserves the right, at its sole discretion, to disqualify any individual who tampers with the entry prod and to cancel, terminate, modify or suspend the Contest or the Internet portion thereof. In the event of a dispute regarding online entry, the entry will be deemed submitted by the authorized holder of the e-mail account submitted at the time of er Authorized account holder is defined as the natural person who is assigned to an e-mail address by an Internet access pro online service provider or other organization that is responsible for arranging e-mail address for the domain associated wi submitted e-mail address. **Purchase or acceptance of a product offer does not improve your chances of winr**

7. Prizes: (1) Grand Prize—A Harlequin wedding dress (approximate retail value: $3,500) and a 5-night/6-day honeymoon t Maui, HI, including round-trip air transportation provided by Maui Visitors Bureau from Los Angeles International Airport (winner is responsible for transportation to and from Los Angeles International Airport) and a Harlequin Romance Packag including hotel accomodations (double occupancy) at the Hyatt Regency Maui Resort and Spa, dinner for (2) two at Swan Court, a sunset sail on Kiele V and a spa treatment for the winner (approximate retail value: $4,000); (5) Five runner-up pi of a $1000 gift certificate to selected retail outlets to be determined by Sponsor (retail value $1000 ea.). Prizes consist of those items listed as part of the prize. Limit one prize per person. All prizes are valued in U.S. currency.

8. For a list of winners (available after December 17, 2001) send a self-addressed, stamped envelope to: Harlequin Walk Do Aisle Contest 1197 Winners, P.O. Box 4200 Blair, NE 68009-4200 or you may access the www.eHarlequin.com Web site through January 15, 2002.

Contest sponsored by Torstar Corp., P.O. Box 9042, Buffalo, NY 14269-9042, U.S.A.

PHWDACONT2

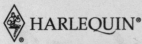